The Macaw Muttered

ALSO BY
Rachael Rawlings

———

Dearly Departed
Dearly Remembered
Dearly Beloved
The Parrot Told Me
The Cockatoo Called

The Macaw Muttered

Rachael Rawlings

Hydra Publications

ISBN-13: 978-1-942212-59-1

Hydra Publications
1310 Meadowridge Trail
Goshen, KY 40026

www.hydrapublications.com

DEDICATION

To my Dad, who persevered and came out stronger in the end.

Chapter 1

Genevieve slipped off her lab coat and hung it on the hook next to the door, placing her purse and keys in the cubby just next to it. Her work ID was still clipped to the lapel to be removed just before washing. The picture showed the pale oval of her face with her hair pulled back into a tidy bun, the only color her blue eyes that darkened to nearly black when she was deep in thought. The ID was still in good condition, even though it was nearly five years old. She hadn't changed much in her appearance since then. In fact, the lab coat was probably the same one she had bought when she had first gotten the job. She would unclip the badge for laundering on Wednesday and again on Friday, leaving the ID next to her keys. Neither had ever been misplaced. She checked for pens and papers that might have been tucked in the pockets of her coat and slacks, and finding them empty, she scanned the array of equipment for her job. Neatly lined up and each in their specified place. Good. They would remain until the next morning when she needed them again. She headed up the stairs, going first to the small second floor bedroom where she slept alone in the queen bed, the covers smooth like an expanse of pale milk, the precise number of throw pillows, four to be exact, laid out in a pleasing pattern of creams and light green. She kicked off her crepe-soled shoes, very practical and easy on her feet after a long day standing and stowed them in the closet, to the left, not the right, lined up just so, toes pointed forward. Next, she went into the bathroom, slipping off her work clothes and dropping them into the hamper by the sink. On the counter, folded, were the clothes she had laid out the night before, well-worn jeans, a tee shirt, white socks, slip on athletic shoes ready to be pulled on at a moment's notice. She used the facilities and dressed quickly, returning downstairs just ten minutes later.

The efficiency was pleasing. The neatness of her life soothed her. She stopped at the foot of the stairs to straighten a picture that was just slightly tilted. OCD? Perhaps. But it wasn't anything that was crippling her, so she would live with it.

The knock at the door made her jump. It was loud, demanding. And who would that be? She certainly wasn't expecting anyone. Thursday was girls' night for a glass of wine and gossip. This was Wednesday, a day of rest, usually an evening of a simple sandwich for dinner and then curled on the couch with a good book. But when the pounding was repeated, she tiptoed to look out the peephole, not for the first time cursing her five-foot height.

The man on the other side of the door looked peeved. She could see the taxi parked behind him, the sign emblazoned on the side 'Ready Taxi'. She yanked open the door, trusting that she could handle this impatient man.

"Yes?" her tone was not friendly, and she hadn't meant it to sound that way.

"Genevieve? Genevieve Glass?"

"Yes," she said again, calm, composed.

"Good. I have this for you. No need to sign or anything." He backed off one step. He wasn't a big man himself so not threatening at all, and his khaki pants and white shirt looked like his attempt at a uniform. This late in the day, his clothes were rumpled and a five o'clock shadow marked his slightly sagging jaw, making him look old and tired. But she wasn't paying attention to him any longer when he picked up the large animal crate and held it out toward her.

"I don't-" she began, but he interrupted.

"Look, lady. I was told to drop this thing off with you. I needed to see you take him. That's what I was paid to do. If you want to argue, you're going to have to get in touch with the pirate." He didn't wait for her to take the crate, just put it gingerly down in the doorway. "Have a nice night," he said under his breath, and turned.

Genevieve stared at him frozen for a moment. "Pirate? Jack!" She started after the man as he stalked across her well-manicured lawn. "Wait! How am I supposed to find him? This pirate!"

"Don't know, lady." The man was climbing into his taxi, slamming the door and starting the engine before she made it to the sidewalk.

"Hey!" She called, but he obviously wasn't listening, and didn't care to. She dropped the hand she had automatically raised as though hailing a taxi, feeling foolish on her quiet suburban street. His engine had made a choking sound, but now it had caught, and the roar increased as his foot hit the gas pedal. She watched with silent dismay as his car jerked away from the curb, moving a little too fast for her neighborhood street, and disappeared in the near distance. She looked at the crate at her feet. No way was this happening, but there it was. She bent down and caught the handle of the crate, feeling the weight of the creature within.

"Ah, Hemingway, what have you been up to now?" she asked, and took the container indoors, letting the door swing closed behind her.

In her sparse little living room, she sat the crate on the coffee table and looked through the bars. The eye that studied her was dark, with a patch of white skin surrounding it, striped by tiny bright red feathers. The rest of the colorful bird was shadowed in darkness. She heard a low growling sound and shook her head. She let out a sigh. She knew somewhere in her garage was a cage that Jack had unloaded on her almost a year ago. It was a 'just in case' situation, he had said, and she had reluctantly agreed to store it, partly because she didn't want to take the time to have it hauled away. She guessed she would need it now.

An hour later, she had cleared an area in her living room for the cage, wrestled the it into place, assembled it, and was sitting on the couch looking into the crate with the creature eyeing her from within. The cage was enormous, but it took a big cage to hold a creature of this size. It had taken her time to dust it off, but like most of her belongings, she kept her garage in top shape with only minimal dust and cobwebs. There was only one perch that came with the cage, but it was anchored it to the cage wall. There was water in the dish, but no food. She would have to go out tonight and buy some. Genevieve bent and opened the door of the crate backing away as the bird strutted out.

Hemingway. It had seemed for most of her life that wherever Jack was, Hemingway was there too. Since she had reached adulthood, she had rarely called Jack "father". Dad as a title seemed inadequate. It hadn't felt right, as though calling him Dad gave him a bit too much credit when she carried that seed of resentment, that little girl bitterness, that she hadn't quite been able to shake. So it had become Jack. And every time Jack had blown into town to stay with his wife and daughter, he had brought the bird with him. When she was grown, and he had come to visit Genevieve in her neat little house, he had brought along the damn parrot. All her life, Jack would turn up unexpectedly, accompanied by this creature, wreak havoc, and then leave just as suddenly.

Hemingway stepped gingerly on the table; clawed feet wide spread on the glossy surface, and eyed her. They had a love/hate relationship, she and this bird. He loved her; she hated him. She grunted to herself, a wry smile on her face. No, that wasn't fair. She didn't hate the parrot. He was a mess. He was loud, obnoxious, and he talked just like Jack. But she didn't hate him. It was very hard to hate something that adored you that much.

As if to prove her point, the giant bird cocked his head and seemed to recognize her for the first time. He rushed toward her, slipping a little on the polished tabletop, and landed in her lap. His head immediately went down to press against her abdomen, presenting his neck for her to stroke. She put her hand out and ruffled the bright red feathers on his head and neck. She watched the dark eyes squint in pleasure. A flood of memories came back as she felt the papery soft texture of the long feathers against the pads of her fingertips. Hemingway was a green winged macaw, or so Jack had told her, and as a child, one of her best friends. She hadn't always agreed with the literary name. When she was a child she had just called him Rainbow because of his excess of brilliant colors, and the name seemed much more suitable for him. They had grown up together, she and Hemingway. Jack had

4

gotten the bird as a chick when she was just a baby herself, so she had always known him, and he had always known her. And he loved her with all of his birdy heart.

"Okay, Hemingway, where's Jack?" she asked, but the bird just made a funny purring sound of pleasure. He would be no help. What talking he did was usually greetings, exclamations, and often bad language picked up from Jack and some of his friends. Intelligent conversation was not the Hemingway's forte.

She found herself squinting into the distance when she thought of Jack's companions. He so rarely was at home, if the little cottage outside of the Louisville suburbs could be called his home, that it was a challenge to find him anyway. Added to that was the fact that he didn't have Hemingway, who tended to draw more attention than his owner. And generally, if the trip were planned, he would find one of his dozens of friends and leave Hemingway in their care. To ship the bird here in a crate like some unwanted poultry was unheard of for Jack. And that scared her. Because if Jack had felt he needed to leave his treasured companion so abruptly, it had to have been for a good reason.

Genevieve briefly thought about calling the police. She could just imagine the call. Ma'am, when did you last see your father? Well, that would be about three months ago. And under what circumstances? He had just dropped by to give her a chunk of money he had inherited from a friend of his who had passed on. Genevieve had taken the money to the bank immediately, feeling squeamish about having it. When Jack had money, it slipped through his hands like so much water stored in a leaky bucket, so giving it to her was his way of protecting her inheritance, or so he claimed. Not that she doubted the story. She had known his wealthy friend, a warm hearted eccentric and one of many of Jack's unusual cadre, but still, the visit had struck her as strange. And although he had sent the bird to her without warning, she had no reason to believe he was actually missing or in trouble. He could be on vacation, for all she knew.

"You have just a few days," she told Hemingway, as his dark eye closed in pleasure as she gently stroked his feathers. "After that, I'm going after Jack."

The next day she was climbing into her car when her cell phone rang. Luckily, she kept it in the outside pocket of her conservative leather purse, so it was easy to retrieve. She didn't glance at the screen, but automatically took the call.

"Hi Mom," she said, slipping into the driver's seat and tossing her satchel into the seat next to her.

"Baby!" her mother's voice was all warmth.

Genevieve felt a smile ease her expression as she pictured her mother in her kitchen, surrounded by walls climbing with papered red and yellow cabbage roses. Her mother was her rock, her oasis of calm, her stability, her heart. And she called, like clockwork, at 6:15 every night. But today Genevieve was dreading the conversation just a little. Because today, she was going to have to talk about Jack.

"So how are you?" she asked automatically, listening as she switched on the car's engine with an efficient click. Her car was perfect, tuned and running like a top, as her grandmother would have said, another part of her perfectionistic nature.

"I went to the grocery and saw Barbara. You remember Barbara, don't you? Lived up the street and had all of those cats? Well she just got remarried a month ago, after losing Ted, such a tragedy, but now she is so much happier, and she just seems to be glowing. Just glowing!" The words bubbled up like balloons, loosely tied with string, one after the other, connected but not tightly bound. That was her mother's thought processes, a mass of information just waiting to be shared. Genevieve's mom was constantly meeting up with old neighbors, church acquaintances, and friends, gathering the tidbits of their lives, and reporting back with births, deaths, marriages, vacations, and the occasional scandal, although she didn't like that type of gossip.

Genevieve made little sounds of assent as she drove, hearing the buzz of her mother's voice but missing much of the content. She was trying to think of how she was going to bring up the subject of her father. For a happily married couple with thirty years under their belt, they had the strangest of relationships.

"So what's going on with you, sweetie?" her mom's voiced pierced her thoughts, popping her ballooning concerns like a pin.

"Um, well, I have an unexpected visitor," Genevieve began cautiously.

"Really?"

"Hemingway was dropped off yesterday," Genevieve admitted.

The silence on the other end of the line was the only show of surprise her mother would give her. Not much disturbed her mother's composure.

"Really," her mother said, her voice now just a shade deeper.

"Yes, he was delivered by taxi. I've tried to call Jack, but haven't been able to reach him. I don't suppose…"

Her mother didn't wait for her to finish the question. There was no need. "You know how your father is," she said firmly. "He may be in town and not have let me know, but he'll come around eventually. I'm so glad you're getting a chance to visit with Bow."

Genevieve sighed. Just like her mother to put a silver lining on it. She wasn't worried about Jack; she never was. And she still called Hemingway by his childhood name, Bow, after the rainbow he resembled. It was as if the bird was her traveling brother, stopping by to visit and share old memories.

"Yes, well, Bow is a bit of a surprise," Genevieve began. "And I think it's strange Jack just left him here. No note, no call. Just the bird in a carrier. So I've decided I'm going to take a few days to take him down to Florida if I don't hear from Jack soon. I'm sure one of Jack's cronies will have an idea of where he is, and will watch after Hemingway for Jack. And frankly I can't watch after that bird, Mom. He's just too much."

"You're going to drive down to Florida? Alone?"

Her mother may have been raised when women's liberation was blooming, but she was old fashioned in some ways. It was fine for Genevieve to get her doctorate and make good money. It was fine that she was an independent and successful woman. But her mother would have much preferred for her to do that while juggling a husband and two sticky toddlers. And the idea that a single woman might take a road trip was just unheard of. And frankly, Genevieve knew that Jack, for all of his eccentricities, would have stood by her mother's side and totally agreed with this.

"Yes, alone. I can drive, and my car is great." She was turning into her driveway now, feeling the familiar pride at how cozy her home looked, with its little peaked roof and gingerbread accents. It had been a mess when she had bought it, 100 years old and deteriorating like an aging lady graying and withering. But some paint and carpentry, the help of a great general contractor and some talented renovators, she had brought the place back to life. And she had tackled it alone. Just like she could tackle this little trip.

"Well now, I'm not sure if that's such a good idea," her mother said, her voice hesitating. "Perhaps one of your friends could go with you! Make it a vacation!"

Genevieve noticed her mother wasn't telling her not to go. She wasn't saying Jack was okay, and that the trip was unnecessary. Genevieve put that little observation in the back of her mind for future pondering.

"I can drive it with no problems. It's a familiar road; I've driven it a dozen times over the years." Of course, that was usually with Jack. Trips to visit his friends, to meet up with shippers who had brought in some good stash of antiques for his buddy Topper, to catch some time out on the ocean in that little boat. Deep sea fishing, beach combing, and walking in the Florida sunset had been her memories of Jack.

"You know; I think a friend of mine has a son that lives in Florida. She said he was up visiting, but was planning on heading back. Maybe he could catch a ride with you. Or you could ride with him!" she seemed to be warming to the subject.

"Um, no. Mom, riding with a strange man isn't necessarily safer than driving by myself," Genevieve interrupted, visions of a blooming beer gut over Hawaiian print shorts settling into the leather upholstery of her sleek car popping into her head.

"It's just a thought," her mother said mildly, but Genevieve could tell she was warming to the idea. Before she could get any more entrenched in trouble, Genevieve switched off the motor.

"Sure, Mom. Well, I'm home, so I better get in there and check on Bow." She looked a little fearfully toward the adorable little place she called home. That giant bird could do some damage. She needed to something about him.

Chapter 2

Genevieve looked with dismay at the floor. What a mess. The last thing she wanted to do was clean. It had been a long day of shuffling papers and putting out proverbial fires. Her job was satisfying but hard. Day in and day out, not only acting as a consultant to a prestigious university, but running the challenging pharmaceutical branch specializing in specific neurological chemicals. This position often included answering questions, researching, sharing her knowledge with the board, with her colleagues and maintaining meticulous data collection, analysis, and reporting of results. It was exhausting.

And now she was on her hands and knees scrubbing bird poop from the wood floors. It was times like these when she would have loved to lounge on the couch for just a moment, wrap up in a blanket and pull out a good book. But that wasn't going to happen. And she suspected that if she looked up, Hemingway would be proudly perched on the top of the cage watching her like a king surveying his kingdom and all of his minions.

"Stupid bird," she muttered, but without rancor.

Her temporary roommate eyed her from his perch on the door of his cage where he liked to stay when he wasn't following her around her house or terrorizing the neighborhood with his ear splitting screams. She was just waiting for one of them to call and complain about the noise. They lived far too close for them not to have noticed the yells. Then again, with the amount of time the bird spent talking, long diatribes about how beautiful he was, and such a fine boy, and what a wonderful singer, it was a wonder the neighbors hadn't visited just to see if she had an insane person staying with her.

It had been six days. Six days of cleaning up after the bird, watching him waddle after her when she went to her bedroom, laughing at him as he smeared banana on his beak, and then berating him for wiping it on her clean couch. He was a lot of bird. A lot of noise, a lot of personality, and a lot of cleaning.

"This is it," she scolded him. "I'm going on a date tonight, and I don't want you making a sound until we leave. I don't want to have to explain you, or Jack for that matter, to Wayne. He's a lawyer. He's reasonable, very nice. And he wouldn't understand Jack, or you, or any of this." She found herself looking around her, surprised she was having such a serious conversation with the bird. But she was right. She and Wayne had started dating just three months ago, and in that time, she had seen Wayne as a suitable companion. He might be a little pompous, ready to discuss his latest case he had won, or to describe in infinite detail the new car he had earned by making his firm extremely successful, but he was steady, and stable, and smart, and, well, suitable. She didn't want Hemingway, and by extension, Jack, to mess up what she viewed as a possible long-term relationship in her life. She wished this idea didn't make her stomach twist.

She finished cleaning up and stood, stretching out her back. She didn't feel like going out tonight, but one of Wayne's partner's wives was having a little get together, and Wayne wanted her to come. It was a mutually beneficial relationship. She could decorate his arm better than most women. While she wasn't pretty in a traditional sense, she was striking with her delicate bone structure, aristocratic bearing, and luxurious dark hair. And the fact he could introduce her as Doctor just sweetened the deal for him.

She climbed the stairs slowly, glancing at her watch. Time had gone quickly. She had less than an hour to get ready. She was practical in her preparations. She would take a quick shower but keep her hair dry. It took far too long to blow it dry after washing. Just taking it down and brushing it out usually was enough to make it shine.

10

Then she would slip on the tasteful black cocktail dress she had bought just three weeks ago. True, it very much resembled the one she already had in her closet, but the other one was two years old and it was time to get something new.

Next, she would throw on her low-heeled pumps and add a light application of makeup to brighten her complexion that tended to be too pale, and add a pink gloss to her lips. She had nice pearls that would be perfect with the dress. In all, it was a conservative yet classy ensemble that was perfectly suitable for a dinner with the partners in a law firm. Just like Wayne. It was suitable.

She stripped off her work clothes, too aware of the limited time, and took a brief shower, seventeen minutes to be exact. When she was dried off, she put on the thin slip with just a wisp of lace and stepped out of the bathroom. And stopped. On the floor, looking thoughtful but happy to see her, was Hemingway. She blew out a frustrated breath. She knew better not to leave him out, but he just wasn't a part of her routine yet, and apparently in her hurry, she had forgotten about him. Oh, she remembered the important things, like feeding him and changing his water frequently, but she had completely forgotten to put him back in his cage and close the door after finishing her cleaning job, and now here he was, looking downright overjoyed to see her, but with a suspicious swath of fabric in his beak. Black fabric, slightly shiny, she frowned and looked at the floor of her bedroom. The white carpet was immaculate, except for, yuck, a large spot where the bird had relieved himself as he waddled over the rug.

And the only other thing laying out was her dress draped across the bed and her shoes. Oh, no! Her shoes were no longer tucked neatly next to her bed. They were tossed in the center of the floor and looked as though someone had tucked the left one into a blender and put it on chop. Gashes and slashes marked the shiny leather, and the satin inner lining was now hanging in the bird's beak like some trophy he had received.

"Hemingway, no!" she cried, bending to take one end of the fabric. The bird didn't give it up, but enjoyed an energetic round of tug of war before she gave up and let him carry it with him.

She picked up the shoes, and without more than a glance at the damage, tossed them in the garbage can in her bathroom. There was nothing she could do about them now. They were ruined and the only thing she had to replace them with were some practical flats she usually wore to work.

She frowned at the bird as she laid out the other pair of shoes.

Wayne rang the doorbell at ten minutes before seven. When she swung the door open, she fully intended to block him from entry. She didn't need the questions. Besides, he had been in her home before. He had commented about how cute it was, a rather condescending tone to his voice, but she didn't care. She loved the place, and his opinion wasn't going to ruin that.

"You wouldn't mind if I grabbed a drink, would you?" he asked as soon as the door swung open.

She hesitated. Was it worth an argument? Probably not. She shrugged and stepped aside, looking at him critically. He was immaculate in a charcoal gray suit, a red tie, and newly buffed shoes. His hair was perfect as well, and it seemed a shame to risk ruining all of that perfection, but she let him in. She suspected he wanted something more than just a glass of water, but if he was hoping for something alcoholic, he was going to be disappointed.

"Sure, come on in," Genevieve said, gesturing him in.

"We are due to Sean's house in thirty," Wayne said, strolling into her living room.

"I have soft drinks and tea," Genevieve said nodding.

Wayne's expression showed his disappointment. "Tea then."

Genevieve nodded, leaving Wayne in the little living room while she went to pour him his drink. She just prayed the bird wouldn't draw any attention to himself. She couldn't have hidden him if she tried. The cage was just too big, but for now, it wasn't an explanation she wanted to get into.

"Are those the shoes that you're wearing?"

Genevieve cringed a little. Then her chin went up. She didn't like the shoes either, but she would have never talked to him with that tone of voice. The irritation rose quick and sharp.

"My other ones got ruined. Unless you want to buy me another pair, these are what I'm wearing," she said her voice cold and crisp.

"No need to get snippy," he said, his eyebrows raised. He needed to get his eyebrows done. They were almost touching over his nose. How had she not noticed that before? Or maybe part of his toiletry had been skipped. She knew he regularly got his nails done. She frowned. She didn't even get her nails done on a regular basis. For an occasion, yes, but why did he need to?

She shook her head and continued on into the kitchen. She grabbed a glass from the cabinet and added ice. The tea pitcher was in the refrigerator, and she had gotten it out when she heard a familiar low whistle followed by a voice, "Now watcha got here, Dolly?" It sounded like her father, like Jack.

"Genevieve, what is this bird doing here?"

She carried out the glass, now getting cold against her fingers. She had been concerned about this, but now, not so much.

"That is Hemingway. He's come for a visit." She wasn't going to give him any further information. She was still too irritated to care what he thought.

"How long?" He went closer to the cage, his pug nose that she had thought cute just yesterday, too close to the bars.

"I wouldn't get too close," she admonished him. "Hemingway can be a little mean sometimes."

"You have a pet that is mean? What is that? And whose is it?" He pulled back, his eyes going to the floor of the cage. "Is that animal waste?"

She had been disgustedly mopping it up just an hour ago, but now she was offended by the comment. It was as though she was seeing this man through different eyes. Oh no, maybe she was seeing him through Jack's eyes. But whatever the reason, he was coming up lacking.

"It's an animal. It doesn't go outside to relieve himself." She thrust the glass at him.

"I can't believe you have him in your living room. Why not the garage? Wouldn't that be much more sanitary?"

She felt herself bristle. It was fine if she wanted to complain about the mess, but not for Wayne to criticize! This was Bow, her childhood friend, who had participated in his fair share of dress up, of tea parties where he had worn a dress, for God's sake. No one was going to put her pet in the garage.

"No," she said harshly. "Wayne, how can you be so ignorant? He's a tropical animal. You can't just stick him in a garage! The drafts are terrible for birds and the fumes alone would kill him."

He turned slowly, his eyebrows again coasting up. For the first time, she noticed his hairline appeared to be receding. Soon, his eyebrows would be nowhere close to his hairline. "Really. So now you're Jane Goodall?"

"Is that the only animal expert you've heard of?"

He took a deep breath. "Someone is being a little rude," he said, looking toward Hemingway, but obviously meaning her.

Hemingway climbed the bars slowly, beak over foot, his dark eye surrounded by the chalk white skin studying the man next to him, until he was well above Wayne in his expensive suit. Genevieve could almost imagine he was aiming. She knew what he was going to do. She had seen him, deliberately when he was bad, do this trick before. It wasn't a common one for macaws, but Hemingway was an exception.

The spew of bird droppings wasn't anything like the polite little mounds left by wild birds in the driveway. It was a giant splat of greenish goo that hit on the front of Wayne's coat, splattering in a warm shot, smearing to Wayne's white shirt and the bottom of his red tie.

She had never heard Wayne cuss. He just didn't do it. But apparently this was enough to make him start because the string of words he spat out in every direction was both foul and personal. When his hand raised as though he were going to strike the cage, Genevieve cut in.

"I wouldn't do that. I think you should just leave."

He turned slowly, hand still raised. She didn't for a moment ever think he would hit her, but at that second, with that look on his face, she began to think he might. She stepped toward the cage. She wasn't going to go down without a fight, and by God, Hemingway fought dirty himself.

14

He saw her expression, then he looked at the cage where the big bird had lowered himself back to the perch, head forward, feathers puffed in an aggressive stance.

"If I leave," Wayne said, slowly, coldly, his eyes glittering in a way she did not like at all. "If I go, I won't be back." He straightened, looking at the filth on the front of his jacket and shirt. "But if you ever hope to see me again, you'll get rid of that thing."

Genevieve gathered her temper. Best not leave it in too much of a mess. "Wayne, I don't think this would have worked out anyway." She turned toward the door and held it open. "Tell Sean that I give my regrets." She had it back, her composure.

"Fine," he said, face still tight. He handed her the glass, untasted and now unwanted.

She stood back and watched as he strolled out the door. She closed it after him, not waiting to see him climb into his Lexus. He would have to go home now. He needed to change. She wondered if he would send her the cleaning bill. It would be like him to do that.

She sighed and closed the door. Well, she still had a date for the night. She and Hemingway would have popcorn and a movie. It suddenly sounded more fun anyway.

Chapter 3

Genevieve shut down her computer and heard the comfortable whir of the fan slowing. The work day was done; and now it was time to head home. She had promised Hemingway she would be chasing after Jack if he hadn't shown in a few days, and it was nearly a week and a half. She knew she needed a plan, so she had gone to her boss at the lab two days before to get the ball rolling.

"You want to go on vacation?" The incredulity in his voice had said more than his words.

"Yes. I'm just closing down the Norzan study; the preliminary report will be on your desk by the end of the day. From what I understood, the clients didn't need the final report for another four weeks."

"But you're planning on going on vacation?"

She looked at him, feeling a thread of impatience. True, her last vacation had been a few years ago, but his reaction was totally uncalled for.

"Genevieve, do you realize the last time you missed a day of work was two years ago? And the last time you had a vacation was, well, according to HR, you've never taken vacation." He sat back in his cushioned office chair, which made a squeak of protest. His short broad fingers knit behind his head as he leaned back to look at her, pit stains in full view.

"I was off for Christmas," Genevieve responded slowly, her mind scrambling back. Had she not been on vacation since she had started the job?

"That was the usual holiday break. This is a real vacation, right?"

"I'm going to Florida. So yes, I'm calling it my vacation," she responded firmly.

"You have months of time built up, and if the latest report is in, then you're welcome to go. You're correct about our due date. We still have some time before turning in the final numbers, but when they hit it will be all hands on deck." He nodded, almost to himself, "besides, I have Larry and Rick to answer any questions if they come up."

"You almost sound like you'll be glad to be rid of me," she said frowning. Her boss, Bob, was also ten years her senior, permanently sweating, and the nicest guy she knew. She couldn't resist teasing him just a bit.

"I am positive the wheels will keep turning without you," he said calmly.

She knew he was right. Larry was another one of those guys, a heck of a nice guy, solid and dependable and would have her back if anything did pop up. In his middle forties, he had been around long enough to put out any fires, and with one daughter in college and another in a small private high school, he knew that the success of the study would help firm up that financial backing he needed to complete the girls' education.

Rick was younger, a little more of a loose cannon, but wildly intelligent. He had worked his butt off to make the study go, and she was confident he would do anything to make sure it stayed in the green. Rick had a plan in mind, a plan that involved moving up the corporate ladder, of big offices and bigger wallets. He wouldn't let the project fail.

"You have my cell phone number if something comes up," she said, her hand automatically going to her pocket to feel for the familiar lump of her phone. Leaving, even at this point in the project, was difficult for her. She knew the business. It was true their research was going to cause a shock wave in the pharmaceutical business. Not a big one, but enough of a stir to make some big names sit up and take notice. She certainly didn't want to hurt their chances of seeing the project through.

"I do," her reassured her. "Just have a nice time. Relax. Put your feet up. Get a tan."

She nodded, but in her mind she was already mapping out her little trip. Operation 'Find Jack' was already started. She had gone through maps, downloaded names and numbers for all of his friends, and had gone to her mother's to pick her brain.

"I'll try," she promised.

And now the computer was closed up, the office door was locked, and her files carefully locked away as well. The information was confidential, and worth no small amount of money, in truth. But the work would go on without her, and she had made it to the parking lot. She hesitated at her car door. In the sunshine, the concrete and glass edifice looked exactly like what it was, a pharmaceutical laboratory. But it was home to her from 8 til 5, or 6, maybe 7 or 8 when she was busy, and let's face it, she liked her job. She liked the order, the systematic examination, the one day at a time. It was a routine she thrived in, and just the idea of heading out by herself, driving to Florida with only a giant bird at her side, had her shivering just a little.

And that was aggravating. She was an excellent driver. Her car was in top shape, just back from its monthly tune up. She had already made reservations for the little hotel she would stop in on her way down, right outside of Atlanta. It had a five-star rating and an excellent reputation, the perfect selection according to her research.

She used the unlock button on her key fob and listened to the musical beep. She was ready.

Genevieve had just finished her second cup of coffee and was feeling utterly content when a knock sounded at the door. She stood as Hemingway gave an enthusiastic, "Hello."

"I've got it," she said to the bird, smiling at herself. Silly. He was making her act downright silly.

When she opened the door she totally anticipated her mother standing on the other side, long gray hair in a ponytail braided down her back. The visits were common and always welcome. Her mother had a habit of stopping by once during midweek and then again over the weekend if Genevieve hadn't made her way out to visit her childhood home. Now her mother breezed in with

18

a hint of sunshine and the smell of herbs clinging to her skin. The peasant dress that she wore was typical of the half dozen she owned, and she was likely to have another half dozen in storage. Her mother bought them in bulk from a local seamstress who specialized in patchwork quilts, knitted sweaters, and restored vintage clothing. The fact that her mother still wore the hippie clothes she had sported in the 60's was just one of the little details of Genevieve's childhood she had dealt with.

What threw her was the tall man standing next to her mother, his light brown hair curled attractively to his nape, his big hands tucked into the pockets of jeans that had seen better days.

"Mom?" Genevieve stood in the doorway, still glancing at the man as her mother closed in, arms open for a hug.

"Baby," her mother said, the scent of growing green things enveloping her. She pulled back, holding Genevieve by her upper arms. "You look wonderful."

Genevieve sighed. As strange as her upbringing had been, there had always been an excess of love.

"I brought someone to meet you," her mother continued with that breezy way she had, easily maneuvering her way past her daughter, bringing with her the strange man. "Let's go on in. I'll put some tea on."

She was being manipulated, Genevieve had no doubt. But as aware of the situation as she was, she also knew with a sinking feeling she wasn't going to win this one.

"Sure," she said faintly, following the two of them into the house and closing the door.

Her mother headed unerringly to the kitchen. Almost every memory Genevieve had of her mother centered around that particular room of the house. Even if she was thinking of her mother puttering in the garden, her hands black with soil, it was for the privilege of harvesting the herbs and vegetables that would be transformed into something magical when they ended up in the kitchen. Memories of sitting on the porch in the cool mornings, hot tea in hand, had again originated in her mother putting the copper kettle on to boil and adding whatever mysterious leaves she needed to make the most delicious steeped brews. Even the honey that had sweetened the tea had come from their own hives for a few years. The living mounds of bumblebees flourishing in the backyard had been yet another adventure she had enjoyed in a childhood full of flex and change, freedom and responsibility.

Genevieve had her own copper pot that her mother found on the top shelf where it perpetually waited. Genevieve herself had long ago switched to the more potent and less healthy caffeinated options that coffee provided, but that hadn't prevented her mother from gifting her with her own teapot when she had moved into her new home. The flavored teas had been dropped off with regularity since then, and when she was feeling especially stressed, Genevieve had succumbed to the lure of home, and made some of the tea, breathing in the fumes as though she were cuddled next to the warmth of her parents.

As the water gushed from the faucet to the pot, Genevieve's mother looked over her shoulder and smiled cat ate the canary style.

"Baby, you know I worry about you traveling alone, and when I mentioned it to Dean here, well he told me he was planning on heading back to Florida. You flew up here, didn't you dear?" She had turned her pale blue eyes from Genevieve to the man who had followed them into the kitchen and was now standing, hip against the counter, watching them with raised eyebrows.

Genevieve frowned. The look was familiar. She and her mother looked nothing alike, and her mother had teased her, calling her their little foundling fairy when she was a little girl. At times, she was almost convinced she had been a changling child, and with Rainbow as her best friend, she was pretty sure she had some strong magic in her. Age had sobered her somewhat.

When she was twelve, she had seen a picture of her paternal grandmother, and the fantasy of her mystical parentage had been blown. She looked just like her father's mother. There was no doubt she was just like any other girl, just as human, just as boring, but never as beautiful as her mother. It had made her angry at the time. She had wanted to look like her mother, with that long pale hair and soft blue eyes. Instead, she had dark brown hair and equally dark eyes, now turning a deep sapphire as her mind raced.

With that thought, she watched her mother, the master manipulator, turn those lovely eyes on Dean.

"Yes, Ma'am, I did."

"Did you get those round trip tickets?"

"No, no, I did not." His voice was delicious, deep, with a tinge of a Southern drawl. Oh, he was charming all right. He was handsome in a careless way. And he was amused.

"Mom," Genevieve interrupted. "I'm sure Dean would like to continue on his trip in peace. He doesn't need to babysit me, and I am perfectly capable of making the trip on my own."

Her mother had moved to the stove and fired up the gas burner, placing the kettle on with a sure confidence. "I know, dear. But I've talked to Dean," her eyes went to the mostly silent man leaning against the kitchen island. "He needs a ride to Florida, and he knows his way around there. He might be able to help you find your father."

Genevieve held her tongue. She knew how her mother worked. The sweet insistence would continue and eventually Genevieve would wear down. It happened almost every time. Almost.

"We can talk about this later," Genevieve said. "Dean, would you like to sit down?" She gestured to the table, and Dean nodded. He was catching on that the conflict was between her mother and her. Luckily, he was smart enough to sit back and watch.

He moved well. Genevieve sighed inwardly. She would bet her mother was counting on this pretty boy to convince her to take someone along on the ride. She knew that her mother wasn't trying for a love match. She just wanted someone to ride along with her daughter, someone big, someone who could help in an emergency.

The tea was steeped perfectly, a tray of sugar cookies was added to the table as if by magic, and they sat down together. The silence had been filled with casual conversation about the weather locally, the weather in Florida, and the difference between the two. Then they talked boats and sailing, beaches and which were the best, all the topics visitors to Florida liked to discuss.

Genevieve was sitting down her cup when she heard a loud squawk from the other room. Revelation. Perhaps she wouldn't have to stop her mother's plans. Perhaps Hemingway would take care of that for her.

Smothering an evil grin, she excused herself and went into the living room. Hemingway was living up to his Rainbow nickname, his feathers puffed up in excitement. No doubt he was hearing the familiar voices and was anxious to join them. And that worked just fine for Genevieve. There weren't that many people Hemingway loved, and she doubted Dean would be his type. She knew the bird well enough she could generally tell if he was going to do something violent to their guest. As long as she was between them, the bird and the man, they both should be safe. However, that didn't mean Hemingway would be quiet. Or nice. Or neat.

She opened the door to the cage and the bird climbed out. When she put out her arm, he stepped up like a total gentleman, climbing closer to her so he could press his feathered head against her chest. She melted a little.

When she strolled into the kitchen with her 'brother', her mother was talking quietly to Dean. Her expression brightened when she saw the bird, and then it changed. Suddenly, Genevieve saw that her mother had been covering her emotions and in reality, she was worried. Worried because Jack's best friend and constant companion was here, and he had disappeared with no word.

"There's our boy," her mom said softly.

Hemingway lifted his head, turning so that his bright eye was studying the people at the table. Genevieve brought him closer, taking him to the chair opposite Dean, flanked by the two women.

"Dean, this is Hemingway." Genevieve looked at the man, searching for a sign of his feelings. "Hemingway, say hello."

The sound the bird produced was somewhere between painful and horrible. Genevieve grinned.

She was ushering her visitors out an hour later, silently cursing her luck, her circumstance, and the fact her mother had so successfully, so completely won that round.

"I thought I told you Dean was an animal lover," her mother had said apologetically after Genevieve had hustled her into the living room to have a private chat.

"No, mom, you didn't mention that," she had hissed, watching as Dean expertly handled the bird, seemingly unintimidated by the giant beak.

And Hemingway, the traitor, had loved every minute of it. He had been overjoyed to see her mother, typical, but had been cautiously friendly to the new man at the table, which definitely wasn't like him. Normally, a new man would need lots of time, and lots of patience to get within beak range of the bird with any confidence of keeping his fingers.

Dean was a natural with animals, and something in his calm assurance was enough to have the big bird relaxing with him.

"Genevieve, you wouldn't think I would send you on this trip with just any man. Dean's mother and I are good friends. I've heard about him for years. He's single, responsible, successful, and Hemingway likes him." Her face was losing some of the sweet motherliness and her tone was threaded with steel. "You don't need to travel all that way by yourself. I don't care how confident you are."

Genevieve grimaced. "Fine," she said softly. "I'll think about it. This doesn't mean I'm going to date him, you know that, don't you? I have a boyfriend." Even as she said it, she flinched. The verb was wrong. She had a boyfriend, but that was definitely past tense. Of course, only with her mom would she call a grown man a boyfriend. There was nothing boyish about Wayne, or Dean for that matter. She let the comment lie for a moment and then added, "But I just want to know one thing for sure, you don't have any other tricks up your sleeve do you?"

Genevieve's mother was still grinning when she returned to the kitchen.

Now she stood in the doorway, lost in thought as she watched Dean walk her mother to the passenger side of the car and open the door for her. She knew for sure that Wayne, for all his starched shirts and polished shoes, did not have that kind of gentlemanly manners. Her mother slid in the seat and Dean shut the door for her, a small smile on his face when he turned toward the door. Genevieve blushed when she realized he had seen her watching. Well there was no help for that. He sketched a wave in her direction, and tipping her chin up, she returned the gesture. It was her house, after all, her mother, her plans.

A demanding squawk from behind her had her turning away from the scene. "Hemingway, you traitor," she muttered under her breath as she shut the front door. Great time for the bird to develop manners.

Chapter 4

"His name is Jack, Jack Glass," she said slowly into the phone, listening to the buzz on the other end of the line. "No, I don't know when he arrived. I'm just trying to figure out if he flew with one of your pilots."

There was a scuffle on the other side of the line. "Looks like a pirate, right?"

"Yes! Yes, that's him. That's Jack." She held her breath. Maybe this was the break she had been waiting for.

"Yeah, I know him. Josh takes him out for rides. Don't know when they went out last though. You're asking about earlier this month?" The man on the other phone spoke slowly as though time had no meaning in his world.

"Yes, I think he might have gone out two and a half to three weeks ago."

"Hmm. Where did you say he was going?"

She huffed out a sigh. "I didn't say. I don't know. All I know is he left town and now I'm trying to track him down."

"On vacation is he? Why don't you wait until he turns back up? Jack gets around."

"I don't want to wait," she protested. "I need to talk to him now. It's important."

"Okay, okay," he mumbled. "Let me get your name and number. I'll talk to Josh when he gets in, have him call you. He can tell you when he last talked to Jack. Where they might have gone. You said you're his daughter?"

She had had to admit that much. The man knew not to give information out to just anyone. Of course, she could have lied, but in this situation, the truth seemed best.

"Sure," she said. "I'll give you my cell phone. I'm going to be leaving town myself in two days." Even the thought of that was enough to make her stomach churn. She had her trip planned down to the minute. She knew exactly where she was going, where she would be stopping, what the mileage was like, where the best restaurants, restrooms, shops, and hotels were. She just didn't know about her traveling companion. She carefully read out her name and number, spelling it out slowly so she knew for sure the man had the right information for her. She thanked him before she hung up, turning to see Hemingway hanging on the cage side.

"Okay, so now for the hard one," she told the bird.

Dean answered after the first ring. That told her he either was waiting for her call, or was one of those techno-centric people that carried their cell phones on their hips and could answer a call like a quick draw artist with a revolver. She doubted the second, so she went with the first.

"Genevieve, I'm glad you called," he said warmly, said it in that voice that could melt the coldest heart. He would make a wonderful salesman. Women would buy whatever product he had to offer just to hear that silky deep sound. And auditory caress, that's what it was. And terribly unfair.

"I didn't know if my mother had been contacting you, and I felt like I should get in touch with you directly," she said feeling her face heat up.

"Well, your mother hasn't actually ever contacted me. It's been a collaboration between your mother and my mother that got the ball rolling. Once your mother heard I was planning on heading back to Florida, and my mother caught on that you would be driving alone, the maternal instincts took over. Those two women can be a pretty formidable pair when they get something in their minds."

"My mom has always been like that." Genevieve felt her muscles easing at the light tone in his voice. "She somehow always manages to get her way without ever seeming to place even the slightest pressure on anyone. It's a gift."

"It's a superpower," he responded and chuckled.

Genevieve was smiling. "So I'm leaving on Monday. I've taken off for my vacation, just a week so far, but my schedule has been cleared for longer if I need it." She paused. "I don't know what you thought of my mother's idea. I don't want you to feel obligated to be my bodyguard. I have made it clear to my mother I would be perfectly safe traveling alone." She paused to take a breath.

"I'm sure you would, but your mother is right. I don't like to fly; hate it as a matter of fact. I would much prefer to drive, so I would be available to ride along with you. I could even take the wheel if you're a trusting sort. I saw your car when we stopped by. It's a beaut. But I totally understand if you'd rather go by yourself, and I can always rent a car." He sighed over the phone. "I don't want you to feel like you have to accept my company, but I'm available."

Genevieve was not a spontaneous person. She had thought about the pros and cons of having Dean ride with her. And after careful consideration, she had decided for sure that the cons outweighed the pros. He was a stranger. There were so many things about him she didn't know, and not the least of them was how safe he was. She was acutely conscious of keeping herself safe. And the long car ride would be uncomfortable with even the closest of friends. To go that far and with someone she barely knew, a stranger really, was crazy. So the answer had to be a firm but polite 'no'.

"Yes," she said, the words slipping from her mouth as though she had absolutely no control of her senses. "Yes, I'd love for you to ride with Hemingway and me."

Carol was Genevieve's closest neighbor and the one she trusted beyond anyone else. She already had a key to the house, but she had instinctively known Genevieve would be more comfortable if they reviewed the instructions in person. When Carol had suggested she come over to take a look at things before Genevieve left, Genevieve had heaved a sigh of relief. It took only a few minutes for them to complete the tour, but Carol stayed for a cup of coffee.

"So this isn't any kind of professional conference?" Carol asked looking skeptical. "No classes, no lab visits, no tours of rival facilities?"

Genevieve smiled. "Um, no. They don't usually have tours set up for these kinds of facilities. No, this is totally a personal trip."

"I gather that this had something to do with the enormous bird in the living room?"

Genevieve hadn't let Hemingway out to visit, although by his behavior, she was pretty sure he would adore Carol. Sometimes he was incredibly easy to win over.

"You might be right," Genevieve admitted. "Hemingway is my father's bird, his constant companion, really. And I need to find out what's going on with him. It isn't like my father to drop off his best friend and disappear, but that's just what he did."

"Oh, Genevieve, I'm sorry. I had no idea it was a family problem," Carol's soft blue eyes filled with concern. "But I'm sure he's fine."

Genevieve smiled a little weakly. "I know. My father is just one of those kind of people. He comes and goes as he pleases, and he doesn't think of what he leaves behind." She bit off any more words before she started sounding petulant. "And thank you for helping me with this," she added.

Carol smiled back, the fine lines on her face rearranging themselves into a beautiful grin. "You know since the boys moved out I have too much time on my hands."

Genevieve nodded. Carol's two boys who were both in their mid-twenties had moved out just a few months ago. Their shared apartment was only a half hour away, but Genevieve knew that Carol missed them desperately. She had complained of time on her hands, so Genevieve had been pretty confident she would enjoy stopping by the house to get the mail, water the plants, and check up on things.

"I appreciate this though," Genevieve insisted. "It would be hard for me to leave without knowing someone was taking care of the house. You know how much of a control freak I can be."

"You like things to be kept nice. I don't see anything wrong with that."

Genevieve nodded. As long as they had been neighbors, they had an agreement, helping one another by trading home improvement pointers, telephone numbers and referrals for good plumbers, roofers, and other professionals. Genevieve had even helped watch over Carol's house when she had gone out of town for a family reunion. Now Carol was returning the favor.

"You know; I've never actually met your father." The words hung out there, and it was up to Genevieve to explain if she wished.

"He's not around all the time. He likes to travel; always has. He kind of blows in, causes all kinds of ruckus, and then blows out. My mother is a saint."

"Your mother is so sweet," Carol agreed. The two women had met on a few occasions, Carol even staying to have a cup of the notorious tea.

"Mom doesn't seem to think there is anything wrong with the way Jack treats us. She has always been perfectly content to be a part time wife. I just think that growing up, it was hard for me to have a part time father." Genevieve didn't like a lot of self-reflection, but when she realized in college that her neatness was headed toward an obsessive/compulsive bent, she had gone to a college therapist to bare her soul. She would never bring it up to her mother. She would never want her to know Genevieve hadn't been just perfectly happy growing up. But the therapy had done her good. It had revealed some little quirks she hadn't realized until she had talked about it with someone who was totally objective. The love hate relationship she claimed to have with the bird, her therapist had commented, might be a little more of a reflection on how she felt about her father. "I love Jack, don't get me wrong," she said hastily. "He's just a force of nature. He loves me, and he loves my mother like crazy, but he'll never be the kind of father that stays at home, fixing things when they break, mowing the lawn, you know, dad stuff."

Carol nodded. "It's hard when you look around at everyone else's lives and they look so good. Suddenly you look around and think, why not me? But you know, there are always things that are going on behind closed doors we don't know about. The grass isn't always greener on the other side."

Genevieve nodded. She knew exactly what Carol had meant. Life hadn't always been fair to Carol and when her husband had died of complications from heart surgery at 36, she had been left with two rambunctious boys to raise and little else.

"I know," Genevieve said and smiled. "Jack is Jack, and I have to get over wishing he was someone else. He isn't going to change, so I need to appreciate his good qualities. But for now, I just want to find him!"

Carol stayed for another half hour, filling Genevieve in about her sons' most recent hiking trip. When she left she had a list of suggestions and phone numbers, all in alphabetical order, written in Genevieve's precise handwriting.

Genevieve had packed her car the night before, and packing up Hemingway was surprisingly easy. He was good at the transfer from the cage to the crate, but Genevieve thought, he probably had done it hundreds of time for Jack.

She was outside of Dean's mother's house by eight in the morning. The August sun was out and shining brilliantly, the temperature comfortable, the tank full of gas. She was ready to go.

Dean must have been standing close to a window because he was opening the door before she had ever switched off the engine. He had a single bag, a duffle that looked like it had been around for many years, worn and scuffed on its canvas sides. He approached the car in loping strides, his long legs eating up the lawn easily. She had opened her car door and gone around to the back when he reached her.

"Good morning!" His smile was bright and in the sunlight with his hair illuminated revealing sparks of gold; he was terribly pretty.

She frowned. That was not a good thing to think about this near stranger.

"Is that your only bag?" she asked, watching as he dropped it unceremoniously into her trunk.

"Yep. That's all I need." The front door of the cozy bungalow popped open, and Genevieve looked back towards the house. An older woman was standing in the doorway, dressed in a bright blue running suit with the University of Kentucky emblem. Her dark hair was softly curled around her face.

"Dean! Did you forget something?" She was smiling, and recognizing the bright grin with dimples, Genevieve realized she indeed resembled her son. She also noted she had met her before as one of the members of her mother's pinochle group that met monthly to gamble away a sliver of their retirement fun-money and share decadent desserts.

Dean had slammed the trunk closed and was looking back toward his mother.

"I don't think I did," he said, but started back towards the house.

His mother approached, a bundle in her hand. "You left something important," she said to her son, her smile turning soft and indulgent, her greenish eyes casting a quick wink. She nodded at Genevieve. "That's Dean," she said and nodding playfully, directing the comment to the younger girl. "He's always forgetting something." She held out what appeared to be a battered wallet, and after Dean took it and stuffed it in his pocket, turned back towards Genevieve. "I'm so glad you decided to take him with you. He's been fussing about the plane ride for days. And this way you'll have some company."

Genevieve nodded, feeling distinctly uncomfortable with her reluctance to take him. His mother's grateful smile made the guilt surge and she had to look away. "Yes, well, it's a short drive." She realized as soon as the words were out she sounded stiff and uptight. But that was how she felt, truth be told. Unconsciously she bit her lip.

"We've got this all under control," Dean teased his mother. "She has the directions tattooed on her back and her attack bird in the back seat. We're bullet proof."

His mother shook her head. "Just so you have everything you need. Do you have cash? Your phone? How about a charger? Do you have plenty of gas?" This last question was directed in Genevieve's direction. The older woman was digging into the pockets of her running pants and pulled out a bundle of money.

Good grief, Genevieve thought as she pulled off a few bills and thrust them into her son's hand. Surely she wasn't paying for gas.

"You pay for the next fill up," she said firmly.

Dean shrugged. "Mom, we have this discussion all the time."

"And I insist," his mother said quickly. "And make sure you stop for meals and walk around a bit. You know that falling asleep while driving is one of the leading causes of car accidents."

"We've got this," Dean insisted. He had shoved the money into his pocket and had closed the distance, catching his mom in a firm hug.

Genevieve saw the other women's arms encircle her son's waist and felt her heart clench. She was an only child, and she knew that moving away from her mother would be next to impossible. This separation must be so hard for Dean's mother.

"I'll call along the way. My phone is charged. I have money. And I love you," Dean said, giving his mother a final squeeze before letting her go.

"Fine," she sniffed in response and gave them a watery grin.

After several more warnings, Dean's mother came up to Genevieve and hugged her too, catching the younger woman off guard.

"We're huggers in our family," Dean's mother explained unapologetically. "And I hope to see you after you get home. You'll have to come to our group one night," she added.

They left her still standing in the driveway, arms crossed over her middle, a forced smile on her face.

Chapter 5

It was an awkward first ten minutes as Genevieve climbed into the car and buckled up. Dean had slid in next to her, his long legs looking a little jammed against the glove compartment. She had always thought that the car had plenty of space, but it seemed to be rapidly shrinking now that someone was in the seat next to her.

Dean seemed to be busy organizing his pockets because he now had out his wallet, the cash his mother had given him, and several other receipts and papers. When he caught her glance, he grinned.

"She always insists I take cash. Stubborn. I've got a nice little account built up for her. Haven't told her about it yet, though."

Genevieve nodded. So that was what he did with the money? She supposed it was a good idea, if he actually meant he was keeping the money in the bank for her to use later. It was none of her business, truthfully. If he needed a little help from his mother, and she was willing to give it to him, then that was fine, she guessed. It occurred to her she actually didn't know much about this man. What kind of job did he have? What did he do when he wasn't visiting his mother? She knew he lived in Florida. How long had he been there? It was obvious he loved his mother, so why had he moved so far away? For a job?

"So do you need to be back to work at any particular time?" she asked, merging into traffic on the southbound interstate.

"No, I've still got a little more time. I don't take a lot of vacations, so when I do, I tend to take a few weeks at a time." He was tucking all of his things back in the bulging wallet.

"Sounds nice," she said vaguely, distracted by the motion of merging into another lane of traffic.

"And your mom said you never go on vacation. She acted like this was pretty unusual for you." He paused, and when she didn't respond, he continued. "You're seriously worried about your father?"

Her attention narrowed and she sighed inwardly. "Jack may be a little unpredictable, but he's always taken excellent care of Hemingway. And he always comes back to visit mom and me. It's not like him to drop Hemingway with no word, no visit or explanation." She shook her head, feeling a little like she was talking to herself. "I just need to make sure he's okay."

"Your dad doesn't live around here?"

She frowned slightly. How to explain. "Jack has an apartment in Florida, where he lives when he's down there, and when he's here, he stays with mom. He travels a lot." Her voice seemed to fade on the words. It had always been Jack's way, this split life.

"So he travels for work?"

Was that true, she wondered. Was that why he traveled? For work. "No," she corrected thoughtfully, "he travels for himself. I mean, at one time it might have been business, but he's retired now. He just does some trading while he's there. That's one way he makes his money these days. Honestly, Jack hasn't had a regular job for years. He's just one of those people who lives by the seat of his pants. He's just been lucky. When he needs money, he just falls into it."

Dean's face was expressionless, but Genevieve hated to think he believed her father was some shiftless loafer. He wasn't. Jack was, just Jack. He did work. There wasn't a job he wasn't willing to take on. He did construction, he did farming, he did restoration, he did buying, selling, trading, and dealing. He was talented and creative. He always had money to share. Perhaps he wasn't wealthy, but he was comfortable, and he always made sure she and her mother had never gone without.

"Jack has made his way through odd jobs for most of my adult life. When I was younger he had more steady work. But now…" she shrugged.

"And Hemingway?"

She was relieved he had changed the topic. Hemingway, while still an oddity of her father, was definitely safer.

"Hemingway has been around since I was a toddler. Jack bought him from a breeder in Florida. It was a total impulse, and we're lucky it turned out as well as it did. We knew nothing about parrots at the time. Mom had grown up with dogs, and Jack had never had any pets. Hemingway was a crazy chance, but Mom ended up falling for him," she broke off hearing the shuffling from the back seat. Hemingway had been in the front next to her for the ride to Dean's house, but she had moved him back when she had stopped by the driveway. She figured the bird was sulking now because he had been unusually quiet.

"You said your mom fell for him, but what do you think?"

"Of Hemingway? He's irritating, loud, messy." She shrugged. "I personally would never have a pet like that." She realized she sounded incredibly prissy and added, "But I can't hold it against him. He's been with Jack for too many years." She smiled a little grimly.

"And Jack is a bad influence?"

She smiled at the thought. Really, the statement was true. Jack was loud and messy. "Maybe," she replied.

"So you aren't exactly like your mother. But it sounds like you're not much like your father either."

She nodded slowly and grimaced unconsciously. "I decided a while ago I wanted to live my own life my own way. So my way hasn't been too much like my parents."

"Yeah, that I understand. I have tried to do the same. I don't really live like my parents did."

Genevieve realized he had been asking all of the questions, and she didn't know anything about him.

"So what about you? How do you live?"

"I have a great rented house close to the beach. I wear shorts almost every day and run on the beach every morning. I have a collection of dogs. It's not exactly how I grew up."

"And you grew up around here? In Kentucky?"

"Um, we started in Georgia when I was little, and moved to Kentucky when I was five."

"So you did grow up in the area mostly," she encouraged. From then the conversation led to which schools he had attended, from elementary to middle and high school, and gradually she realized he had pulled her back into her own story. She wondered what he might be holding back but decided to worry about that. Everyone had things they didn't want to share.

Three hours later, her back was beginning to ache and they opted to try for a short stop. She wanted to get something to drink and walk around for a bit. She worried about Hemingway, but knew she couldn't get him out. She had the strange little harness Jack used when he wanted to take the creature out of his crate, but she knew well she would need to practice putting it on Hemingway before she tried to actually take him outside the confines of a building. She was pretty sure the bird could fly, but she didn't know if he could ever find his way back to her if he did take flight.

She pulled off at one of the many little pit-stop towns that boasted a McDonalds and Dairy Queen, three gas stations set one next to another, and clustered around the interstate as though it was the lifeline to their existence. And perhaps it was, but Genevieve knew that most likely beyond the curve in the road, there was the true town with an elementary school, a line of stately homes and post office.

When they pulled in and parked, she switched off the engine and stood for a moment in the breeze. Hemingway was making some disgruntled sounds in the back, so she swung open the back door and started rummaging through the duffle bag she had left on the floorboards. She needed snacks for him, she decided. She pulled out a little container of pellets mixed with a few seeds. In a baggie she had some slices of apple, and she put the combined goodies in his little travel bowl and slid onto the seat beside him. She closed herself in with him by pulling the heavy car door until the latch engaged. She carefully opened the door to his crate, and making sure he couldn't step out, tucked in the bowl and shut the door. She sat back to watch him for a moment, amused as he approached his snack eagerly.

36

She glanced around and saw Dean's figure in the distance. He was walking slowly, a cell phone to his ear, talking and gesturing as he spoke. So far, he had been a great companion. He carried on a good conversation without being too chatty and was also comfortable with occasional silences. The fact that his voice was the smoothest hum of music was just a bonus. He seemed to be intelligent and had a good sense of humor. So she figured it would work just fine. She doubted they would make it much past Georgia for today. She had already made reservations for a second room in a hotel she had researched. And that was good. They would be comfortable tonight and would be well rested after their drive today, so tomorrow they would make Florida in plenty of time for her to visit at least one, if not more, of Jack's usual haunts.

Of course, she would also need to move into her temporary lodgings since she didn't plan on taking Hemingway everywhere with her. But then again, she was pretty sure the bird would be more of a welcome visitor with Jack's companions than she would be.

As Hemingway finally decided to trust her and eat some of the offerings, she climbed back out of the car. She left the door ajar and let the breeze cool her slightly sticky skin. She took a few nice deep calming breaths, smoothed a few wrinkles out of her pressed shorts, stretched her arms in a slow motion, touched her toes, and she was refreshed.

When Dean returned to the car, she left him to watch Hemingway and ran to the restroom. After she had used the facilities and washed her hands, she stopped to look at her reflection in the mirror.

Her dark hair was smoothed back and tied in a ponytail, her makeup minimal, her clothes a little rumpled from riding so long. But she looked fine. And why did she care about how she looked? She shook her head at her reflection, catching herself in the gesture just as an older lady with a halo of red hair pushed through the door. The woman's darkly outlined eyes widened at Genevieve's movement, and she ducked quickly into a free stall. No talking to herself, Genevieve silently scolded her reflection, and hurried back into the lot.

The hiss of the tires against pavement was starting to have a mesmerizing quality. The sun was finally sliding down to peek behind the tree line, and Genevieve knew for sure it was just past 6:30. She didn't need a watch to tell the time. Her sense of time was impeccable and always had been. Now she wished she didn't know how late it had gotten. A traffic stall due to minor road construction had slowed them down. Then there had been the bottleneck because of a car pulled to the side of the road, and the requisite slowing so that strangers could gawk. Irritating. According to her meticulously researched timeline, she should have made it to the little town just south of Atlanta by now and be sitting down at the restaurant. She had even planned what she was going to order. Of course, she didn't always stick to those precise plans for meals, she wasn't truly OCD, okay, maybe she was a little obsessive compulsive, but she often chose to stick to her plans. It was comforting.

Dean had sunk into a silent thoughtfulness. When he spoke, Genevieve was jolted out of her thoughts.

"You've got to be feeling tired by now. Why don't we stop to get a bite? Then we can drive a little farther."

It occurred to Genevieve she had made the reservations for the night, the two single rooms with a double bed each, but hadn't thought to tell him.

"The hotel! I didn't tell you where we were staying."

"It's fine. I'm sure they still have rooms, if I need to get one. No problems." His voice was mild.

When she glanced his way she saw the quirk of his lips.

"No, I mean, yes, you need one. But I already put in a second reservation for your room," she blushed as she stumbled over the words just a bit.

"Great. That works just fine. So we can stop somewhere close by and then finish the drive after dinner."

"Sure," she said softly. "Good." So she didn't eat at the restaurant she had chosen. That was fine. Where she ate wasn't that important. And then she would make it to the hotel, the highly rated one she had chosen, with no problems. Back on track. "Where do you want to eat?"

"Let's just follow our nose," he responded.

"What?"

He grinned. "We'll just look for something that seems good. Just hunt around until we stumble on a diner or something. Maybe some downhome southern cooking?"

She looked at him doubtfully, but reluctantly agreed.

"If you say so."

They picked a possible area to stop and Genevieve slowed the car. At the end of the exit they turned left at the bottom of the ramp, heading towards the glittering lights of small town America. They hadn't chosen where they were going to stop with any logic; they just followed the road until Dean spotted a dinner that boasted 'mama's fried chicken and mashed potatoes'.

She pulled into the half-filled lot, and she switched off the motor.

"I don't want to leave Hemingway out here in the car," she said frowning. The poor thing had been stuck in the crate for way too many hours.

"No, he goes in with us. He'll be fine in the crate." Dean seemed supremely confident with the statement. Genevieve didn't figure many places would allow animals, even crated ones, but with Dean acting like it was an everyday common occurrence, she figured they might be able to pull it off.

"I guess the worst they can do is make us get our meal to go."

Dean climbed out of the seat, unfolding his long legs and swinging open the back door before Genevieve could protest. Sure, it was her bird, but if he wanted to carry the crate inside, she wouldn't complain.

Wordlessly she swung her door wide and slipped out. Her legs felt heavy. She took a moment to gather her thoughts and stretch her limbs before using the automatic lock on her key fob. Let the excitement begin.

The little restaurant was actually pretty nice. Granted, the floor was slightly sticky and the plastic coated menus had unidentifiable stains, but the sandwich that Genevieve ordered was piled high with tender roast beef and a slab of cheddar cheese. The toasted white bread was almost definitely homemade.

Dean had surprised her. He had chosen an omelet that looked delicious. Cheese and fresh vegetables spilled out of the perfectly finished eggs. When he had caught Genevieve looking at his dish, he had grinned and offered her a bite.

Sharing food was not one of the things she liked to do normally. She worked in a lab, and thus was a little squeamish about the chance of contamination of any sorts. However, she was on vacation, by God, and there were some things that had to be let go. She took a small bite and thanked him.

"This is good!" she exclaimed.

"So you don't go to many mom and pop places?" Dean asked, taking a large bite of the omelet.

"Not really," she admitted. "I have a handful of places I go to routinely at home." She looked thoughtfully at her meal. "I always order the same thing when I go there, too. I mean, I know it's going to be good. I know I'm going to like it. It's just hard for me to switch sometimes."

"Sure," he said mildly, "but you never know what you might be missing if you don't try some different things."

She nodded as the waitress approached and refilled her coffee cup. She had another hour and a half to drive, so she figured the caffeine would be a necessary evil at this point.

As the waitress was straightening, casting a flirtatious little glance in Dean's direction as she stood, Hemingway emitted his characteristic raucous cry and she jumped back, her hand over her heart.

"What is that?" she asked in a strangled voice. Genevieve suspected she would have added some more strong language if she hadn't been currently on the job.

"Sorry," Dean said easily. "That's our companion bird. He had to come in with us. We just couldn't leave him alone in the car." Dean's smile was absolutely mesmerizing. Genevieve realized it might just be of use, though. At least they weren't likely to be thrown out.

"Is that a bird?" The waitress, a twenty something with artificially darkened hair and red lipstick was now bending toward the crate on the floor.

"It's a macaw," Genevieve said. "His name is Hemingway."

"Is he your pet?" The waitress's eyes had risen to Genevieve, then darted to Dean.

"He's mine," Genevieve responded, choosing to avoid the tangled explanation of why she was traveling with her father's bird.

"Oh."

"Your food is very good," Genevieve said, changing the subject and hoping the girl would not ask more questions, and maybe with luck, would move along.

"Um, thanks." The waitress paged through a little pad of receipts and tore out a page, laying it face down on the table. "You can pay whenever you're ready."

Genevieve let out a sigh as she walked away, and Dean leaned over with a chunk of his meal to give to the bird. "You were a very good boy," he told the bird, and Genevieve heard a laugh in his voice.

"He scared her half to death."

"He just wanted a little attention. Maybe a little bite of our meal?" Dean glanced up, a lock of hair falling attractively over his forehead.

"He's rotten," Genevieve said, but her tone had softened.

Chapter 6

The final leg of their journey seemed twice as long as any other part. When they finally pulled up to the hotel, Genevieve could feel her shoulders sagging with relief. Driving wasn't easy, especially if you weren't accustomed to sitting still that long, concentrating, and worrying at the same time about what the guy in the seat next to you thought of your driving, or your hairstyle, or your conversation. She hadn't been so self-conscious for years. Normally at the lab, she was supremely in control. She kept her hair in a bun, her lab coat pristine and pressed, slacks and blouses that hugged her frame, and her mind was on the work and little else. Sure she had friends she went to lunch with, that she talked with or took breaks during the day with. But for most of her time, she was the boss, and she was running the show.

Now she was doing the same. After all, they were in her car, she was driving, she had mapped out the route, and she had chosen where they would stop and when. She could admit she was a control freak, but it worked for her. Granted, the dinner hadn't been according to plan, but it had turned out to be just fine, and she was glad they hadn't decided to go on.

Now the hotel rose with a sleek stucco façade. The lights were artfully placed at the base of tropical plantings, and the door was open and welcomingly lit from within. Genevieve sighed with relief. She was here. They were finally here.

She pulled up close to the door and put the car in park. They climbed out together, leaving Hemingway in his crate still buckled in the back seat. She locked the door after them and strolled toward the doorway. Dean held the door open for her and she passed by him.

Check in was easy and quick, all computerized with tidy little key cards. Their rooms were across the hall from one another, not because they had requested it, but out of coincidence only. Genevieve was relieved actually. Then she scolded herself for falling into her mother's way of thinking. She was perfectly capable of taking care of herself. She didn't need any man; she didn't need anyone to be caring for her.

She and Dean returned to the car with their keycards in their hands to get luggage and Hemingway. She hadn't wanted to leave him in the car, but parked under the trees as it was with the windows rolled down to let in the faint evening breeze, he was fine. Besides, when she had made the reservations, she hadn't included the fact that she had a parrot with loads of attitude and an incredible ability to destroy furniture. She knew the hotel might frown upon this kind of visitor, but she figured she could keep him busy enough for the evening, and when night came, she would crate him again.

Dean carried his duffle bag only. He packed lightly, he explained, and then grabbed Hemingway's crate with easy grace. She had her bag, perfectly packed for maximum efficiency and her purse, which was equally orderly. She took out the bags as well as Hemingway's supplies and joined Dean. Together they went back into the hotel and walked directly across the lobby and down the hall. The last thing she needed was for Hemingway to let loose one of his earsplitting calls, so she hustled along as though to urge Dean to walk just a little faster.

Once in the hall, she used her card and listened to the smooth click as the lock disengaged.

"Okay, so I planned that we would head out around 7. Does that sound alright with you?" she asked Dean as she stood in the doorway.

"Sure," Dean replied. "Do you want me to put him in your room?"

Her hands were full so she nodded and stepped back so he could duck in around her. The rooms were just like she liked them, neat and almost sterile. The walls were painted a bland beige, but were unmarked. The smell of cleaner was in the air, and judging by the mingled aromas, the snow-white bedding had been bleached to a higher level of cleanliness. Another uncomfortable side effect of working in a lab, she knew the potential microscopic companions that lurked in hotel bedding, so the type of cleanser was important to her.

Dean took the crate to the desk which was laid out with brochures and mysterious slips of paper labeled for their convenience. He slid the crate on the top and bent to look in at Hemingway.

"You'll be okay for the night?"

Dean didn't look tired, but she felt exhausted and wanted nothing more than to turn in for the night. He was astute enough to read it on her face, so he slipped out, leaving her in the comfort of solitude.

Blessed peace, she thought with relief. Except for Hemingway. The bird had been pent up for the entire day, so Genevieve took pity on him and let him out. After giving him fresh food and water which she laid out on the desk, she unpacked a few of her belongings, laying her plastic encased toothbrush next to her tiny bottle of toothpaste, placing the little sample bottles of her own shampoo and conditioner in the spacious shower, adding all the other items she would need for bathing, and lastly digging out her nightgown to wear.

She looked at Hemingway as he serenely sat on the desk and considered leaving him there. But no, if there was a backfire of an engine, or an errant knock on the door, he might startle and take flight, running into windows or mirrors.

When she bent and told him to step up, he obediently put one clawed foot on her hand, and then followed it with the other, using a slight flapping of his glorious wings to help him balance. She took him into the bathroom with her and looked around the marble sink top. She knew what Jack would do. Jack would take the bird into the spray right along with him. He had always had the bird perched on the curtain rod when he bathed, and sometimes Genevieve had done the same when she was in elementary school and the novelty of having her feathered friend flapping and squawking above her hand been fun.

When she got older, she had seen the bird as part and parcel of the whirlwind that was Jack, and she had become disenchanted with them both.

Now she switched on the water, and using her free hand, had the bird step up again so she could put him on the rod that bridged one side of the tub to the other. Hemingway stepped onto the curtain rod as though they had done it a hundred times before and immediately fluffed his feathers as the spray touched him.

She climbed into the tub and closed the shower curtain, careful not to shake the bird from his perch. For a long moment she just luxuriated in the heat. She usually took quick showers, fifteen minutes including shaving her legs. She was efficient in that as well as everything else she did. But tonight was different. She was bone tired and the worry, although she didn't want to admit it, was wearing on her. She had checked her phone a hundred times today, and not once had she seen Jack's number appear. He had, for all intents and purposes, vanished as soon as he had packed up and sent the bird to her. And she wanted to know just where he had gone and why he had left with no explanation, no warning, and no plans for his return.

After a prolonged bathing session where she splashed the bird a little and smiled as the water beaded up on Hemingway's feathers as though he were studded with pearls, they both left the shower. She had put on her nightgown and wrapped her hair in a towel. She padded barefoot over to her suitcase and pulled out a pair of fluffy socks. She added those to her outfit, and then sank on the bed with the bird still slightly damp and wrapped in his own towel. He shook off the cloth with a quick birdy shudder and strutted across the bedspread. She had pulled it down to the bottom of the bed and folded it neatly before going into the bathroom, as was her habit. She would replace it in the morning when she made the bed. Foolish, she knew, to make the bed when someone would be in to change it in a few hours, but she couldn't stand to leave a room with the bed unmade.

She leaned back against the headboard for a moment, closing her eyes. It was almost 10:30, early yet for sleep, but that's exactly what she felt like doing. And really, they were planning on an early morning so perhaps she should grab her rest while she could.

Hemingway had made it to her lap, and, like a puppy, had cuddled his head against her stomach. She smiled again and gently stroked his feathers. His dark eyes surrounded by thin white skin lined with tiny red feathers closed with pleasure. She felt her own eyes do the same.

She woke just an hour later, finding the bird still sleeping on her lap, and her head turned at an odd angle making her neck ache. She gently picked Hemingway up and took him back over to the desk. She couldn't let him have the run of the room. Luckily, in his sleepy state, Hemingway went docile and quiet into his crate, and Genevieve latched it behind him.

After she settled back in her bed and laid down, pulling the covers up to her chin, she found that although she was still incredibly tired, sleep just wouldn't come. She lay awake in the dim light, listening to the dry shuffles of the bird as he settled down. The far off sound of motors made her turn her head, but instead of them retreating into the distance, the sound grew louder.

She frowned. How inconsiderate! The drumming of the powerful engines was now very close, and she surmised they must be residents as well. She sighed. But at least now that they were here, they would turn off whatever machine was making such a racket and come inside. Except they didn't. The sound continued, waxing and waning as the vehicles circled the parking lot, but still uncomfortably loud in the darkness. Genevieve slid out of bed and padded over to the window. From her first floor vantage, she could see the stab of a headlight as a trio of motorcycles swept around the lot. What were they waiting for? She watched in silence as the lights dimmed and disappeared only to slide into sight again as they rounded the corner. She counted five slow rotations before she heard the distant laughter rising above the sound of the engine. They weren't parking at all. They were just having fun, riding their toys out in the parking lot for the fun of it, unmindful of the people trying to sleep inside.

Genevieve checked the clock. It was after midnight now. Her plans for getting up early to start the remainder of their drive were looking less and less appealing. She thought about calling the front desk to complain, after all, it had been more than a half hour now since she had woken to hear the noises, but just as she went up to the hotel phone on the bedside table, the engines started to cut off, first one and then the others.

In the blessed silence, she breathed a heavy sigh of relief and headed to bed. And then she heard the laughter. It wasn't a cheerful sound, not happy at all, but rather mocking. The next sounds were the raised voices of people arguing, a harsh angry conversation. The words were slurred but the tone was not. An occasional curse could be heard above the general shouting. Men's voices, angry voice, probably drunken voices seemed to slip through the window and into her room as though there was nothing blocking the sound at all.

She thought about putting a pillow over her head, but then decided she would try to drown out the sound with some white noise. Without turning on any other lights, she went to the bathroom and switched on the exhaust fan. The sound was a low buzz, enough perhaps to cover some of the noise, but still quiet in its efficiency. She sighed. It was the best she could do for now.

As she slid back under the covers, she heard the voices moving. Good. Maybe they were coming inside, going to their rooms to sleep off whatever they had to drink. But her hope wasn't going to be granted. They rowdy crowd moved the arguments from the parking lot into the lobby, and from there into the hallway. Next, doors were opened, some slammed closed, but the raised voices now filtered in through the walls and door instead of the window. They had taken the fight into their rooms and were continuing at full volume.

Genevieve closed her eyes tightly trying to ignore the sounds. But it went on and on, and she wondered if the people were ever going to give up and go to sleep, or pass out, if anything would make them shut up!

The clock was reading 1:00 AM and the crowd added music to their arguing. She assumed they were still fighting given that the doors were still opening and slamming closed, their voices strident. She was so tired, and her head was starting to ache. She tried to ignore the sounds and thought again about calling the desk. Surely they could hear all of this! She couldn't be the only one lying awake in the dark.

She heard the police come next. There was a single whoop of the siren as though informing every one of their arrival and then the added voices. The banging on the doors sounded different this time. There was the ring of authority in the tones the newcomers used, and the music was cut off abruptly.

She listened with a little more interest to the fight now. The former opponents were now united against the officers and were complaining with indignation. Only a word or two was clearly audible, but it was enough for her to understand what they were saying.

She wasn't sure if the police actually arrested any of the crowd, but after only a half hour of debate, a blessed quiet descended on the hotel. She rolled over and looked at the clock. It was 2:17 in the morning. She groaned quietly and laid on her side, willing sleep to come quickly. And of course it didn't, the last scene registering in her tired brain was the hotel clock glowing 3:07.

The sound that woke her was terrifying, a loud cry followed by the furious flapping of an angry bird. She jolted upright and looked over to the crate. It was still there on the desk, but now it was vibrating with movement from the creature within. Hemingway was scared or angry, and he was making a racket.

"Stop, bird," she moaned, and stumbled to her feet. She was at his little crate in a second, debating whether or not she should let him out even if it wasn't time to get up yet when she saw the crimson splotches on the brochures she had left next to the crate. She bent close in confusion until it registered that she was seeing blood.

"Hemingway?" she said, her voice catching as she pulled the latch free. The bird rushed out, and she could see the blood. It was smeared on the sides of the crate, it darkened his feathers in patches, and a line of it was on the pale skin next to his beak. "Oh, no," she breathed. She knew enough about birds after having him in her life for so long to know that bleeding wasn't good. The animals just weren't large enough to survive much blood loss. And from the look of it, he had lost some blood and was continuing to bleed.

She picked him up hurriedly and held him against her chest as she looked around the room. She snatched the towel off the chair and headed to the door. They needed a vet. If he was bleeding, they needed help now. Her father hadn't left her with any supplies to take care of the bird, and now this.

She was across the hall before she realized where she was going, using her free hand to slam on Dean's door. She hadn't stopped to put on clothes, and stood in her granny nightgown, her hair wild.

He pulled open the door after a muffled, "wait a second," and some corresponding shuffling in his room. When he peered out at her, his normally smooth hair was mussed and he wore just a pair of sweatpants, with bare feet and bare chest.

She didn't have time to check out his attire, however, and burst, "Hemingway is bleeding!"

"Okay," he said calmly, and before she could say anything more, held out his hands and took the bundled bird and towel from her. She numbly noticed she had smears of blood on her fingers and the back of her hand.

Dean took Hemingway into the room and started unwinding the towel. With sure fingers, he picked through the bird's feathers. "He broke a blood feather," he said matter of fact. "Can you get my shaving kit from the bathroom? I have some tweezers in there and some blood clotting powder."

She nodded and automatically went into the bathroom, which was a mirror image of the one in her room. Sitting on the sink where she would have left her miniature bottles of lotion and face cream was a battered leather bag, gaping open revealing messily squeezed toothpaste, a toothbrush wrapped in a plastic lunch bag, a comb, deodorant, and other necessities. At the bottom of the bag was a small tin that said "quick stop" on the lid and a pair of no nonsense tweezers. She took both to Dean and watched amazed as he deftly found the broken feather that still had a blood supply to it, used the tweezers to yank it out quickly, and applied the powder to the wound.

"How did you?" She lost her voice as she realized the bird was calming, eyeing Dean cautiously and settling in his hands. It looked like Hemingway was going to be fine and her heartbeat was finally beginning to slow.

"I'm a vet, remember?" he asked, his brows raised almost to the lock of hair falling over his forehead.

"You're a vet?" She couldn't have heard that right.

"Yes," his voice was low and soothing as he gently wrapped the bird in the towel again and held him towards her. "You hold him for a minute. Be calm. You'll help settle him down."

She took the frail bundle from him and cuddled Hemingway close to her again. "You're a vet," she said again.

"Sure." A dawning realization came to his eyes, and his lips slowly curved into a devastating smile. "Didn't your mother tell you?"

"No," she said a trifle grimly. But it certainly explained a few things. Like why her mother was sure he would make the perfect traveling companion for she and Hemingway, and why he hadn't blinked when she had presented him with the enormous bird on that first day. It felt like a maternal set up.

"Hmm, she must have forgotten to mention it," he observed. The smile still quirked one side of his mouth as he watched her hold the bird. "We'll make sure the clotting holds," he said after a moment, "and then I'll clean him up." He seemed to see her for the first time and the smile became a grin. "So what happened to you?"

"What happened to me?" she almost growled. "Besides the bird waking me up at the crack of dawn with his panicked screaming? And the noise that went on half the night." Seeing his puzzled expression, she shook her head. "Didn't you hear those idiots outside last night?"

"A little, but I can sleep through almost anything. Comes from sleeping on a cot in the office while all of the critters settle down."

"Well I didn't go to sleep until three and now it's," she looked over his shoulder to see the alarm clock on the bedside table next to his rumpled bed. "It's six," she said, and almost cried. She hadn't gotten three hours sleep in all, and now it was time to get up and get ready for the rest of the trip.

"What time are we set to leave?" he asked casually, running a hand through his rumpled hair. The movement made his chest and arm muscles flex in a very interesting way.

"Seven," she said wearily. She was so tired she couldn't even enjoy the view.

"But we don't have to leave at seven," he said gently, "right?"

She purposely avoided the question and found herself looking at her bloodied hands contrasted against the white of the towel. She grimaced in distaste and her stomach rolled a little with the sight. "Can I go wash up?"

"Sure," he said. "I'll take our friend."

She handed the bird over again feeling a little like she was abandoning a hurt child. But at least she knew Dean would be able to take care of the bird. And far better than she could.

She went back into the bathroom and turned on the sink, adding the hot water generously, until she could feel the warmth sink into her skin. As she used the little unwrapped slab of soap that the hotel had provided, she watched the suds turn pink with the bird's blood and felt a little sicker. It could have so easily been a disaster. It was a miracle the bird had done so well with Jack and all of his adventures. She finally turned off the water and glanced up at herself in the mirror. Oh Lord, she hadn't considered how she looked when she had rushed out of her room. Her hair fell in tangles down her back, and her eyes had dark circles under them that contrasted nicely with her chalk white complexion. Without makeup, she was ghostly. And to make matters worse, there were streaks and smears of blood on her oversized nightshirt, not a lot in any one spot, but enough of the rust colored stains on the floral patterned cotton to look like she had just been an active participant in a bloody crime.

Great, just great.

She gave up any idea of improving her appearance and returned to the room. Dean was sitting on the side of the bed, cuddling the bird and talking to him. The television had been switched on and some early morning sports show was playing softly in the background.

"Why don't you go back to bed for a while? There is no way you should be driving when you're going on that little sleep. We have the rooms until 11."

She thought about her neat schedule, ruined. But then she thought of the hours on the road and knew he was right. For her to drive feeling like she did just now was stupid and dangerous.

"But Hemingway," she said softly.

"I'll keep him here. I need to watch over him anyway."

"Are you sure?"

He smiled. "Go. Rest. I'll keep him until you're ready to pack up."

She nodded, not even thinking about arguing the wisdom of his plan. So they would be later getting in Florida. At least they had a better chance of making it safely.

"Thanks," she said, pushing her hand through her hair.

"Sure," he responded and followed her to the door.

Wordlessly, she went out the door and across the hall to her own. She realized then that she had been lucky her door hadn't sprang shut behind her and locked her out. With a final sigh, she closed the door behind her. After changing into a fresh nightgown, she crawled back under the covers.

Chapter 7

At 11:00 she woke automatically. It was a knack she had, being able to set an internal alarm that unerringly woke her. She never overslept, and she was rarely late for anything. Being late might lead to rushing, and rushing led to mistakes. She would not tolerate mistakes.

Now she climbed out of bed and took a quick hot shower, back to her usual brisk pace. After she was dressed and packed, she went across the hall to check on Dean and Hemingway.

Dean opened the door as soon as she knocked, and she smiled when she saw the bird perched comfortably on the back of the desk chair, as regal as ever.

"He looks good," she said to Dean, crossing to the bird and giving his cheek an affectionate rub.

"He's fine. Recovered well and he only bit me a little bit when I tried to check him."

"Oh, did he get you!" Genevieve exclaimed, chagrined that the parrot would hurt someone who was trying to help him.

"Didn't break the skin, and I'm used to it by now. Unlike most humans, my patients bite. It's part of the hazards of working with them."

"Well, I'm sorry he was acting like that. Sometimes he seems like he has very little common sense. Biting the hand that feeds you." She shook her head as she directed her words to her avian companion. "Bad manners and bad language. That's what Jack has been teaching you."

Dean just smiled at the comments.

Genevieve pulled her gaze away from his admittedly attractive smile and looked around the room. While her room looked as though no one had actually slept in it, bed made neatly, towels folded on the side of the tub, furniture all pushed back in exactly the same positions she had found it, the chair lined precisely with the legs of the desk, Dean's space did not fare so well. There were towels in a crumpled heap on the floor at the foot of the bed, probably a little bloodstained from the bird's injury, and his sheets and blankets were still rumpled in a comfortable nest she had roused him from when she had barged into his room with Hemingway. The desk chair was pulled out and moved in front of the television, presumably so that the bird could perch there and see the flashing screen. The television still droned in the background, and the remote was tossed in the center of the unmade bed. Luckily, Dean had at least gathered his belongings, and his bag were packed and placed by the door.

"Are you both ready to go?" she asked. She had taken a few additional minutes to rinse out the crate to get rid of the bloodstains, and it sat open in her room. She wasn't sure how happy Hemingway would be to be loaded back in the carrier, but there was no way she could allow him to be loose in the car. If they were in an accident, he would never survive the impact, not to mention the fact that he might distract her with his movements.

"Sure. He's fine, I'm fine. We've been watching the sports channel. We don't agree on teams, but we've decided it's easier to agree to disagree."

She looked at him with raised eyebrows but made no comment. He was funny that way, making casual jokes, supremely relaxed and seemingly sure of himself even in the face of what could have been a disaster of a night.

"Okay, well, I can grab his crate if you think he's okay to go back in."

Dean nodded. "He'll fine. The bleeding stopped almost immediately. I've checked him a few times since."

She ducked out of his room and returned to her own. There she gathered her packed bag, purse, and the crate, and took them all out into the hallway. She closed the door behind herself, honestly relieved to be leaving this place. It would have been a fine place to stay, just like she had planned, had it not been for outside circumstances. Who could have predicted that a rowdy bunch of motorcyclists would have decided to end their party here? And even the police coming hadn't quieted them down completely. And of course, Hemingway could have panicked at any of their stops, injuring himself. His accident had absolutely nothing to do with where they were staying at the time. But even so, she was happy to hear the finality of the click of her door closing as she went back into Dean's room.

He had left his door slightly ajar and was gathering the few belongings he hadn't already packed, stuffing his wallet into his hip pocket and unplugging his cell phone. When she set the crate down on the floor, he went over to the bird and expertly had him step up onto his arm and then into the crate as though they had done it a hundred times before. Hemingway may have loved her, but he obeyed Dean much more easily than he did when she asked him to do something.

Checkout was completed by noon, and by the time they had hit the road, her stomach was aching because she was so hungry. They stopped at a local sandwich shop on their way to the interstate and both bought a wrapped sub sandwich to go. Their meal was a quick fifteen minutes in the parking lot, giving Hemingway a stray crust and bits of veggies, and then they topped off the gas tank, Dean insisting on pumping the gas and paying.

The afternoon sun was a little hazy as they got back on the interstate, the sun shimmering in a veil of high clouds. The clouds thickened as they drove, and by two o'clock, the sky was darkening with blanketing gray and the threat of rain.

"We're due for a toad floater," Dean commented, referring to the weather app on his cell phone.

"A what?"

"Toad floater. Lots of rain."

"Hmm," she responded. They had gotten out of southern Georgia just thirty minutes before, and she could feel the difference already. Florida had that kind of heat that soaked into the earth and seemed to rise, consistent and ever present. The roads were gradually beginning to flatten out, and the dense vegetation had taken on more of a tropical look, with palm trees interspersed between giant oaks hanging with a webbing of Spanish moss.

"You have to watch the rain here in Florida. It comes up hard and fast. But it doesn't last as long as the rain up north, at least not usually."

She nodded. She had visited here often enough to know the weather patterns were different from home. That didn't mean she wasn't startled when the first big plops of rain hit her windshield, leaving spatters that spread as broad as her handprint before she turned on the wipers. The deluge continued, and she gritted her teeth and switched on her headlights to try to combat some of the dense rain.

"You might want to turn on your emergency lights," Dean observed, his voice raised to be heard over the rattle of the rain and the buzz of the tires. "Helps the people behind us see the car."

She nodded tensely and hit the button, watching the steady blink that signaled that the lights in the front and back of the car were flashing their warning. She had slowed to a steady pace, and cursed silently as a few cars flew by her. In the right lane, she approached a line of slower moving traffic but decided not to go around them. Instead she hung back, watching the glow of their taillights as they guided the way through the torrent and puddles of water.

Their pace was set and steady and she relaxed slightly. The rain waxed and waned, sometimes lightening into a heavy drizzle, then becoming more intense again. The sky seemed to be clearing in the distance. As the rain struck in a last rush of heavy rain, a tumble of dark rubber caught her off guard, and before she could dodge the obstacle, it was under her wheels, hitting the undercarriage and body of the car with hard thuds and bumps.

She cursed out loud this time as she felt the steering wheel tremble in her hand, but she kept the car from swerving into the other lane. Now her heart was thudding with the rain, and she could hear another noise, a broken sound, coming from beneath her.

"Something's wrong!" she cried out.

"It's okay. There's an exit right here. We'll go on down to the nearest gas station. She'll make it that far."

Genevieve white knuckled it until she pulled off onto the exit and then slowed to a crawl as she pulled onto the county road. Finally, the rain had let up enough for her to see. The town reminded her of the one she had visited to see her grandmother years ago, a widening of the road with two fast food restaurants near the exit, two competing gas stations, but the promise of more civilization just a half mile down the road.

She pulled into the first gas station, something no-named and locally owned and shut down the car's engine. Her hands were shaking. She knew her neat little plan had met a severe snag.

The gas station they had chosen had only that, gas, and some snacks, soda, and other caffeinated beverages to keep truckers on the road. It did not have any type of mechanic, but the guy manning the register knew someone. Of course. So with the small town wheels rolling, word got out to Buck, from Buck's Auto, that some motorists needed a tow and repairs. It seemed that the slab of mysterious material on the highway had actually been a blown tire from some eighteen-wheeler.

"Happens more than you think," Buck assured them as he hooked up her car to the tow truck, leaving it dangling like a stranded fish on a line. "Smaller cars hit the reinforced tires, and it wrecks the undercarriage. We'll have to take a closer look, but I imagine we can get this fixed for you pretty quick."

Genevieve nodded a little weakly. She was standing in front of the little gasoline station store, her bags at her feet. Dean had Hemingway in one arm and his duffle slung comfortably over his shoulder.

"You guys can climb in the back," Buck continued, a drop of heavy rain sliding from the rim of his ball cap to fall in a warm splat on the already soaked pavement. "I'll take you into town, and you can find somewhere to hang out unless you want to just stay at the garage with me."

"How long do you think?" Genevieve began, but she knew in her gut he was unlikely to have an idea what repairs would run until he got a closer look at her car.

"Well, ma'am, I'll get a better idea when we get 'er up on the lift, but I can tell from the way she's leaning a little that we're going to likely have to replace that bumper. It's not likely to go back like it should."

"So you'll need to order that part?" Dean's voice was even as he shifted in place, Hemingway scuttling around in the crate with a squawk of impatience.

"Yep, looks like." Buck's eyes had slid from Genevieve with her hair hanging damply down her back, her once crisp blouse and jeans now wilted in the damp, to Dean and his companion. "So that's a macaw, right?"

"Yes," Genevieve said cautiously.

"My grandpap used to have one of those. He was blue and gold." Buck's eyes went to Dean. "Good luck with that," he said, a smile just touching his lips.

"Yeah, they are a challenge, sometimes," Dean said, reading the message behind the words. "So if you have to order the part, how long does it usually take to get it in?"

"Depends on the make and model," Buck responded, "sometimes a few days, sometimes a week."

Genevieve felt the breath whoosh from her chest. This was not good. There was no way this was going to end well. "But," she began, but Buck was turning back towards the truck.

"We'll know more in a bit," Buck said throwing open the back door of the extended cab and ushering them inside.

Genevieve closed her mouth and nodded. One thing at a time, she reminded herself, and climbed up in the seat.

The back of a truck cab proved to be much tighter a space than any of their previous situations, and Genevieve found herself tucked up next to Dean with no space between them. The bags were piled around them, and Buck's assistant who had remained in the truck for the entire time, still sat in the front seat, unmoving and silent. He was a gangly youth, somewhere in his early teens, and appeared to be immersed in the music that could be heard scratching through his earbuds.

Genevieve had stuffed her bag at her feet and had her purse in her lap. Dean's bag was similarly tucked next to his tennis shoes and Hemingway's crate, which hadn't looked so large in the back of her car, now seemed to take up every extra inch of space. Dean had shifted until his one arm was along the back of the seat, his other arm steadying the crate. They were pressed close, hip-to-hip, but Genevieve couldn't say she minded. The rain had given her a bit of a chill, and his warmth felt good through her damp clothes. He smelled good too, which was more than she could say for the hard working Buck.

The engine of the truck roared to life and they were off, settling into a slow pace, headed for the garage. The little town itself wasn't much larger than the off ramp extension. There was a grocery store, a cleaners, a little strip of shops locally owned, one selling Avon, and a few restaurants boasting homemade goods. Genevieve was sure they would end up dining in one of those before the day was over.

At the garage, Buck expertly maneuvered the truck and its catch into a space and threw the engine into park. "If you all want to wait in the room over there," he gestured to a wide glassed-in room with a plastic sofa and low coffee table, "I'll get a look at her and give you a ballpark estimate."

Genevieve and Dean climbed from the truck with their bags in tow and went into the waiting area. It smelled of cigarette smoke and burned coffee. She hesitated before sitting in one of the six straight-backed chairs pushed up against the wall. She knew there would be a wait. She checked her watch and then pulled the cell phone from her pocket. There were no messages from her mother, and worse, no note from Jack. Still no word. Still no relief from the worry. Jack wasn't a great communicator. She would spend weeks not hearing form him, only to have him arrive totally unannounced on her doorstep, a bakery bag in one hand and a giant coffee in the other. It was the same while she lived at home. A full week with Jack in residence was an event. It rarely happened, and when it did, she was almost relived when he left. A little bit of Jack, his enthusiasm, his booming voice, his expansive nature, and his continuous stream of motley friends dropping by, was plenty of fun for a ten-year-old looking for a break from the humdrum week of school. But for a twenty-five-year-old with a high pressure job and an OCD complex, it tended to be a little more than she could take.

But at this moment, she would take it all back just to get a note from her father.

She watched listlessly as Dean took a sat in one of the chairs opposite and set the crate on the table. She wondered what they would do now. If the car was out of commission for a few days, would she just stay here? Should she go on to southern Florida, perhaps rent a car? She had places to be, and although most of her schedule was in her own head, she still knew there was a deadline looming. She would have to return to work at some point. As happy as they were to see her take some time off work, as soon as a new project came up, they would need her.

And she needed to be there for her mother. And if they didn't find Jack? Her stomach clenched, and she turned her attention to the bird shuffling around in the crate. She slowly got up and opened the outer flap of her neatly packed case. Treats were there. And the poor bird had been through a lot.

After another thirty minutes had passed while she gave the parrot treats though the grating of his crate, Buck came in.

"Well, now, I think I have some good news," he began, and after that statement, she pretty much lost track of the conversation. She was generally a smart competent woman, but the workings of a car engine were not something she was familiar with. When she realized she would never master the task of car maintenance, she had done the practical thing and purchased a comparatively expensive car for that reason. The reliability of it had insulated her from some of the upkeep that plagued the cars of her childhood years. And now as an adult, although she gamely tried to comprehend what was going on with the machine, she knew that she was woefully lacking in that area. As she listened to the discussion, she just hoped that Dean might be able to translate some of the lingo into terms she could deal with, preferably an end price and a timeline. With this thought, she also decided she needed to take a few courses in car maintenance as well.

"So how long?" she said, pulling out of her own thoughts.

"If the part gets here tomorrow, we can have you on the road the day after."

"Two days then," she affirmed.

"Yes, ma'am."

She pressed her chilled hands together, grappling for control. This was doable. Two days from her schedule would be an inconvenience, but she could handle it. Today was already a bust.

"Okay, then let's order it."

After the secretary, who was also Buck's wife, dropped them off at the little bed and breakfast around the corner, Genevieve hesitated on the sidewalk. Dean had agreed that waiting on the car would be the best thing at this point. There was no sense trying to take the car to a bigger city to get it fixed when Buck seemed to know what he was doing. Dean went on to explain that he had tinkered on his fair share of vehicles in his youth, so he seemed to have at least a working knowledge of a garage. And his conclusion that Buck was fully capable of handling the repairs settled the matter for Genevieve.

Now that her decision was made, she realized that perhaps what was good for her wouldn't be good for Dean. He had already put his life on hold for the time he had spent visiting his mother. To prolong the vacation might not have been in his plans. She slowed on the walk up to the front porch of the quaint wood sided cottage and caught Dean's arm lightly, removing her hand as soon as he turned to look at her. "Dean," she said a little stiffly. "I realize you might need to be back to work quicker than I can get you there," She said as they paused at the front door. "If you need to get back, I wouldn't be offended if you rented a car and left. We're only six hours away from your hometown. I'm sure I can make it the rest of the way by myself."

"I don't have a time that I have to be anywhere," Dean responded in that frustratingly calm tone.

"It's going to be two more days," she began, but he was shaking his head. For the first time she saw a flash of emotion there in his expression, and she quieted.

"I came back to see my mom because this time of year, it's what we do. We have to be together to remind each other why we are here, why we're going on. After I visit her, I always need to decompress a little, and mom knows that. She wanted me to ride with you for some reason, and now I can see why. This trip is good for me. It's a vacation from my present life, my busy work and day to day stuff, but it's also a vacation from my memories, and I know they would have chased me all the way back to Florida if I had just rushed home." He ran a hand through his hair, his eyes suddenly years older. "I think that I needed this time away. So no, I'm not rushing to get back. And yes, I want to stay with you for the rest of the trip. As long as you'll have me."

Genevieve hadn't heard him speak like that in all of their time together. Sure, they didn't know each other that well, but riding for hours on end with someone in a closed car had a way of making an acquaintance progress rather quickly to a friend. The earnestness, with just a tinge of pain, in his speech made her pause.

"Then I'd appreciate it if you stayed with us," she said, her eyes dropping to the shape of the bird in the crate.

"Okay then," he said, and held open the door for her.

Chapter 8

The bed and breakfast was charming. Genevieve walked into the little bedroom, the old wooden floors creaking under her shoes, and laid her bags on the quilt that covered the single bed. It wasn't big, but it was homey and clean.

Dean had been given the room next door, and they would share a bathroom. The older home had been built in the mid 1800's and updated over the years to improve plumbing, heating and air conditioning, but little else had changed.

She realized a minute later as she flipped open her suitcase and saw the spare bag of pellets that Dean had taken Hemingway into his room, and she hadn't noticed. She was still feeling awkward from their earlier discussion. After what he had said on the walkway, she was torn between wanting to ask him for an explanation, and wishing that she had never seen that expression in his eyes. She stood still, gazing blindly at her open case and ruminating on his words. Her mother had not given her any clue that there was a specific reason for his visit, and she wondered if she had even known. But apparently there was a whole lot more to the story. Dean was obviously going through a difficult time, and his relaxed manner and calm demeanor were hiding something much darker, much sadder.

She sank to the bed and glanced around the room. There was a phone and an outdated box television. She doubted there would be free Wi-Fi, and she hadn't taken her computer from the trunk of her car. Perhaps that hadn't been wise, but she would be able to stop off and grab it if she needed to. It wasn't likely Buck would abscond with it anyway. So she was a little limited. While she was here she could make some phone calls, but beyond that, she wasn't sure what she could do. And Dean? She didn't know if she should try to give him space or continue on as they had been, connected at the hip. Not that it was just her decision to make. Perhaps her best bet would be to ask him. That was what mature adults did.

She took a few extra minutes carefully unpacking her bag. Even if her time line, her careful schedule, was thrown off, she could still maintain the niceties of home. Feeling more civilized with her clothes neatly laid out in the drawers and hung on hangers, she took out her little toiletry bag and placed it on the dresser, picking out the little bottles and lining them neatly on the surface. She wouldn't spread out her things in the bathroom like she might if she wasn't sharing it. Just the idea of Dean looking through her limited supply of beauty products was somehow too personal.

"Stupid," she muttered to herself and zipped up the bag. When everything was arranged to her preference, she pulled out her cell phone and started going through the contacts. She had some of her father's best friends programmed into her phone, but she had a second, longer list tucked in a notebook in her purse. She pulled out that notebook and laid it on the desk next to her elbow.

For the next hour, she called some of her father's best buddies and constant companions, concentrating on the three men he most habitually accompanied when he was in Florida. She got immediate responses from two of them, men that she had already talked to just three days before, and they again regretfully told her they hadn't heard from Jack. She could hear the worry in their voices and it made her just a little more nervous. When she had called before, Casper, her father's friend who owned a local restaurant in Florida, had stated that he was sure Jack would be by soon. Jack never came into town without grabbing at least one meal there, and he was confident he would see him. However, Casper didn't sound so sure with this second call.

"He's not called you or your mama?" Casper asked, his voice gruff.

"No, neither of us. And I still have Hemingway."

He huffed a sigh. "Okay, girlie, give me a day and I'll make some calls," Casper said slowly. "My wife is away on a vacation with her girlfriends, or I would leave the place to her and go out and have a look myself. But just now, I can't get away."

Genevieve was nodding. She hadn't even known Casper was married until he mentioned it during their last conversation. Of course, she hadn't seen him in a good five years since Jack had dragged her down to Florida to attend a fairly outrageous birthday party for Mac, one of Jack's best friends. And the whole gang had been there then, a motley group of men and women Jack had collected over the years. Even her mother had attended for a few days, even though she hated Florida, the damp and the heat.

Her second call went out to Nub, one of her father's old buddies from the marina. He lived on a boat most of the time with a tiny apartment on land he visited only when the weather was at its worst. His real name was Jonathan, but his friends had taken to the nickname when he had lost one of his fingers to the local wildlife. He didn't deal with crocs anymore, but was known to take people out on his boat for some deep sea fishing.

His real job was not quite so adventurous. A tax preparer by trade, he now was mostly retired and only did the accounting side of the job when he chose to, or when one of his good buddies asked for help.

He answered the phone almost immediately and Genevieve wondered if he might recognize her number from her last fruitless call. She felt a surge of encouragement. Perhaps he had heard from Jack and was waiting to give her a message. Perhaps she wouldn't have to worry about her errant father any longer. Perhaps his words would melt the knot of concern that had lodged in her stomach and refused to move.

But she was disappointed. He hadn't heard from Jack, not for a month at least. No news. No more information. No clue to where Jack was. Beyond that, he was out of town himself, off for a conference up north.

The third man she had tried to contact was Abraham Macintosh, or Mac, as Jack always called him. Mac was an avid collector as well, a dignified gentleman that cared for Jack and tolerated Hemingway. When she had called the first time and received no response, she had left a message asking for him to give her a call back. On the second attempt, she had added to her message, explaining that Jack had left Hemingway with her and she was getting concerned. On the third attempt she had merely hung up when no one answered. It seemed like he was as missing has Jack was. That little piece of information made her pause.

A light knock on her door had her jumping off the bed, and she realized she had become tense sitting there worrying about her father. But she had done what she could from the confines of the hotel room. She had alerted Jack's closest friends in Florida, she had tracked down what few leads she had, and now all she could do was wait. She knew that once she had arrived in Florida, she would be repeating these attempts at conversation, but this time in person. She could go to the restaurant to see Casper, to Mac's home by the ocean, and to the other haunts Jack frequented when he was there.

At the door, she paused to straighten her now dried clothes. She ran a hand self-consciously over her hair, smoothing down the stray strands that were now only slightly damp. Dean was standing in the doorway, tall and easy in the same jeans and slightly rumpled shirt he wore so well.

She frowned. She didn't know exactly how he did it, but he had a casual air of elegance despite the wrinkled attire. Even his stance was totally at ease, but she had the feeling that at a moment he could take control of almost any situation, and she realized with a pang that she would miss him once they got to Florida, and he returned to his normal busy life. Not that she wasn't perfectly capable of taking care of herself. But in a strange place, it was nice to have someone to bounce ideas off of, to know where you were and miss you if you weren't around.

"Hey," she greeted.

"Hemingway and I have had a discussion, and he has promised to be on his best behavior if we agree to take him out for a walk."

"Really? Meaning that he didn't bite you when you let him out of the crate?"

"He didn't bite me when I let him out, and I was able to get the harness on him."

She blinked in surprise. When she had found the harness among her things at home, an older one that Jack had left with her along with some toys for the bird, she had tucked it into her bag along with his food container. She had no intention of putting it on him until they had arrived in Florida. She knew from experience that many people opened up when faced with Jack's most loyal companion, and the proof that she indeed had been left with the bird in Jack's absence would convince people to talk to her. She hadn't been sure how Hemingway would react to her attempts at putting the harness on him. He generally was a gentle as a lamb with her, but she wasn't going to take anything for granted. She had seen him draw blood on several occasions and knew just how powerful that beak was.

But now that Dean had apparently been successful at putting the harness on the bird, she couldn't see any reason why they shouldn't take him out with them, at least for a little while. The rain had let up, the clouds thinning and leaving a . gray pearly sky like the inside of a conch shell.

"So you have all of your fingers still?" she asked.

He had up both long fingered hands showing her the lack of scars. "I do," he responded smiling.

"Then that sounds like a great idea," she said, "let me just grab my keys and phone."

Taking a bird on a harness was not like one might picture it. Hemingway perched on her arm, occasionally climbing to her shoulder to run his beak through her hair, preening her as he would one of his flock. His wings were clipped enough that he could glide to the ground of he wanted, but not soar into the distance. He was a big bird, a tough bird, but he would never survive in the wild. Domestication had robbed him of his independence.

In Florida, big parrots were a more common sight than here in the northern area, and certainly more than in Kentucky. But even so, as she walked, she was receiving numerous curious and some incredulous stares. Children pointed, teenagers snickered, and she had to admit that walking next to Dean in the damp daylight, she didn't care a bit. The air had warmed slightly, the sun was just breaking thought the clouds, and she was making a concerted effort to just enjoy the moment.

"So have you gotten any word about your dad?" Dean asked as he walked next to her, his hair ruffled in the breeze.

"No, I did talk to Casper, one of his good friends that he always sees when he heads down here. Casper has a restaurant, and Jack likes to go there and show off Hemingway. Casper even has a place for Hemingway to perch when he visits. But he said he hadn't heard anything from Jack. He said he would make a few calls himself. Hopefully someone will know something about were Jack was headed, even if they didn't actually see him."

"So you're sure your dad was headed to Florida? You said you didn't talk to him when he headed out of town."

The thought had occurred to her. There was no solid evidence that Jack was in Florida. There was no proof he was anywhere. He might have disappeared somewhere in Kentucky or close by Indiana. But Genevieve doubted it. Jack did travel, but his trips were much more limited since the death of Topper, his worldlier friend. With Topper, he was likely to have traveled anywhere. They had been in and out of the country, crossing state lines like cracks in the sidewalk, seldom staying in one place for more than a few weeks before going on. Their home base had always been in Kentucky, but they had made a comfortable living traveling, Topper finding endless trades and bargains along the route.

Now Jack seemed content to go from Kentucky to Florida with occasional detours into neighboring Tennessee, Georgia, Indiana, and Ohio. He had certain areas he liked to frequent, and as he grew a little older, was becoming just a little more predictable.

This made his recent behavior even more of a mystery. While he was known for his travels, he was consistent with his communication. They had gotten postcards and calls when she was a child, but as she aged and mobile phones became more of a prevalent piece of technology, he had adopted that as well. Granted, he texted only in response to someone's bidding and rarely used any of the other functions of the phone, but he could be reached when they needed him.

Thinking back, she realized that as angry as he had made her for his disappearing acts, he was consistent at being there for the important things. He hadn't missed a birthday, a graduation, and would come flying back when her mother had called, like when Genevieve had been hospitalized for her appendix or when she had won the scholarship for a full ride to the University.

His absence picked at her, slowing her thoughts and making her feel somehow incomplete.

"Jack is predictable in his unpredictability. He tends to come and go easily, but he always stays at the same places. He has his usual haunts, and he has certain people that he regularly checks in with. I've talked to most of them already, and they are as baffled as I am. So no, I'm not sure it's Florida, but when Jack heads out, it's usually this way and I guess I've chosen this as a good place to start looking for him."

Hemingway shuffled a little on her arm and then climbed to her shoulder, fluffing his feathers impressively.

"What about this guy? Does Jack always take him when he goes on these trips?"

Genevieve nodded. "He usually does. The only time I've seen him leave Hemingway behind, with me, or mom, or one of his friends like Topper, is when he knew that it wasn't safe for him. For instance, he didn't take him to Alaska when it was too cold. They were doing some backpacking, and he was sure the bird couldn't take the weather. But besides that, he brought Hemingway into almost every adventure he had." She thought of the times she had been jealous of the massive bird. Wouldn't she have liked to travel all over the world? Wouldn't she have wanted to go on cruises, on train rides, on adventures?

"And he hasn't called, or texted?" Dean was glancing her way.

"Jack uses his phone sometimes, but it's an older model. Most of the time it works, but there are some messages I missed. But I have checked, and even if he missed me, he wouldn't have forgotten to let my mom know what was going on."

She huffed out a breath. Sure, she could be a little resentful of her father, but maybe she needed to let a little bit of that go. Dean seemed to understand a little bit of her emotions and was silent. They had progressed away from the bed-and-breakfast and toward the center of town. There was the typical Main Street with older buildings tucked one next to the other to meet in one unified brick façade, doorways and storefront windows sheltered from the sun by practical yet decorative awnings. A few doors down was the Town Square where the main roads crossed with one another, the signs declaring names like Oak and Magnolia. So not main street per say, but still the same idea. On the opposite side of the crossing was a substantial square building, the face split with traditional pillars, the almost unnecessary sign labeling it as the courthouse. It had a comfortable little town feel, and even the pedestrian traffic seemed to be part of the ambiance as though they had been added to the set as decoration. There was the young mother was a toddler by the hand, the other hand steadying a stroller where a pink faced baby slept in oblivion to the sounds around her. There was the harried looking middle aged man carrying a sack with some mysterious purchases and rummaging through his pockets for the keys that went with the dusty sedan parked next to him. There were the two older men, walking slowly, lost in a conversation, both wearing blue jeans and long sleeved flannel despite the rising heat.

Hemingway, and by relation, Genevieve, seemed exotic and strange in this setting. She said nothing as they continued across the street and into the city property.

"Wanna sit down?" Dean asked, his head nodding towards a wide bench under a picturesque gazebo by the steps of the Courthouse.

"Sure," she said and followed him to the bench. When they sat, Hemingway decided to descend from his perch, and confidently hopped from her arm to Dean's.

"Well, hi," Dean said to the bird, a small smile curing his lips. "Decided you would forgive me for the harness now that we've been outside?"

Genevieve found herself looking fondly at the big bird and shook her head. Sure, he was cute when they had him in careful control on the harness in the sunshine. It was the shrieks of displeasure when he was in the cage, and she refused to give him her breakfast at six thirty in the morning that grated.

"So you said you've had him for most of your life?"

Genevieve smiled. "I was just a kid when Jack brought him home. I think mom was hoping for a puppy, but Jack had his own ideas of what would be a good companion for me. Not that he knew anything about birds. He had never owned any before. We just had to learn as we went. We're lucky we didn't mess up along the way. Birds are surprisingly fragile." She slanted a look at Dean, and then felt flustered at his direct gaze. "But I guess you know all that. Being a vet, I mean."

"I work with all kinds of animals, but I have to admit, I'm not specifically an avian vet. I have treated my fair share of birds, but I've treated far more cats and dogs."

"So that's what you see the most?"

"Sure," he said nodding his head, "but I have my fair share of exotics. Especially in Florida. Less horses than in Kentucky, at least in my community, but more lizards, snakes, things like that."

"Do you miss living in Kentucky?" she asked curiously.

"Sometimes," his eyes were downcast, looking at the sleek feathers on Hemingway's head as he gently stroked the bird's cheek. "I moved down here a couple years ago. I needed a change." He glanced up at Genevieve, and she read sadness there. He looked away for a moment and then seemed to rouse himself. "But I have a great practice going now. I'm working with two other vets, a married couple that is just wonderful. Their business was already going well before I ever got there, but now," he shrugged, "we've got a great staff, and the place almost runs itself."

"Is that why you were able to take off for so long?" Genevieve hadn't meant to ask the question, but once it was out, she wanted to hear the answer. She herself was always so disciplined when it came to work. With her own vacation causing such a stir, she wondered how other people handled the prolonged absence from their jobs.

"Yeah, I've got my clients covered," he replied. "We have a vet tech who's good. She's helping take some of the slack." He looked at the bird and smiled. "Lillian would love to get her hands on you," he told Hemingway. "She has several birds herself, not as big as this fellow, but I'm sure she would have one if she could."

Genevieve was surprised at the odd feelings she had when she listened to him talking about this unknown Lillian. Was it jealousy? How in the world could she have that kind of feeling toward this man? She barely knew him. And besides that, this Lillian might have been sixty years old with grandkids and a husband that helped her collect the menagerie.

"So what kind of birds does she have?"

He looked at Genevieve and she was struck again how expressive his eyes were. "She's got two tiels, a green cheek conure, and a caique." His voice warmed as he spoke of her. "She lives alone and had a tough time finding a rental house that she could keep all of the animals in. I'm not crazy about the neighborhood, but she seems to get along okay."

Genevieve had an almost irresistible urge to ask if this paragon of animal lovers was more to him than a co-worker. It was obvious by the way he spoke of her that he liked and respected her. And why wouldn't he?

"So does she have family in Florida?" It sounded like she lived alone, so the husband and three kids were out, but Genevieve hadn't given up on the idea of a feisty older lady.

"Her parents live in Tennessee, but they were originally from Puerto Rico. She has two sisters, both married with little kids. Lillian doesn't get to see them as much as she would like to since they live up north."

So much for the older lady idea. If her sisters had little kids, chances were that Lillian wasn't too far off their age. Which would generally put her close to Genevieve's own age, since most of her friends were either newlyweds or parents of young children. She felt another pang, but this time it was for the little loss she felt when she thought of her friends in their little families, moving on, moving away from her.

"She sounds nice."

"Maybe we can stop by so she can meet you and Hemingway. She's always wanted a big bird, and she would love to see him." He fluffed the bird's feathers with his fingertips and Hemingway closed his eyes with pleasure. "She'd like to meet you too," Dean put in, almost as an afterthought. Genevieve looked at him, and would have sworn she could see a little color in his cheeks. Was he embarrassed? She stowed the thought away.

"Are you ready to head back?" she asked, changing the topic.

"Sure," he agreed, and stood. "Want me to carry the bird?"

"No, we're good," she replied, realizing she was feeling little strange, a little sad, and wanted the closeness of the animal. Hemingway loved her. No matter what else happened on this trip, meeting Dean's friend, searching for Jack who had run off from all of them, Hemingway still loved her above all.

Chapter 9

Dinner was at another charming little place in town, a pizza parlor where the cooks made their own crust and tossed it in front of an open window into the dining area before putting it in a giant industrial oven in back. The food was good and any of the awkward feelings from earlier were lost. Hemingway was left behind in the room with his own meal of pellets and a few seeds for treats in the crate. He had made his displeasure known as Genevieve slipped from the room, growling low in his throat and then throwing out some random curse words from his embarrassing large vocabulary. When Dean asked if they could have some slivers of vegetables to take back to their pet in the room, the waitress obliged with nary a strange look. She must have heard odder requests in her time. Genevieve wondered if the gesture was because Dean had heard the complaining.

Genevieve took the vacation spirit a little farther and ordered a glass of red wine to go with her meal. She wasn't driving, and she wasn't in any danger of imbibing too much with the single glass to sip on. Besides, the wine had a pleasant warming sensation and she felt some of her tension ease.

"So do you have any plans for tomorrow?" Dean asked, and she took it as a leading question.

"Not really. I'm waiting to see if I get any calls, but until we get the car back, I can't do much about Jack," she replied. "Did you have any ideas?"

"Well, I was asking one of the ladies at the desk if they had any advice about what we could do around town, and they gave me a few suggestions. This pizza place was one," he said, one eyebrow quirked to accompany a slight smile.

"Okay, so that sounds promising. What else did they suggest?"

The rest of the dinner was spent making plans for the next day, which comforted Genevieve. She liked to be planned; she liked to know exactly what she would do from one day to the next.

From there the conversation turned to what she was planning when she got to St. Petersburg, so she reviewed her ideas of where she wanted to visit, Jack's usual haunts and his friends, and what she hoped to find. Dean was silent, perfect for bouncing ideas off, nodding at the right time, and then adding in his own suggestions. He was astute, she noticed, thinking of things she hadn't, so by the end of dinner, she felt back in control. She had a plan, a new, albeit amended scheduled, an idea of what needed to be done. Now all she could do was pray that all of her work would pan out and she would find Jack, safe and whole.

Breakfast the following day was strong hot coffee and pastries at the local coffee shop before they hit the sidewalk. They wiled away the morning going to antique shops and quaint little gift boutiques where Genevieve ended up buying a pair of earrings for her mother as though getting a gift for her would somehow make her mother feel better in the absence of her flighty husband. Dean had an affinity for pocket watches, and Genevieve was impressed to see the amount of knowledge he had about them. They stopped to examine several, but he didn't buy any of them. Genevieve wasn't sure if he collected them, or just had an interest in the antique timepieces, and tucked the information away for a later conversation.

After lunch at the local diner, they caught a ride with one of the hotel workers to a local site where they grew a variety of citrus trees and had a honeybee hive to provide the rich condiment. It seemed that Dean's silky voice and charm could talk even the middle-aged hotel clerk to drive them to the out of the way site. On the way they learned a large chunk of the woman's life story, about her children, three, her husband who worked for a trucking company, Dan, and their beagle she had had to chase down this morning when he had darted out the front door in pursuit of a squirrel, Ducky. Her rendition of the chase had Genevieve nearly in tears of laughter, and she thoroughly enjoyed the ride.

The whole trip was pleasantly scenic. The road was mostly lined by citrus groves until they came to the actual shop location. The surrounding area was dotted with gardens and several gift shops selling the produce, live plants, and bakery goods as well as hundreds of products made from the honeybees' creation.

As their new friend headed back into town and they stood in the warm sun and watched the little Toyota sink into the distance, Genevieve sighed softly. It was one of those crystal moments when you'd like to freeze the day, to take a slice out later to savor the precious seconds of peace. The scent of citrus was in the air, perfumed with dozens of blooming things, and she stood next to the undeniably handsome Dean, who just happened to be a nice guy.

Genevieve was pulled from her reverie when Dean started forward. He paused for a moment for her to catch up. The front of the store was surrounded by a maze of gardens, and as she walked, she pointed out the flowers the bees might choose, listening for the soothing buzz.

"I can't imagine living close to this place," Dean observed looking a little nervous as the insects sipped from bloom to bloom.

"Why? Do you think that the honeybees are going to dive bomb you? They aren't interested in you unless you're wearing flowers in your hair," Genevieve quipped.

"Hmmm, funny. You don't know what they're planning," he responded darkly.

"I do," she argued. "We grew up with hives in the back yard. I've helped harvest the comb."

He turned and looked at her then. She knew she didn't match the description of a beekeeper. She didn't have the rugged appearance of someone who spent lots of time outdoors puttering in the garden, but the expression of disbelief on his face was just a bit too much.

"Really? And what other interesting hobbies do you have?"

"I know how to grow herbs and make medicinal teas, I know how to milk a goat, and I know how to can and make my own jams and jellies. You can't live with my mother and not acquire some interesting abilities."

"Your mom is so cool!" he exclaimed, and Genevieve grinned. Yep, her mom honestly was cool, and she had to reluctantly admit, so was Jack.

The reminder made her think of her silent phone. So if she went by the old adage, no news was good news, then she was golden. Not that it was completely silent. She had several texts from Rick, none bringing up any problems at work, but all hinting strongly that he needed to know when she was going to be back in town.

"Let's go into the shop. I might get some of the honey to give to mom when I get back home." Dean nodded and together they wound their way through the rest of the gardens and into the little shop to complete their purchases. Genevieve insisted Dean try different flavored honey sticks and to nibble at a honeycomb. She was grinning when he chose a few of his own favorites to buy for home.

Their next stop was a little outpost that sold plantings from the garden area, and Genevieve walked among the herbs, feeling more at home. The scent of mingling herbs and spices soothed her. She was trying to settle her racing mind, trying not to worry about the hours that were going by.

She checked her cell phone every quarter hour, stifling the urge to pull it out more often, but there were no calls from her father, from his friends, or even from her mother. They ate snacks at a table in the shade, drinking homemade lemonade with just the right blend of sweet and sour. When they caught a ride back into town, and she returned to the room in the early evening, she took a quick shower and let Hemingway out of his cage. While he chewed contentedly on some of the gifts she had gotten, the fresh fruit being his favorite; she checked her email from work. There were only a few short missives from her co-workers with questions that were relatively simple to answer. It appeared that they were getting along just fine without her.

The rest of the emails were spam, but she decided she had far too many on her smart phone and began to go back in the inbox and delete the advertisements for products, the useless messages from cell phone companies and forums she didn't want to subscribe to, and requests from social media sites.

She was still deleting and in the middle of the selections from two months ago when she saw she had a message from Jack. Her hands grew icy. Had she unknowingly committed the worst omission? Had she gotten a message from Jack that would have explained his absence and ignored it? She couldn't remember ever seeing it before, but here it was. She touched the emblem and waited as the email loaded. The reception wasn't the greatest here and it took time for the email to process.

But the message wasn't what she expected at all. It was attachment with no heading or text to explain. She tapped the little icon and a picture filled the screen with no word of explanation. Instead, it appeared to be a photograph of a document, that when expanded, was taken in such poor lighting that it couldn't be read. She'd have to open it on her computer if she wanted to see it clearly. And her computer was in the trunk of her car, useless to her now. She blew out a sigh in frustration. Had she been at home, her computer would be charged and ready to be used. But here, she hadn't bothered to take it out of the car's trunk.

She squinted at the little phone screen. It was going to drive her crazy to not be able to access the picture, but she knew by tomorrow they would be back on the road.

"Okay, Hemingway," she said, watching him strut across the desk. He had eaten all but tiny sticky scraps of the fruit they had bought him, and had then started to demolish the pad of paper the owners had left on the desk for their convenience. She knew that a bird's play toy was not the original purpose for the paper, but if it kept him from chewing on something more valuable, she could handle it being sacrificed. Her eyes went to her phone. It wasn't quite five o'clock. Would anyone be in at the garage? They should be. Traditional closing hours would be five, and perhaps if she called, she could get the laptop before the garage was locked up for the night. And then what? She knew that the coffee shop that they had eaten their breakfast in had free Wi-Fi. It seemed even in small towns, there was a fair share of hipsters who needed the additional caffeine to work on their computers. It may not have been a Starbucks, but the resemblance had been there.

She found the number from the garage on her incoming call log on her cell phone and hit the button to return the call. She had spoken to the man earlier in the day, pleased when he noted that they had the part and would be working on the car in the afternoon. She wondered if the car was ready, but knew that even if it was, there was no way that she would want to pick it up tonight. It would be better to wait til the morning when she and Dean could go in together.

But for now, she just wanted to get in the trunk.

"Hey ya," the voice said, a casual greeting.

"Um, I was calling about my car."

"Ya, sure. Are you Ms. Glass? Cause the car's not quite ready."

She glanced out the window, mentally assessing the time. "Yes, well, I thought that the car might not be finished, but I wanted to get something out of the trunk."

"Okay, sure," was the casual response. "I'll be here another hour at least working on her. You want to come on over?"

"That would work well," she responded, seeing the warm spray of sunshine out the window. Plenty of time to grab her computer, run by the coffee shop to plug it in and get on the Internet, check out her email messages, and be back before dinner.

"Then I'll be here," the voice affirmed.

It took her a few precious moments to convince Hemingway that he wanted to go back in his cage. But after that, it was only seconds to lock her room. She hesitated outside Dean's closed door. They had been virtually connected at the hip since this trip began, and now she froze in indecision. Did she want to call him? She didn't need him to go with her. She was perfectly capable to go back to the garage and get the computer. None of that was a problem. But would he come over to her room to try to speak with her? And if he did, would he be worried when he realized that she wasn't there? She wasn't accustomed to having a traveling companion, so it suddenly seemed like a dozen little questions were coming up with each turn of their plans.

She approached the door and knocked softly. When the door swung open, Dean was standing in his bare feet, the sound of the television humming in the background.

"Hi," she greeted and then continued quickly, "I am headed to the garage to get my computer. I'm going to take it over to the coffee shop to check something out. I didn't want you to come by and find me missing."

He was nodding. "Sure, you need any company?"

"I'm good," she said, then bit her lip. Had she insulted him? "Unless you wanted to get out," she finished weakly.

"Nope, I have the end of the game to watch," he said, his tone easy.

"Okay, well, good," she said, relieved that he wasn't offended either way. "I'll see you later for dinner?"

"6:30 and the Mexican place tonight?"

"Sure," she agreed, smiling back.

"Then it's a date."

Her face was still a little pink when she got out into the humid air. It's a date certainly didn't mean that it actually was a date. Dating was stupid, and she was phenomenally unsuccessful at dating, as her experience with Wayne proved. In fact, her history with men in general lacked. But a date with Dean, that was out of the question. He was a great guy, handsome, charming, smart, funny, and he lived in Florida. He also seemed permanently messy, lost things all the time, and had a true affinity for animals and lots of them. He had spoken casually of his own menagerie, which included not one, not two, but three big dogs. And if one big bird was a mess, then three panting, slobbering dogs would be three times worse.

So no, as great as he was, this was not going to be a date.

The garage was lit from within and the noises sounded like some huge mechanical beast was losing its supper on the concrete floor. Genevieve stopped at the door and knocked, knowing full well that there was no way anyone would hear her.

After a moment looking at the closed door, she tried the knob. It turned easily in her hand and she entered the front office. The lights in this section were mostly off, only dim recessed lamps lighting the way down the hall. She saw no movement in that room, so she moved rapidly toward the garage and the noise. She was surprised that she felt a tiny spidery crawl of fear. There was something deep in her that was scared, but she certainly didn't want to admit it.

A gangly middle-aged man was buried head first into a car parked next to hers that was sitting in all its glossy glory under the florescent lighting. She felt her tense muscles ease. Her eyes traced the pearly gray paint job, seeing no signs of the earlier damage. She wasn't sure what was left to do since most of the damage had been beneath the car, but it looked good to her all the same.

"Hello," she called out, keeping her voice modulated even though she had to speak fairly loudly.

The man ducked out from under the raised hood, head tipped so that he could see her from under his baseball cap.

"Hey ya," he said, his voice familiar from their conversation on the phone. "Ya wanted to get in your car?"

"That's me," she said smiling politely.

He nodded wordlessly and went toward the back of her car. "I think it's unlocked," he said, wiping his hands on a stained white cloth as he went.

She walked with him to the rear of the car and popped the trunk with her key fob. Inside her computer bag looked undisturbed. She ducked in to grab it and straightened quickly.

"The car should be ready first thing in the morning," he said, and Genevieve saw while standing next to him that his shirt was tagged with the name Kevin.

"Okay, Kevin," she replied, starting toward the door. "Thanks so much for getting this done."

He nodded. "You be careful," he said and turned back toward the car he was tending to. Genevieve threaded back out the long hallway and into the front office. It remained empty and still dim, and outside, she thought it looked as the though sun had been extinguished a little as well. When she slipped through the door, the wall of humid air hit her like a cottony fist. Clouds had increased which draped a gauzy film of moisture over the sun as it steadily slipped to the west. It wouldn't rain, but it would stay humid and uncomfortable.

Genevieve walked briskly back down the sidewalk her computer bag in her hand. She felt better having it with her like it was another lifeline to her normal routine. At the coffee shop, she found a table and pulled out a chair, sliding into the seat nearest the wall. She suddenly couldn't wait to start the computer and pull up the email from Jack.

She opened the laptop bag and pulled out the computer, looking at the slightly battered surface of the case. The computer had been hers for over a year and she had used it daily since she had picked it up from the local electronics outlet. She had the cord out and plugged in before positioning the laptop on the little table. Around her, the place was comfortably quiet with just a few other patrons hunched over their own electronics while they drank coffee or tea from plain white mugs.

"Here we go," she said softly, and listened to the whir of the fan as the computer booted up. The screen flickered to life and she waited for it to finish loading while she thought of her evening plans. A date? Well, no, but it would be nice.

The computer finished loading and she rested her hands on the keys, quickly tapping out her choice. With the program called up, she started scrolling through her emails, skimming through several days' worth of unread missives. When she finally reached her target date, she slowed her scanning. And it wasn't there. She frowned and scanned back over the emails, more slowly now. But it wasn't there. There was no email from Jack.

She went into her other email account on the off chance that she had been checking the wrong one, but she knew that wasn't true. She used the work email for almost everything, her Gmail account only for less important messages.

Nothing from Jack. She went back to the work account and switched over to the folder choices, picking the trash bin. It was empty. She felt a strange shivery feeling and frowned. She was the only one that used the account. She was the only person with any interest in the contents. So where did it go? She knew she hadn't pulled up her email and emptied the trash bin. She was systematic about her habits, and she only emptied it every two weeks on Friday afternoons. And she hadn't done that this last Friday. Besides, if she had, she wouldn't have seen the message on her phone earlier.

She grabbed her phone and pulled up the email app knowing that if the main account had been wiped then the phone's app would be gone as well. And just as she had suspected, there was no message from Jack. She muttered a curse and studied the phone more intently. It matched the computer. Somehow, the email message had been deleted and then the deleted emails had been emptied from the server, all very recently. She knew that there was most likely a way to retrieve the message, but she wasn't sure how to do it.

Her eyes skipped over the other people in the coffee shop, suddenly feeling ridiculously suspicious. So she knew for certain she hadn't gotten rid of the email. She knew she hadn't deleted it. But if not her, then who? Who would want to erase such a mundane thing? Who would care to clear out a note from Jack? Of any of her messages, the one from Jack would have been the least interesting of all of those received. After all, the chemicals she dealt with daily were of possible interest to other chemical companies. Espionage was not unheard of, even if it wasn't as dramatic as what might be portrayed on the television.

But the email from Jack had just been that picture. And now it was gone. She felt a surge of unease again. She had seen the email just an hour ago if that. And between the time she had gone to get her computer and had settled at the coffee shop, the email had disappeared. Erased. She refused at this point to even ponder the possibility that the email had been deliberately taken off the server. After all, there was absolutely no reason for anyone to be looking at her emails. And no one could get into her account. It was password protected, just like every other worker's account.

She rested her chin in her hands and looked at the screen. She wasn't likely to find the explanation here. Whatever had happened must have been some sort of quirk of the system. No doubt with some technical help, she would be able to find it again.

If she could just persuade herself to believe her own thoughts.

A few minutes later she noticed that the woman behind the counter was observing her a little too closely. It took her a moment before she realized she was taking one of their tables and hadn't thought to buy anything. She got up immediately and went to the counter, ordering a fancy coffee she didn't want, but that smelled delicious when she finally took it back to her table.

She tried not to think about the email and took another half hour looking though the few notes she had from work. She checked on the progress of their latest, and hopefully completed project, and shot off a few questions to her fellow workers.

There. She had done what she needed to do. She took a sip of the coffee and sighed. Very good.

While she had the computer accessing the Internet, she took a few minutes looking at maps from St. Pete's. She had already planned out her route. She knew exactly where she planned to go, who she planned to talk to, but there were still a few people she hadn't been able to contact. She was hoping that once she got there and was able to talk to some of Jack's friends, they would have some ideas of other people she could talk to.

After another fifteen minutes, she returned the heavy mug to the front counter and took the computer bag with her back to the hotel. It was almost time for dinner, but she had enough time to clean up.

It wasn't a date, but she didn't want to be a mess, after all.

Chapter 10

The Mexican restaurant was definitely not a chain establishment, which appeared to make Dean happy. The more original the menu, the better he seemed to like it. All the wait staff in the dining room spoke rapid Spanish, and Dean ordered in the same language.

"You speak Spanish?"

"I had some in school, but I've learned quite a bit more with my new practice," Dean said, plucking a tortilla chip from the basket and breaking it up into small pieces. "And Lillian tends to drop into Spanish once in a while so it helps that I understand what she's saying. Especially if she talking to me, or about me."

She pondered the comment silently. It wasn't as though this was the first time he had mentioned Lillian. They worked together every day, and he had said he admired the woman. And here it was again, the reminder that he had friends, or more than friends?

"It's a good skill, knowing two languages," she observed.

"What about you? Do you have any hidden talents?"

She shrugged. "Not really." Should she mention that she had a near photographic memory while she was at school, recalling much of what she read without effort? That she had scored in the highest percentiles in all standardized testing, resulting in accelerated progress though school? "No, I don't know that I do," she said slowly.

"But you grew up with bees," he said smiling that charming quirky smile. "And your mom makes tea and your dad is a pirate. I think you win in the skill set."

"Well, of course. I didn't think about it that way. But yes, I can harvest honey, dry herbs and spices, and tie dye almost anything."

"Hmm," he said. "A woman of many facets."

"That's me," she said lightly.

They walked back to the bed and breakfast under the silver moon. It was one of those nights where the breeze barely stirred the leaves on the overhanging trees, but the heat had lessened. Genevieve felt like she would be happy if the evening stretched for just a few moments more. It was such a peaceful feeling, full of the scents of damp earth and tropic blossoms, a lovely Florida warmth.

If she hadn't had to worry about Jack, she might have stayed one more day. She might have lingered here for as long as Dean would stay, taking in the local charm, and the undeniably attractive companion.

She smiled to herself. It was impossible, silly, and not like her at all. No, she couldn't consider that she wanted to stay here with Dean, that she wanted to stay here at all, she amended to herself. Besides, as handsome and charming as Dean was, she could see how differently he lived his life. At the dinner table he realized he had forgotten his wallet and insisted on jogging back to the room to retrieve it. While she had stayed behind sipping on a soft drink and checking her emails for the millionth time, he had made it to the inn and realized he had forgotten his key with the wallet. Genevieve could almost picture him charming the middle-aged lady they had waved to as they exited earlier. She would have, no doubt, melted under that smile and the smooth music of his voice and immediately provide him with another key to access the room.

He had been back just minutes later, long enough for Genevieve to sink back into discontent and unease. But after he sat down, he had easily gotten her mind off of her worries, admitting he habitually forgot his wallet, his keys, his cell phone.

"For my senior prom, I forgot the keys in the car," he said smiling, "and then locked it. It was after the dance, and well after one in the morning, when I had to call my dad to come pick us up." He shrugged, "my date ended up going home with one of my buddies."

"She wasn't very nice," Genevieve sputtered, thinking of her own sad prom night, a set up date with the cousin of one of her best friends. He had been a great guy, but head over heels in love with his college girlfriend and consistently distracted the whole evening.

"She was fine, but pretty furious. She ended up dumping my buddy a week later. Heard she was married and has two little ones now."

"Your mother kind of implied that you forgot things," Genevieve observed.

"Yeah, well, she would know. It's amazing that I managed to get through school," he said lips quirking slightly. "I mean, I had the brains. I could understand the information and I could pass the tests. But I missed due dates pretty much all the time so the teachers were constantly asking me for stuff." He shrugged. "My poor mom and dad were always getting calls from the teachers. We had lots of conferences."

Genevieve listened with interest. She had met his mother and knew only that his father was gone. She didn't know what had happened to him, but she knew her mother had mentioned that his mother lived alone. She didn't want to ask.

"What about you? I bet you did great in school. All A's, all the time."

Genevieve smiled without comment. Of course, he was right. She had graduated from elementary school, high school, and even college with great scores. Her mother hadn't had to attend teacher/parent conferences at all. But grades had been Genevieve's least concern in school. She had been the quiet girl, the one that ruined the curve, the one that buddied up with teachers because the other kids didn't understand her, and most didn't care to. After all, the people that knew her family had a totally different reason for snubbing her. Her mother was a hippie; her father was a pirate. What else was there to know about her?

So the fact that Dean had been forgetful as a child, and yes, as an adult as well, seemed like a relatively small problem to her.

"My mom had me tested when I was in eighth grade," he admitted. "ADHD. It's pretty popular now, as far as a diagnosis, but then it wasn't as well researched. And I don't have the hyperactivity part it. I just have the attention problems." He smiled a self-depreciating little twist of his lips, "but now I have people that look out after me."

"Like your mom?"

"Guilty," he said. "And at work, I have the vet techs and assistants."

"So you've figured it out," Genevieve replied, trying to keep the tone light.

"I have," he glanced at her, "except for those times I forget my wallet and have to leave my dinner date sitting by herself."

Genevieve felt her cheeks heat. Dinner date? Leave that one alone, she scolded herself. And as she walked next to him now in the silvery moonlight, she sighed inwardly. No, not a date. But that didn't mean she couldn't enjoy the moment.

They parted into their separate rooms, Genevieve ducking through her doorway without any pause. She knew she was being a coward. She didn't want to linger. She didn't want to invite any more familiarity, not when the word date had been associated with their evening. Because if she paused, if she gave it a chance, how might that change their relationship? Or worse yet, what if she had read far too much into the discussion, and he had meant it to be exactly what it had been, a dinner between two people, almost strangers, who had been forced together?

After she had closed and locked the door, she realized again she had forgotten Hemingway. As she had finished getting ready, Dean had come over and taken the bird into his own room. "He'd want to listen to this ballgame," Dean had said, gesturing toward the other room.

They had left Hemingway in Dean's room while they went for dinner, and there he remained. He would be bunking with Dean for one more night, it seemed. She wasn't about to go and ask him if he wanted her to take the bird back.

She checked her computer bag, noting that the computer was still tucked inside. It would do her no good at this point without any Internet connection, so she left it where it was and began getting ready for bed.

When she settled into bed, she again pulled out her phone. She plugged it in for power and pulled up her email. She paged through the messages one at a time going back a week, then two, then three. After she had gone back a full four weeks she noticed an email that was from Jack, but she knew what it contained. She opened the message and smiled at the picture he had sent, himself and his friend Mac standing on the side of the dock, the boat behind them, a leftover from their adventures with Topper. She felt a surge of sadness. Topper's death had left Jack at loose ends for many months, but he was slowly getting over the loss of his best friend. The picture showed that he was finally returning to some of his old haunts. But that wasn't the message she had been looking for. She sighed. She knew she had seen it, the blurry document. But it was gone.

Morning came far too early, but Genevieve felt like they had been hanging around for a week, not just a day in the little town, and was anxious to be on the road. She called the garage first and was greeted by Buck's jovial voice assuring her that the car was running as good as new. He again mentioned how much he liked her car, and she smiled to herself. This admiration for anything on wheels had to be a male thing.

Dean's door was still closed and she hesitated just outside. Should she tell him that she was going to pick up the car? Normally she wouldn't hesitate to take care of such a chore on her own, but since he had helped her with getting the repairs set up, she felt like he might be interested in seeing the outcome.

She raised her hand to knock on the door and heard Hemingway exclaim, "Shut up, ya old bugger!"

When Dean opened the door, his shoulders slumped with relief. "Thank God it's you. He's been hollering all morning, and I thought we were about to be evicted!"

She shook her head, "Bow, what are you doing?"

The giant parrot was perched on the foot of the bed, his feathers on his head fluffed and his eyes pinning in excitement.

"Bow?" Dean asked curiously.

"Rainbow," she muttered, realizing she had dropped the bird's nickname. "I called him Rainbow when we were little."

"You have the most unusual brother," Dean said, and she glanced at his face to see his expansive grin.

"That is putting it mildly," she said, and dropped on the foot of the bed, letting the bird tumble into her lap to cuddle against her. "So why have you been a bad boy?" she asked the bird.

He cocked his head and looked at her, his eyes alert to her every movement. "Aww, good bird," he murmured to her.

She stroked her hand over his head, feeling the silky feathers beneath her fingers and smiling. "Are you ready to go find Jack?" she asked the bird.

But he didn't respond.

Considering the trouble they had experienced getting to that point in their journey, the rest of the way had been almost frighteningly easy. They had grabbed breakfast at the diner they had visited before and headed out with full cups of coffee to start their journey.

The car was ready, sparkling clean and lovingly prepped. Genevieve was thrilled. They had gotten the car in pristine condition for her, and the OCD part of her brain rejoiced in the spotless carpeting, the sleek leather polished, and even the muted shine of the tires.

She had paid a reasonable bill for the repairs and thanked Buck profusely.

"Well, now, the fixin' was easy enough, it's the gettin' the parts that takes a little time," he responded he patted the hood fondly. "It's a nice car, and you look to be nice folks. I'm glad you're happy with it. Make sure you come back by on your way through."

Genevieve thought that she just might. There was something cozy and fine about the little town in the middle of nothing. It wasn't exactly a tourist attraction like many of the other places in Florida, but it had been a great place to spend a couple days.

"I will definitely try," Genevieve responded, nodding her thanks again.

They were ushered with some ceremony into the car, tucking their bags in the back and Hemingway in the seat behind the driver. With a purr, the engine came to life and they pulled the car out into the sunshine.

They only stopped one other time to stretch their legs and let Hemingway flap around the car a little. Genevieve didn't want the big bird to cause any havoc on her pricy car, but he was a perfect gentleman, taking snacks delicately from their fingers and muttering a soft thank you.

It was a full sunny afternoon, the heat floating off the pavement in waves, when Genevieve pulled into the very practical, very pedestrian hotel where she had chosen to stay. It wasn't on the beach; she wasn't planning on going into the ocean in the near future. It also wasn't one of the full-featured posh spas that catered to the sophisticated tourist. It was a place to stay that was neat, clean, safe, and practical.

Dean looked skeptical as they pulled into the parking lot. "Remind me again why you chose to stay here? I know dozens of better places, on the beach, a lot more character."

"I checked this out before I left home," Genevieve said quickly. "It has excellent ratings."

"Ratings," he muttered. "Okay, and you want me to come with you while you check in?"

"No, I'm good," Genevieve said. She had wanted to come by, leave her bags, inspect the room, and make sure there were no more problems before she dropped Dean off at home. Why she felt she needed to delay, she refused to think about. Besides, if something did go wrong, he was a local and could give her suggestions if she needed an alternate place to stay. She had her own list of places she needed to go to seek out her missing parent, but having a local source would be helpful if she needed him.

"If you want to just wait with Hemingway, I'll be out in a second."

It took fifteen minutes for her to take her bag in, check into the supremely unremarkable hotel room with a king bed and faux wood furniture, and drop off her computer, suitcase, and hanging clothes. She was an efficient packer, so it only took her a few minutes to get it all in place. She hustled back outside to the car where Dean and Hemingway sat under a tree. Dean was in the driver's seat flipping through something on his cell phone, the windows were down, and Hemingway was making some surprisingly birdy sounds.

"Okay, I'm good to go," Genevieve greeted them both.

"Sure." Dean swung out of the car and strolled to the passenger side of the car. He had added a hat to his attire and the breeze blew the few tawny curls around the edges of his baseball cap. "Now we get to go to my side of the world," he said and a smile crinkled his eyes.

"Do you want me to just drop you home?"

"You're not going to come in for a drink?" He glanced at her and smiled again. "Thought you might want to meet my guys."

She knew he meant his dogs. And she knew she should be dropping him off and moving on as soon as possible. The sooner she found Jack, the sooner her life got back on track. But for some reason, that wasn't appealing to her as strongly as it should have.

"I'd like to meet your guys," she responded, and turned out of the parking lot.

Dean's house was tucked behind tropical plantings and waving palms, a pale green sided home with broad windows overlooking a fountain in front. The gardens were a little on the wild side, lush with heavy stemmed plants with large blooms and deep green leaves. It wasn't what Genevieve would have chosen, not the neat and tidy cottage she preferred, but on closer inspection, she realized what it reminded her a little of her mother's home.

"This is nice," she said as they pulled into the drive and she parked the car. In front of her was a cherry red VW bug, not the newer model with the little bud vase attached to the dash, but an older car that had been lovingly restored.

"Lillian's here!" Dean exclaimed. He pointed to the car, "she must have come by to take care of the guys. That is her pride and joy."

"Oh," Genevieve said weakly. She should have suspected something from the look of the car. If she had found out at Dean actually drove that particular car, she would have been surprised. No, maybe surprised was putting it too lightly, she thought repressing an involuntary smile, but she had known the car did not match his style.

"Come on," Dean said enthusiastically, swinging open his door. He didn't stop to get his bags, but strolled to the opposite side of the car and opened Genevieve's door, ushering her out.

She guessed she didn't have a choice now. She slid out, her sandals crunching over shells that covered the area in front of his house, and gingerly followed him toward the door.

"How far is the ocean from here?" she asked, filling her nervous silence with words.

"We're about a quarter mile from the water," he said pulling the door open.

"So do you visit often?"

"The ocean? Pretty much every weekend and some evenings during the week. The guys like to run in the water." He paused. "Well, actually, Henry doesn't much like the water. He would rather stay here if he had the choice. He is not a beach bum like the others."

Genevieve was smiling when she followed him into the house, hearing in the near distance the sounds of barking, skittering nails, and the hum of a woman's voice.

When the door squeaked behind them, the sounds changed, the barking growing more excited and closer as the dogs rushed from the recesses of the house to where they stood in the tiny foyer.

"Henry!" Dean's voice was pure joy as a mongrel with a tufted golden coat came speeding around a doorway. The dog flew toward Dean and threw himself at the man, his feet landing somewhere at Dean's middle as Dean cuddled him close.

Right on Henry's tail was a smaller dog, this one sleek and quick with glossy black fur and large brown eyes. He nosed his way between Dean and Henry, pushing his muzzle up to Dean's hand to get his share of attention.

The rumble from the back of the house had Genevieve turning in some alarm. The next dog was coming, and he sounded big. With a thump, the third dog cleared the doorway, moving fast and clumsy, missing the man and dogs and sailing past on the slick tile floor until he ran into the wall.

"Duke," Dean called out, and the dog righted himself, shook his massive head as though to clear it, and approached with no less enthusiasm on the second go.

As the dog jumped on his hind legs, his paws hitting Dean's shoulders as his hairy nose pushed against Dean's cheek and gave him a long, wet kiss, Genevieve became aware of another figure coming through the doorway. And this had to be Lillian.

Chapter 11

Genevieve hadn't been expecting to like Lillian. At least not right off. She had always been the sort of person to assess a newcomer with a clinical view, measuring them on their words and actions before she ever trusted them with any emotion. And on a purely foolish note, she had heard an awful lot of praise about the other woman. She found she was preparing herself not to like Dean's friend; she was finding she was feeling a little petty that way, but despite these preconceived notions, there was absolutely no way she could have avoided liking the other woman. Lillian was one of those rare souls that exuded light and warmth that made you feel as though you had known her your whole life, and she knew everything about you and still thought of you as her friend. She had approached Dean at full speed with arms wide open for a hug and smacking kiss on the cheek. He had to bend down to accept the embrace; Lillian might have topped five feet but only by a quarter inch. Her sleek black hair fell in a long ponytail down her back, and her almond shaped eyes, deep chocolate in color, were sparkling with enjoyment. She was lovely as well, Genevieve noted.

"About time you decided to come home!" Lillian exclaimed. "Duke thinks he should be able to sleep with me. And honey, that is not going to happen. My bed can't stand that kind of weight."

"Duke only weighs a shade over a hundred pounds," Dean said grinning. Duke, who must have had some Irish wolfhound in him to stand that tall, was leaning against Dean, perfectly content.

"What do you call a shade?" Lillian replied skeptically. "You've never been great at estimating," she continued. The smallest dog was now tucked under her arm; it's eyes rolling in bliss as she rubbed its ears. She glanced at Genevieve, dimples showing on her cheeks as she winked. "Don't believe a word he says! He'll sweet talk you into almost anything, and the next thing you know, his two-ton pet is breaking your bed."

Dean sighed. "Okay, sure," he said, and then turned to Genevieve. "This is Lillian, my friend and co-worker, and Lillian," he looked to his friend, "this is Genevieve."

"Good Lord, like I didn't know who she was," Lillian exclaimed, turning a grin full of white teeth and dimples towards Genevieve. "She was in every single message you sent me for the last week."

Genevieve was caught by the 'week' comment. She had met him a week ago, sure, when her mother had brought him to her house to broach the subject of his joining her little trip down. So he had been sending messages about her for that long? Even before she had decided that he was going to be riding with her? She stowed that thought for later and smiled back at Lillian.

"I've heard a lot about you as well," she said honestly. "And Dean said you like birds, so he figured you would want to meet Hemingway." As she spoke she thought of the bird still shut up in the back seat of her car, windows down, but she was a little distracted by Henry, who had moved on from Dean and was now nudging her leg, hoping to get some attention. She automatically bent to stroke her fingers through his golden fur, amazed at how soft his curls were.

"Is he here?!" Lillian's voice had ratcheted up in excitement with the question. "I want to see him, is he really here?"

"He's waiting in the car," Dean said laughing. "And just like that, we're forgotten." The last he directed toward Genevieve.

Lillian didn't hear him since she was already headed out the door, the dogs following in a furry flood behind her.

"We'd better keep up," Dean said strolling behind the dogs and woman out into the dappled sunlight.

96

Lillian had reached the side of the Mercedes and had stopped with apparent indecision. The dogs didn't feel the same hesitation, and the giant Duke had reared back on his long legs and was standing almost upright against the car, his enormous sandy paws against the rear passenger window.

"Duke, down!" Dean's voice was firm, and the dogs all sunk back and stepped away from the expensive car. "Sorry about that," Dean said apologetically as he tugged open the car door. He took a moment to study the window and the car door as though looking for any damage from the dog, but didn't seem to find anything because he reached in and pulled out the crate.

"We'll have to leave the dogs out here," Lillian said as she hurried up to Dean, her eyes all for the crate and the shuffling bird within.

"We can do that," Dean agreed. He led back inside the house, turning left into a large tiled living room instead of returning to the kitchen. Lillian gestured for Genevieve to follow and then closed the door behind the three of them, leaving the panting dogs outside.

Dean stood in the doorway and nodded for Genevieve to sit down. She chose a couch and sat down gingerly. She glanced around for somewhere that they could set Hemingway's crate. In the middle of the room, flanked by two full sized sofas made from some artificial leather material that were scarred by dozens of claw marks, was an equally oversized coffee table that was stacked with old veterinary magazines, car magazines, and a few paperback novels.

"Put him here," Lillian said firmly, scooping up one stack of the magazines and dropping them casually on the floor next to the couch.

Genevieve was busy looking around the space, observing with interest that Dean tended to decorate with lots of dark wood, white tile, and rich earth tones. She wondered what of the furniture his mother had chosen. Or perhaps some girlfriend? Just because he and Lillian didn't seem to have a romantic relationship didn't mean there was another woman somewhere in his life. And that was none of her business, she reminded herself.

Lillian had pulled open the wire door of the crate, and Hemingway was stepping out.

"He's not always nice when he's been cooped up all day," Genevieve warned.

She needn't have worried. Hemingway took one look at Lillian's warm brown eyes and fell head over claws in love with her.

Over coffee, Genevieve listened as Lillian reviewed the week's events in the vet office with Dean, relieved for a moment to be sitting down unobserved. She had her plans, altered yesterday and painstakingly outlined in her professional calendar, and she was thinking of all that needed to be done. She had dates posted in multiple places, on her computer, in her cell phone, on the wall calendar she had hung in her kitchen, and in the planner that she was never without, another addition to her expansive bag of supplies. Once she got back to the hotel, she would have the time to call around again to see if there was any new news about Jack. But since it had only been a day since she had last called, she doubted there would be any word.

She was brought back to the conversation when she saw Lillian had turned her eyes away from Hemingway who lay in her lap like an adoring puppy, to Genevieve.

"Dean said that you're looking for your father? And he comes here a lot?"

When Genevieve nodded her assent, Lillian continued. "You know, this big guy looks familiar. There aren't that many green wing macaws in the area. Maybe I've seen your father and Hemingway before?"

"You might have," Genevieve agreed. She pulled her cell phone from her pocket and tapped the picture icon. She flipped through the photos realizing with a pang that she hadn't many pictures. She didn't take them. And why? Why didn't she take pictures? Was it because she had little going on in her life besides work? It struck her as a little pathetic.

Not a good time to start rethinking her life.

She found the picture of Jack in front of the boat and passed her phone to Lillian.

"That's Jack. The one with Hemingway on his shoulder," she said unnecessarily.

"I have seen him," Lillian said, her voice hushed. "Oh, yeah, I've seen him!" She chuckled then. "He's awesome! Really funny." Then she seemed to realize that this wasn't a fun trip, but that Genevieve was there for a serious reason. "Oh, I'm sorry Genevieve. I can see why you're worried about him." She cuddled the parrot again, Hemingway leaning against her as though they were best friends for life. "I know he never went anywhere without this guy. I remember talking to your dad about Hemingway."

"Where did you see him?" Genevieve asked, her mind catching on the little details.

"Um, it was at a restaurant. It's down by the coast. They even had a place for this guy to perch."

"Casper's place," Genevieve said with a sigh, "it had to be there. Jack and Casper have known each other for years, and I doubt anyone else would have put up with the two of them."

"You're probably right. I don't remember the place, but the seafood was good."

Genevieve looked at the picture on the screen as Lillian passed it back to her. Jack was grinning, big and blustery, his beard caught in an errant breeze the shifted it over his barrel chest. Her own chest ached just a little.

"Where was this picture taken?" Dean asked, leaning close to Genevieve to look at the screen.

"That's at the marina that Topper had his boat."

"Topper?"

"Horace Topper was one of Jack's best friends and sometimes business partner. He was from the Louisville area like we are, but he traveled even more than Jack. He didn't have a family, at least not an immediate family that lived in the house with him, so he traveled more than he stayed at home. But Jack and Topper were very close," she finished smiling slightly. Jack had loved his buddy, and they had mixed business with their friendship with surprising ease. Jack had known Topper was wealthy, but often noted he thought the cash was a burden. Perhaps that was what had made the partnership so easy. Jack had never seemed to want anything from his friend, and even in financial lean times, had refused various loans from his companion. You don't mix money and friendship, he had stated, and Genevieve had to agree.

"Had?" Lillian's word had her coming back to the conversation.

"He passed away last year," Genevieve said. "I've never seen Jack so shook up." She was silent for a moment, thinking of Horace Topper, a kind older man with a big heart. She had gone to the funeral, standing in a slim tailored black suit, her mother in a relatively sedate purple gown that caught the breeze in ripples, reminding Genevieve of the flow of the ocean, standing next to her. Jack stood on his wife's other side. Jack had worn a suit last seen somewhere around his wedding day, and it had fit as Genevieve expected, too tight and too shiny. But that hadn't mattered, not a bit. Topper was gone, and Jack was there to see him go, to shed a few tears, and to give a fond farewell. She would have expected no less.

"Jack and Topper were close. They used to come down here regularly. Topper was an avid collector, so he was always setting up trips for the two of them, going through antique stores all the way through Tennessee, Georgia, and Florida. Jack just managed to benefit from some of Topper's business."

"What was his business?" This was from Dean as he sat back on the leather like couch and stretched out his legs.

"Good question," Genevieve replied. "Topper had a houseful of stuff, things he had collected for years, and he probably had owned ten times that much. He just traded, sold, bartered."

"Antiques?"

"Mostly," Genevieve had been to Topper's house many times, but each time had been a treat when she was a child. It was like an ever-evolving museum because she had seen something new, something usual, something fascinating every time she went. The old house itself, a mansion built over a hundred years ago just off the main road that paralleled the Ohio River to downtown Louisville, was impressive. The items inside were that much more so. "He had old furniture, collectibles, china, jewelry, silver, you name it, he had a little."

"And Topper owned the boat too?" Lillian was looking thoughtful.

"They shared it, but I think it was primarily owned by Topper." Genevieve paused. "They went out together on most trips. Lots of times they had a small group of them. I even went out on some of the day trips."

"Where's the boat now?" Dean's question was casual, but it struck a chord. She hadn't thought of the boat. Surely Jack hadn't gone out on the boat. She shook her head, unconscious that she was making the gesture, but feeling like she needed to shake the idea loose. No, that couldn't be the answer.

"At the marina, I assume," she said slowly, not certain at all.

Dean didn't remark on it anymore, and she shook her head slowly. One more thing to follow up on, she supposed.

Back at the hotel room, she set up her computer on the desk and put the crate in the middle of the bed. She had thought about where she might want to leave Hemingway when she went out on her trips, but admitted to herself she didn't want to go anywhere without him. She would be going by to visit Mac tomorrow. She knew that for sure. She had yet to get him to answer his phone, and it bothered her more than she could say. Mac was an older man like Jack, though not as old as Topper had been at his death. But Mac was in most ways the polar opposite of his boisterous friends. He was neat and reserved, fastidious and cultured. Mac was another collector, although he had held many other jobs in his youth, including a professor at a university in Boston. If Jack had admitted he was embarking on one of his harebrained schemes, he would have at the least told Mac about it, if not asked him to join. She knew that for sure.

If she wasn't able to find Mac, then she would definitely go see Casper. He had spoken to her a few times, but he had a much broader reach than she did, and he would be able to find people that might have heard of Jack's whereabouts. She would probably wait for that visit until later in the day so she could enjoy dinner there. Casper's fish was the best in the city, in her opinion, assuming nothing had changed in the years that she had been away from his cooking.

She booted up the computer and looked through the emails for one final time. She had a note from Larry asking about some statistics they had posted in the report about their product. It had taken her nearly an hour to get on the work server and find the information he had requested, but she found the task soothing. She wasn't a traveler. She liked her routine, her structure, and being here on her own with so much uncertainty had her uncomfortable. Rereading data analysis was comfortable. She wryly considered what that said about her.

A second email was from Rick asking if she had found her father. She was surprised. She had told Bob she planned on going to Florida to track down Jack, but she hadn't shared it with anyone else on her team. That meant Bob had spread the word, at least in a limited way. If Larry and Rick knew, then Bob had been the one to tell them, because she hadn't shared the reason for her leaving, not that she cared to tell them.

Now she tapped her lip thoughtfully with one finger as she looked at the screen. This hotel, unlike the bed and breakfast they had stayed in the night before, had a good Wi-Fi signal. The populated emails were a few days' worth. She flipped through the numerous missives, ads for improvement of home and body, sales of books, electronics, clothes and makeup, things she hadn't signed up for and would have to unsubscribe to as soon as she got up the gumption. Which wasn't like her. Normally she was more focused than this. But worry had her distracted, and that made her unhappy.

She finished looking through her messages and then checked through some files. She pulled up her calendar next, looking at her to do list for the upcoming day.

The rattle and flutter of the bird had her closing the top on the computer and turning to her companion. She was getting a little hungry, but she didn't think she was as brave as Dean. She wouldn't take Hemingway out with the hope of some waitress letting her settle in, and she didn't want to leave him this soon.

"Pizza?" she asked the bird, and he responded with one long, low whistle.

She hadn't wanted to let the bird sleep free in her room, but in the end she had done something she never did at home, fallen asleep watching the television. She had also left the lights on dim, had a stack of papers on her lap, and Hemingway cuddled up next to her. When she woke he was still there, still leaning sleepily against her pillow. She scanned the room but didn't notice anything that made her suspicious of his activities during the night. He must have been too tired to misbehave.

When she went into the bathroom, he followed a few steps behind, and as soon as she turned on the shower, he stepped in flapping and cawing with joy. If anyone was in the room beside hers, she suspected they would be hearing some strange sounds. She just hoped they didn't call the management. It had happened before. When she and her parents had gone on family vacations, an infrequent occurrence since her mother never liked to travel, they had taken Rainbow along. He was her feathered brother, she had insisted with childhood stubbornness, and her father had agreed. Jack loved them both. They both came on vacation. They both had gotten a souvenir before the trip was over. Jack was accustomed to traveling with the big bird, although at the time, Hemingway had spent far more time at home with her mother and her rather than go on the road with Jack. It was only after she had moved out of the house, after she had grown up and grown more distant from her parents, that Jack had started taking the parrot with him on all of his adventures.

On this particular trip, Jack had promised an adventure in the Wild West. They had driven from town to town, from city to city, visiting every little strange and off road sightseeing spot. It had been exhausting and wonderful. As they were settling in for the night at a Holiday Inn next to a picturesque pioneer village they had visited the day before, Rainbow started complaining. Jack had brought in ice cream for the three of them, but had forgotten to bring a treat back for Bow, a rare occurrence, truly. The screeching had brought the people next door from their peaceful slumber at ten in the evening, and when pounding on the adjoining walls hadn't quieted the bird, they had called the manager.

Bow had loved the sounds of their fists hitting the thin walls, and he had responded with enthusiasm, yelling loudly back in what he assumed was part of the family flock call. The management had come to the door, thinking for sure that someone was being murdered by the high-pitched screams being emitted from the residence of the room. After the manager had finally gotten the real story he had been relieved but asked them to leave.

Now, as she watched the bird make a show of strutting and flapping his great wings where he perched on the curve of the shower curtain, she hoped that the same fiasco wouldn't happen again. She didn't want to be evicted from her chosen hotel. And being thrown out was just embarrassing at her age.

After their shower, she dressed in pressed shorts and a sleeveless top. She braided her hair neatly in a rope down her back and laughed as Hemingway came out of the bathroom, still damp and a little matted.

"I'm going to go grab something for our breakfast," she told the bird, and baited his crate with his favorite snack, a banana chip from the natural foods store. She went down into the lobby to look over their free breakfast offerings, and chose some cereal for the bird and a muffin for herself. The coffee was good, so she brought up a steaming cup with her.

After breakfast, she checked her computer once more, and finding only a note from Larry regarding the job, nothing that would need to be addressed now, she headed out into the sunshine. Hemingway was in the crate again, but she had packed his harness. The weather was wonderful, and if Jack had been able to visit his friends with Hemingway loose, then she would try as well. She felt guilty keeping him in the crate for the whole time; she wanted to give him more freedom to move around, but there was no way she was going to have a cage to let him stay in. The size cage that he required wasn't exactly portable.

With a final check to make sure her door was locked, she headed out to the car.

"Let's go see if we can find Mac," she told the bird, and turned on the engine.

Chapter 12

The GPS filled in the gaps where Genevieve's directional memory failed, leading her to the white stucco and glass structure that was her father's friend's home. She remembered it from her last visit in her early teens when the treat of Florida breezes, the hot rays of the sun, and the salty taste on her lips had been sheer joy. Mac had found the architectural wonder that was his home years before she was born, but it remained starkly modern in style despite its age.

The drive was flanked on either side by a front lawn covered in geometric pavers that wound their way between a lush tropical garden, perfectly maintained and in full bloom. Unlike Dean's wild jungle like property, Mac's was in precise order. It should have been much more appealing to her, the geometry and tidiness of it. She wasn't sure she actually felt that way, however.

Shaking her head to dismiss her thoughts, she walked up the drive. The car was parked in the shade, but she took Hemingway with her up the deck stairs. At the door, she looked inside through the window. She could see the greenhouse room through the sunlit glass, the plants grouped in artful arrangements around a central cleared area furnished with a table and chairs set. But the table was cleared and there was no sign anyone had sat there lately. She frowned, recalling that Mac tended to breakfast there, enjoying the room when the heat wasn't as oppressive and the view from the rear windows, those facing out toward the vista of the ocean, was a dazzling display of color.

There was a doorbell of sorts attached to the doorframe and she tentatively pressed it. Hemingway was shuffling in his crate so she wasn't sure if the bell had sounded within. She pressed it again more firmly, leaning closer to the glass to hear the bell chime. Okay, so that worked, she thought, leaning away from the door. She checked her watch, forcing herself to wait for two full minutes before hitting the bell again. She repeated this several times before stepping back, frustrated.

"Okay, he's not here," she said softly. Hemingway didn't seem to be particularly upset. He was still shuffling in the crate, and she heard him make some new noises. Sea birds? Maybe. Or perhaps he was showing some of his location memory. It wasn't unusual for him to make sound effects or say words in one environment or with a certain person and not use it with any other situation. The mysterious avian brain.

She stood still for another moment and rocked back on her heels. Well, she hadn't actually expected that Mac would be there. She had tried to call him many times, leaving messages on the cell phone. If he had gotten the messages, she hadn't heard from him, but she doubted he had. Mac knew her. He also cared for her, she thought. If he had heard the concern in her voice, he would have called back. So the conclusion was pretty natural. He hadn't gotten the message. He hadn't known she had called. And that was because he wasn't home. He wasn't somewhere he could get her calls.

So now she knew that not only was Jack missing, she suspected Mac was missing as well.

When she walked back toward the car, she was frowning. She had hit a dead end with Mac. However, he was different than her father. Mac had a home he stayed in year round. He did not travel extensively. He had roots here, was part of the community, was both well-known and well liked. So perhaps he would be missed as well. She glanced back toward the house. It looked strange and abandoned. From the corner of her eye she noticed a section of greenery cut away from the side of the house, revealing the flash of a window pane. Had a branch broken off in the wind, or cut away by Mr. Mac before he left? A darker thought crossed her mind. Had someone else tried to clear the view to look inside the house? And why?

Logic had her visiting the neighbors first. The lots here were generous for the area, but the nearest neighbors were still close by. The house on the right was painted a bright coral with white trim. The posts were covered with vines that twisted in graceful lines, bright pink flowers breaking up the dark green stems.

The screen door was closed but the inner door was open onto a narrow porch that stretched the length of the front of the house. Genevieve figured there would be another in the back to take advantage of the fantastic views.

She stopped in front of the door and set the crate down by her feet. Hemingway was being quiet, interested in what their next step might be. She lifted one fist to the metal side of the screen door and knocked, the door making a rattling hollow sound.

A moment later the quick clatter of steps on tile sounded within the house and a woman stepped out onto the porch. She was moving fast, wearing a neatly creased skirt, short and showing a length of tanned legs with a pressed top in pale pink. She might have been ready to go on a luncheon date, but Genevieve wondered if she didn't dress that way all the time. She just seemed like someone that might habitually stay in top form. She stood on the other side of the screen and studied Genevieve through the screen.

"Yes?"

"Hello, sorry to bother you," Genevieve said quickly. "I'm a friend of Mac's. Or rather, my father is one of his best friends, and I was hoping to talk to him." She paused, watching the expressions flicker across the woman's tanned face.

"Mac?"

"From next door, Mr. Macintosh."

"I know Mac," the woman replied. Her carefully made face creased in a quizzical expression, her glossy lips pinched. She let the door ease open a crack and stepped back. "Would you like to come in?"

Genevieve nodded, feeling the morning heating up. The porch was open, and a fan was spinning lazily above them giving a welcome breeze. She leaned over and caught the crate by the plastic handle on top.

"Is that a parrot?" the woman asked, bending down to get a better look inside the container.

"This is Hemingway. He's my father's bird," Genevieve explained, feeling the weight of the bird shift inside as he reached out one dark claw to grasp the bars.

"Then you must be Jack's girl." The voice was suddenly warm and easy.

Genevieve felt a rush of relief. Here was someone who knew Jack. Hopefully that would mean that she knew what was going on with Mac as well.

"Yes, I'm Genevieve." She set the crate at her feet again and held out her hand. The woman took it, her palm callused and grip firm.

"I'm Carla. Nice to finally meet you. Jack has spoken of you often."

Genevieve was silent for a moment, unsure of what had made her stomach clench. Was it because her father spoke of her often? Because he must have talked about her a lot for this woman to know of her?

"So you know Jack well?"

Carla smiled easily. "I've met him several times." She gestured Genevieve to a chair and seated herself opposite, tucking her knees neatly together, ladylike.

"Jack's the reason I'm here," Genevieve confessed, putting the crate on the floor. Hemingway made a little sound of protest and she could see him clinging to the bars to get a better look outside.

"You said you wanted to see Mac," Carla observed.

"Jack left Hemingway here with me, and I haven't been able to contact him. I thought Mac would know where he was."

Carla was frowning. "I imagine he does know, but I doubt you're going to be able to catch up with Mac. He went out of town himself a few weeks ago." She nodded toward the neighboring house. "He's asked me to take care of his plants. He has such beautiful property."

"Yes, he does," Genevieve agreed, and her mind was spinning. Jack was out of town; Mac was out of town. She couldn't talk to Mac because he was gone, and gone where? "Do you know where Mac went?"

"Well, no," Carla seemed unconcerned. "He just asked me to run by and water his plants. He didn't mention where he was going." She glanced out the window and then toward Genevieve. "In fact he didn't say how long he would be gone either. Which is not like him. Macintosh is normally precise about these things."

Genevieve nodded. That she could understand. She was planned as well, but of course Jack wasn't and maybe…

"Do you think Jack and Mr. Macintosh went together?" she asked. The timing was just a little too coincidental. Of course, they were both travelers, but for them to be gone at exactly the same time, it was more than that.

"I don't know," Carla said slowly. "I didn't see Jack. I haven't seen him for probably a year almost. But of course, with Topper gone, they don't seem to be out traveling quite as often."

Genevieve studied her. Carla seemed to know a lot about her neighbor. So perhaps they were more than just neighbors. Friends? Definitely.

"If you hear from him, would you let me know?" She patted her pocket, remembering suddenly she wasn't at work, that she didn't have a stack of business cards.

"Sure," Carla said. She saw Genevieve's movements and waved her hand. "Let me get you a pen and paper. You can write out your numbers so I can call you." She stood and walked with quick mincing steps into the house. A moment later she was back. "Just write out your name and number. And if I hear from Macintosh, either he will contact you, or I will." She handed over the pen and paper, and Genevieve wrote out her information in her clear, precise handwriting.

"Thanks for this," Genevieve said honestly. "I've been a little worried about Jack." She stood and handed over the paper. As an afterthought, she said, "I don't suppose you know anything about the boat. Topper and Mac went out on a boat with Jack several times. I just wondered if it was still around."

"Oh, yes." Carla had a little smile on her face. Her face relaxed, the lines loosening around her mouth. "I've been out on the boat myself. It's nice." Her eyes strayed back over to the house again. "But I don't know if Mac has taken it out lately."

Genevieve thanked her again and bent to pick up the crate. Carla didn't seem to hold the same affection for the bird that some of Jack's other friends had. Her brow crinkled slightly as she gazed down at the crate, and her hands curled into a little ball at her middle as though she were holding something tight in her joined fists. She watched them intently as they headed for the screen door. Genevieve went back down the steps gingerly, holding the rail in one hand and the carrier in the other, feeling the sway as the bird shifted within. She glanced up once as she walked across the yard, toward Mr. Macintosh's lot. Carla was at the doorway, back straight and face expressionless. Genevieve opened the car door, her eyes looking up almost without thinking. Carla was still standing there framed in the dim shadow of the porch.

Genevieve changed her mind about her next steps as she pulled away from Mac's home and headed into the sunshine. She was going to the marina. There was something bothering her about Macintosh leaving at the same time Jack disappeared. Were they together? Was this some kind of joint adventure between the men? Genevieve hoped so. Of course, they were known to go on long car excursions, on quick flights to other countries, and virtual voyages across the ocean when the spirit took them. But she felt somewhere in her gut that this time, this time was different. She had an inkling of where they might have gone now, and she wanted to check out her idea as soon as she could.

Before she left for what might be a goose chase, she put in another call to Nub, her father's friend who had been living out at the marina. The last she had heard, he was staying out of town, but that didn't mean that he hadn't heard anything about Mac taking the boat out. When she was finally able to get in touch with him, he told her regretfully he had broken a bone in his foot and had retreated to his little apartment while on the mend. It had been months since he had set foot in the marina. Dead end. It appeared that she was on her own for this visit.

It had been three years since she had been at the marina, loading up on the boat with Jack and his friends for a day out. They hadn't gone far out to sea; it was meant for a few hours only, but she had been thrilled to see the leaping dolphins following, dodging and playing in their wake. Their plans of fishing had less to do with the poles in the water and more to do with sightseeing, showing her some of their fishing spots, and the best places to gather colorful shells and shark's teeth. The men had pointed out their best and favorite views, and she had obediently snapped pictures with her little digital camera. She still had the images somewhere stored on her computer. It was one of those golden days she didn't want to forget.

She had to look up some of the local marinas on her cell phone, finally finding the one she was searching for. She put the address in her maps program and listened as the computerized voice instructed her on the best route to her destination. As she started the car, she noticed from the corner of her eye another vehicle pulling out, a dark SUV, stopping behind her instead of pulling around. She frowned with frustration and pulled away, noting that they tailed her for a few minutes before melting into the background.

The marina was close. It took only fifteen minutes to get there. The boats were lined up liked parked cars, the masts spearing the blue sky, the hulls gleaming in the hot Florida sun. Genevieve only vaguely recalled the boat itself, and knew for sure she would never be able to identify it by herself. She was happy to see that there was a shack, its wooden door hanging open, a few men clustered inside, smoking cigarettes and drinking out of soft drink cans.

She felt a little ridiculous climbing out of her car, her purse slung over her shoulder, the crate gripped in the other hand. She closed the car door firmly and walked over to the solitary building.

"Excuse me?"

One of the men turned, a twenty-something guy with a scraggly beard. His skin was burnished a smooth brown, his hair lightened by the same harsh sun. He had an artful tattoo of a rose winding up his arm, the thorns painted to appear as though they were piercing his skin.

"Yes ma'am," he responded. He tossed his empty can into the trash and tilted his cap back on his forehead, revealing bright blue eyes already surrounded by crinkles from squinting in the sunlight.

"I was looking for a boat," she began, glancing from him to the other men, two older guys in sweat soaked tees and matching beer bellies.

"You wanting to hire one out?" one of the men asked, his voice harsh with smoke. He put out his cigarette and cleared his throat. "I've got a few going out today, but we'd have to check the schedule." He had straightened, has hands hastily tucking in the loose yellow tee shirt, his attempt at looking presentable, she assumed.

"No, no, I need to find one of my friend's boats," she amended. She briefly explained the situation, and to make it seem like she was not totally crazy, she pulled out her phone to show the men the picture. She had to lean over and put the crate on the ground at her feet. When she looked back up, she saw one of the older men was studying the picture obediently, the yellow shirted man that had offered her the ride, but the other was looking with fascination at the crate as a shuffling sound reminded her of her companion. The third and youngest guys' eyes seemed to have rested on her chest where she suspected he had gotten an eyeful as she leaned down to pick up the crate. She willed herself not to blush and sourly hoped he had enjoyed the view enough to help her.

"Is that Hemingway?" one of the older men asked - not the one who had offered her a ride, but his equally sweaty companion who wore a bright red ball cap with the name of some sports team embroidered in loopy white lettering.

She looked at him sharply. "Yes," she said surprised. Good Lord, did everyone know Jack?

"So you're looking for Topper's boat," the man said grinning.

"Yes," she breathed, relieved. "Yes, I'm looking for Mac and my father. I thought they might have taken the boat out." It had been Topper's boat, but after his death, Jack and Mr.

Macintosh had jointly inherited the craft. She wasn't going to mention that if the boat was in place, that she planned on turning it inside out in hopes of finding a clue to the whereabouts of the two men.

"Your father?" The man scooped off his cap and ran a hand over his almost bald head, his eyes squinted in confusion. "Your father wouldn't be Jack would it?"

"Yes," she agreed, nodding. "I'm Genevieve Glass."

The other man's eyes widened. "Jack's daughter," he said, shaking his head. "You haven't been around here for years. Wouldn't have recognized you at gun point."

"It's been a long time," she agreed, and then felt a twinge of guilt. Her father had asked her to visit. He had wanted she and her mother to come down to Florida for trips, for memories. He was a sentimental old cuss under all the bravado and beard. But she hadn't had time to indulge him. She had projects to finish, work to do, her own life to live. But she wasn't going to justify her absence to this man, she thought stubbornly. "Have we met before?"

The man hummed his assent. "Like I said, it's been years. But to answer your question, the boat's not here."

She took a deep breath, not sure how to feel. Was she relieved to have found a possible clue regarding Jack's disappearance? Or was she worried because those old men had taken off in the boat without telling her where they were going? Of course, just because they hadn't told her anything didn't mean they hadn't told anyone where they were off to.

"How long have they been gone?" she asked her eyes scanning the three men.

"Well, now, that I'm not sure about."

Genevieve blew out a frustrated breath and waited as the man gazed beyond her into the splintered light of the sea beyond. "I think he might have gotten some fuel on his way out," he said at last.

"And that would tell us at least when they left?" she asked hopefully.

"Yeah," he said, his eyes squinting, watering a little in the bright light.

"That would be great," she said, feeling a rush of relief.

"Chris, check the logs," the red capped man said to the twenty something who had seemed to check out during their conversation and was gazing out toward the water.

Chris ducked into the comparative darkness of the shack and left the three of them standing in the sun.

"Sorry, I should have introduced myself. Name's Bruce Carver," the man said, adjusting his red cap again. He gestured to his companion in the yellow shirt. "This is Mike Serato." He turned toward Mike. "You met Topper and his friends didn't you? Her dad is the big guy, looks like a pirate, has that damn bird all the time."

Mike's eyebrows lifted toward the brim of his stained cap with the logo of a straining fish on a line, and his lips quirked. "Didn't that bird bite you?"

"Almost drew blood," Bruce said, casting a glance down at the crate as though to make sure it was securely closed.

Genevieve was tempted to tell him he was lucky. If threatened, moody, angry, scared, or any of another dozens of emotions affected Hemingway, he was likely to bite. And he could take a chunk of flesh with him. Birds his sized were known to cause wounds requiring stitches all the way up to broken finger bones. It happened. And she had known him to cause some minor damage, although she couldn't recall Jack ever having to go to the hospital because of his pet. But she kept her mouth closed. Jack was usually adept at assessing Hemingway's mood and warning others. If Hemingway had bit the man, chances are it was at least partially his fault. Of course, she wasn't going to tell him that. After all, she was hoping for help, and she wouldn't get it if she accused him of doing something stupid to get himself bit by the big bird.

The young Chris came back out of the building with a spiral bound book in his hand and held it out for Bruce to take. She could see now that these two men worked at the marina, and she figured Bruce might be the manager of the place.

"Took the boat out early in May with a full tank," Bruce said, his finger on a line in the block print of the log. "So he's been out for about a month and a half. He must have gone into another port for supplies. Seems pretty likely. But like I said, he hasn't been here since unless he crept in at night and no one let me know." He tilted his head thoughtfully. "And you know something, you're not the only one that's been looking for that boat."

"I'm not?" Genevieve's voice reflected her confusion.

"Nope. Man came down here just a week or so ago. Looking for the boat. I didn't know him, so I didn't tell him nothin'."

"Oh," Genevieve said softly, but her mind had started spinning again, and this time, the thoughts were darker.

Chapter 13

Genevieve returned to the hotel with a lot on her mind. Her usual analytical processes were firing, her memory tracing back through the facts rapidly, dismissing some of the outliers, things that didn't seem to be related to her current problem, and focusing on what she considered the most important line of study. Her job had required she analyze data, form hypothesis, and then follow up. She felt like she was closer to the truth than she ever had been since Hemingway had been dropped on her front door, but she wasn't sure how close she was to seeing Jack face to face. If they were out on the boat, Jack, Mac, and any possible combination of cronies they might have rounded up, there was no way to track them down. No way at all. So square one was to figure out where they might be going.

She knew anyone from outside the situation would be wondering what she was doing, going to all of this trouble to find Jack when it was becoming obvious he didn't want to be found. He had managed to drop Hemingway off at a place he considered safe, and then disappear. It looked deliberate. It seemed that Jack wasn't missing so much as purposefully hidden. And who was he hiding from? She thought of the man that had been looking for him at the marina that Bruce had mentioned, but dismissed the idea. Her mind went back to her missing father. Apparently neither she nor her mother had been worthy of his confidence. And here she was chasing down his oldest friends, and Casper hadn't managed to made the trusted list either unless he was a remarkably good liar. And she liked to think that hearing her concern over Jack's disappearance would have prompted Casper to give her some reassurance. Surely if he knew where Jack was, and knew he was safe, Casper would at least have given her some comforting words.

No, she didn't think Casper knew what was going on with Jack. At least, she amended, he didn't know exactly what was going on. But that wasn't to say that Jack hadn't inadvertently dropped a hint about his plans. And perhaps Casper knew something, but was unaware of the significance.

That being said, she still intended to go talk to Casper. He was the only other one of her father's friends she kept up with besides Mr. Mac. She hadn't seen him face to face for a few years, but she had heard updates from her father. She was certain Casper knew all of the other players. And when all the facts were laid out there, there was one thing that kept her anxiety from easing. Her father may very well have taken the boat, with or without Mac, to places unknown. But why had he chosen to leave not a single word with any of his family? Why leave them in the dark?

She checked her watch. It was after 3 o'clock, and she was starving.

She looked toward the crate. Hemingway was perched on the desk. He had demolished his lunch of fruit, some fresh vegetables, and pellets. She had given him an empty tissue box to play with, and he was busy ripping strips of cardboard from it and dropping the pieces like confetti on the floor. She would have to clean that up before anyone in housekeeping came in and saw the mess. He was having such an obviously enjoyable experience, flapping his great colorful wings and bobbing his head in abandon, that Genevieve had to smile as she shook her head. He was like a child sometimes, the crazy bird. It was well documented that parrots had the intelligence of a child too. Granted, it would be a spoiled three-year-old child with a temper, but he still made her smile. She had missed him when she moved out on her own. She had to admit that, although only to herself, but she had to be honest. He was a disaster. He was loud. He was a whole lot of work. Like Jack, he was loveable, but easy to resent when his unpredictable personality got in the way of the order and routine that she liked, or rather needed, to function.

Now she stood with reluctance and went over to the crate. She had his special treats; his favorite nuts set aside to lure him in the crate. He had been a good sport about it so far, staying in the crate for hours on end. She knew Jack kept him out more often than not, wearing him like another accessory, almost always perched on his jacketed shoulder, and daring anyone to protest the presence of an animal in their establishment.

She made the decision then. If Dean could fit the halter on the bird, then she could as well. For this trip, she wouldn't crate the bird at all.

But that wouldn't be a problem with Casper. Casper had known Jack for years, and Hemingway was a regular. He had a table already chosen for the pair when Jack came by, situated out of the main flow of the restaurant just close enough to the window for the big parrot to enjoy the view of the seabirds wheeling away on the drafts of salty heated air.

She hadn't been to Casper's establishment for a long time, but Jack had told her the last time she had seen him he had been out to see Casper just a week before. She closed her eyes and recalled the conversation. She had dropped by the house to see her mother. Soup had been simmering on the stove and the aroma of freshly baked bread had permeated the front room of the house. In the summer, the windows were thrown open at every opportunity, and it had been unseasonably cool that day. She had stepped in through the open screen door and stopped in the front room to shed her lab coat and hang it on the hook by the door, dropping her purse in the little chair next to it. There was a small stack of mail on the chair, and when she picked it up and shuffled through the envelopes, she saw they were addressed to her. Even after years of living away, she still received a few pieces of mail here, and she hadn't taken the time to change her address on a few mailing lists. It was a fragile link to her childhood, but she stubbornly refused to acknowledge to herself there was a reason she hadn't changed her address. Subconsciously, she liked the connection to home. She had tucked the mail into her purse and followed the sound of her mother's voice into the kitchen. She was sitting at the scarred wooden table, the familiar mug of tea in front of her. She had a book open on the table next to her, and a pair of red-framed readers perched on her nose.

"Who were you talking to?" Genevieve asked as she stopped in the doorway, inhaling the delectable scents.

But before her mother could answer, the sound of footsteps thundering down the stairs had gotten her attention, and she turned to see Jack stroll in. Jack, her father; Jack, the character; Jack, the unpredictable.

Hemingway had greeted her first, crying out with a powerful caw before flapping his massive wings and flying straight to her. She had lifted an arm in front of her, parallel to the floor and bent at the elbow, and he had landed neatly on it just like he had hundreds of times before. He wasn't fully flighted. Jack kept his flight feathers trimmed so he could glide to the floor, but not gain enough air to get carried away by a draft into the wide blue yonder. As a child, Genevieve had trained Hemingway, Bow as she called him, to fly to her from any close by surface and land on her arm, to then be pulled close for a cuddle. He didn't do the trick for anyone else, and she still felt a twinge of triumph.

Jack had followed the bird, his arms wrapping around her in a hug that avoided the bird, but managed to squeeze her firmly to his broad chest, the wiry hair of his beard scratching her forehead.

"My girl," he rumbled, and she had returned the embrace a little half-heartedly, she remembered now with a pang. He had smelled of leather and soap, familiar.

The visit had been a repeat of so many before. He had stayed for a week, living in the house as though he was always there, cluttering up the space with his collections, taking care of the dozens of errands and chores her mother had collected for him to do to keep the little homestead on its feet and running. There was a section of fence to be mended, a leaky spot in the roof, a window that wouldn't budge, and something wrong with the clothes dryer.

Genevieve had come by twice to see her parents. The first time had been an accident of sorts, and the second was when her mother had promised a dinner for the family before her father departed for his next trip.

"Where are you going this time?" Genevieve had asked, not that interested. Her mind had been on work, on one of the niggling problems that plagued her project she had yet to iron out.

"Just to Florida for a few days," he had responded. "Going to go by and talk to Casper. You know, that place hasn't changed a bit since you were there years ago," he had told Genevieve, looking at her meaningfully.

"Hmm," was her noncommittal reply. She hadn't time to run out to Florida and hang out with her father's buddies. She had outgrown her traveling days. She had a job now, responsibilities.

"He would like to see you," he had hinted.

Now as she walked in the doorway of the humble restaurant, she smiled a little. Jack had been right. The place hadn't changed, not so much as a stick of furniture had been changed out.

Casper was behind the bar as he always had been, leaning back against the rough wooden surface, his eyes on the television that blinked in strobes. A ball game was on, something with tiny white figures on a broad green field, but Genevieve wasn't looking at that. She was looking at her father's friend, seeing with a pang that like everything else, how he had aged. His face, still browned by the sun, had gained some lines and creases. He still had those characteristic pale shadows around his eyes that came from using sunglasses habitually, although she thought at this age, he might need glasses just to see. His hair was still full and thick, but the brown held streaks of gray.

Around him, the movement of the staff, one teenaged girl with shorts much too short and a tight pink tank top, and an older woman that might have been his wife he had married since Genevieve had seen him last, went on with a smooth rhythm. Lunch was about over, and dinner wouldn't start for another hour. In Florida, Senior citizens tended to dine early, so five o'clock was as likely to be as crowded as seven o'clock, especially during the week.

She walked straight to the bar, Hemingway balanced on her shoulder while she held the strings of his harness in her hand. She did it on purpose. If Casper didn't immediately recognize her, as she had changed a lot in the few years since she had seen him, he would most certainly recognize Jack's favorite feathered son.

With the sound of wood scraping on wood as she pulled the barstool out to sit, Casper turned toward her. She had forgotten how bright his blue eyes appeared in that brown face, or how white his smile seemed as it stretched in a welcoming grin.

"Genevieve! So you made it."

"Hi," she said feeling suddenly younger. She forced herself to stand a little straighter. "I got here last night. I've been hunting around for Jack since then. I guess you haven't heard?"

"Heard what crazy plans he had or where he went?" he finished her question for her, leaning both hands against the roughened surface of the bar. "No, hon, I haven't. I called around to a few of our friends, but no one has seen or heard anything from him for few weeks. Actually, from what I can tell, it looks like the last anyone heard from him was before he left for home. Seems like he went directly from Kentucky on this little adventure."

"I know he was here," she said straightening on the stool and hooking her sandals over the crossbar.

He had grabbed a glass and without asking, had filled it with diet soda, adding a dollop of cherry syrup and a maraschino cherry on the top. He put it in front of her before she asked, and she took it automatically. Her fingers found the cold sides of the plastic straw and she smelled the sharp scent of cherry. After a long sip, she smiled. It was good. It always had been. And she had completely forgotten how she had loved this drink when she had come here with Jack years before. But Casper had remembered.

"So how do you know he was here?" he asked, watching with approval as she drank more of the delicious concoction.

"I was at the marina," she began. "I thought he might have been out to visit Mac, but when I went to his house, Mr. Mac's neighbor told me he had been gone for some time. She had no idea where he had gone, but she knew Jack, so she seemed to know Mac pretty well. She's watching the house for him, the gardens and all." She paused, her fingers unconsciously tracing the sweat beading on the side of the glass. "But then I thought about where they both might have gone. And I thought of the boat. So my next idea was to try the marina."

"It was a good idea," he agreed. "Jack loved taking the boat out. And since he and Mac bought it off Topper's nephew last summer, they've gone out in it almost every time Jack comes into town." He leaned his hands back against the bar. "Went out on it myself a few times," he continued.

"At the marina, they knew it had been fueled and gone out a few weeks ago, but they have no idea where they went and they didn't know who was on it."

"So you know Mac took it out, but not if Jack was with him?"

She sighed. "That's about it," she agreed.

The older waitress approached just then, and Casper introduced her as his wife, Debbie. Genevieve smiled at them, seeing the newly wed glow even after almost a year of marriage.

"Genevieve here is chasing after Jack," Casper filled in, taking a sliver of fruit and holding it out for the parrot.

"Where has that man got to?" Debbie asked. She was smiling, a look that Genevieve had become accustomed to when people thought of Jack. It was the look of curiosity, and a little bit of chagrin, as though they couldn't believe someone was leading the life he led, and doing it successfully. Jack followed the beat of a different drummer, and pretty much everyone knew that.

"That's exactly what I'm trying to figure out," Genevieve admitted.

"And you're taking that bird with you?" Debbie lifted one plucked brow, her teeth, slightly crooked in front, exposed between bright coral lips as she smiled again.

"Hemingway is going everywhere with me," Genevieve admitted. "You'd be surprised how people open up and talk when they see him."

"He is a charmer," Debbie agreed. She looked at the half empty glass of cola in Genevieve's hand, and turned toward her husband. "Haven't you gotten her anything to eat yet?"

Casper's lips twitched. "See why I married her?" He looked at Genevieve. "So what can I get you? The usual?"

Genevieve looked around the restaurant, feeling a little as though she had slipped back in time. There weren't a lot of places where she had a usual order. It had been years since she had been here, but before that, she had enjoyed the same lunch every time she came to Casper's place, a perfectly prepared fish sandwich with homemade tartar sauce and thick cut French fries. Just the thought of it had her mouth watering. "Yes," she said looking gratefully at her father's friend, "that would be wonderful."

She was relocated at Jack's table, the one close to the bar but far enough from the door that the parrot, now perched on a stand with the harness keeping him in place, wasn't tempted to take a quick flight outside. Hemingway even had his own plate and bowl, one filled with water and the other with goodies from the menu that Casper always gave the bird.

She was glad she had come. Casper seemed to have few ideas of what might have happened to Jack or Mr. Macintosh, but he was concerned, and just that made her feel a little less alone.

When dinner was over, she tried to pay a tab but it was waved off. Casper wouldn't take her money, but assured her he would stay in touch and asked her to let him know of any news she received from Jack. She agreed to the same. It had been another dead end, she knew, but she was still glad she had followed up.

The hotel was mostly still when she strolled through the lobby. It wasn't like the place she had chosen when she was with Dean. No circling motorcycles or screaming patrons. At least not so far. The beige lobby was as unremarkable as it possibly could be, and she could imagine Dean's expression if he came in. She was satisfied with her choice, however. This one, at least, was exactly as she expected. She felt a little twinge and thought about how nice it would be to bounce ideas off of Dean. She could have asked him his opinion about what she had learned. See what he thought of the missing boat, and the missing Mr. Macintosh.

She was still lost in thought as she threaded her way down the hallway. Someone had made an unfortunate choice in carpeting, she noted. The rug was an intricate plaid in the ugliest shades of brown and green she could imagine. With the beige walls, she felt like she had fallen into some eighties movie set. And it wouldn't have been a good movie.

She used the card to unlock her door, and breathed in the smell of cleanser and laundry detergent as she walked in. Good. Clean was good.

She dropped her purse and keys on the little table and put the crate on the bed. She flicked the switch on the television, letting the white noise wash over her. She didn't normally watch it at home, but here in a strange city, a strange room, she liked the feel of company. Speaking of company, she pulled her cell phone out of her shorts' pocket and studied the screen. No messages. She opened the contacts app and scanned some of the entries. Dean's was a new one she had added just a few days ago. She switched off the screen and dropped the cell phone on the desk. No way would she be calling anyone else tonight.

She transferred the parrot to the desk as she pulled out her pajamas, planning on an early night. Together they went into the shower, and after a joint bath, she went back into the bedroom, watching with amusement as he waddled after her.

She heard a notifying ping from her phone and checked her email. Nothing new there. But she had received a text from Casper asking her for a copy of the picture she had of Jack. She opened the gallery app on her phone and scrolled through the photos. Not seeing what she was looking for, she backed out of the camera section, and looked at the other icons in the gallery. She noticed a section titled downloads and looked at what appeared to be some photos she had received in her emails. She remembered getting copies of snapshots on her phone from her mother. Most were of a new and exotic orchid her mother had been growing. But when Genevieve looked a little more closely, she saw an unfamiliar picture.

"Oh, my," she breathed. And she knew what it was.

Chapter 14

It took her just a second to think of a way to transfer the picture from her phone to the computer, and she emailed it as an attachment to her private email address. She wasn't tangling with her work address just now. The fact that the original email had disappeared still seemed suspicious to her.

Keeping Hemingway in her sight, she sat at the desk and opened her laptop. She needed to plug it in. She was impatient to look at the picture, but she had to make sure she wouldn't lose the lead again.

After she was connected with a power source, she booted up the computer. As the fan buzzed, she checked to make sure her email had sent from her phone, and then leaned back in the chair. Now, all she had to do was check out the picture.

She felt a wave of relief as the email opened on her computer and she downloaded the attachment. She opened the picture and bent forward to look at the screen.

"Oh, you have to be kidding me," she said softly. "Is this a pirate map?"

It was definitely a drawing of landmasses, the water identified by the characteristic symbols that seemed to be universal to old maps. It had everything except for the ominous "there be monsters". It was also almost certainly hand drawn on a yellowing paper, and the age would be anyone's guess.

But as she scooted away and looked at the shape as a whole, she realized it wasn't the broad expanse of the ocean, but a much narrower and specific area depicted in the black fading ink. And there were none of the common symbols or words either. No X marks the spot. And no labels either.

"So what now?" she asked no one in particular, but Hemingway tilted his head as though he knew she was talking to him.

She tried to enlarge the picture of the map, but it hadn't been taken with a sophisticated camera, probably the shooter on Jack's cell phone which itself was a few years old. It was serviceable, but definitely not high definition. And the lighting hadn't been great. She was pretty sure the picture had been taken indoors and with no flash.

What she wanted to do was to print it out. She wondered if there was some little shop where she could get it done. If nothing else, she could go to one of the multitude of office stores. They would be able to give her a hard copy she could examine more easily.

"Do you think this is where Jack is?" she asked Hemingway. He had strutted closer to her, taking a flapping jump to settle himself in her lap. Now she unconsciously stroked his head and neck feathers as she looked at the drawing. If it was a local map, and she was just guessing that it was, then perhaps it depicted the place where Jack and Mr. Macintosh had taken the boat. And in that case, it left a few possibilities. Were the men still there? They didn't appear to have come home. And if they were there, what were they doing? The idea that it was a map, a very specific map, leads to the natural conclusion that it was a map to a specific destination. And if it was?

"How can I figure out where this is without any words?" she asked the silent bird. It would take her forever to just flip through page after page of maps, even using the web as a source. Of course, if it was Florida, she could ask some natives, but she had a small pool of people to choose from. There were the men at the marina, Casper and his wife, perhaps the neighbor next to Mac's house, and Dean.

Dean. It was incredibly tempting to call on him first. He wasn't a native Floridian, but then again, she had no certain proof that the map was even showing a destination off the

Florida coast. She just assumed it was since they had taken the boat from here.

She looked at the map again. There was no need to make any rash decisions now. She could wait until morning, get a print out of the map, have it in hand before she asked for anyone's advice.

Her cell phone was in her hand, her finger pressing the call emblem next to Dean's name before she had finished the thought.

The veterinary practice where Dean worked was not as Genevieve had anticipated. It was situated in a strip mall on a busy street in a commercial area, flanked on one side by a Subway restaurant and the other side a cell phone dealer. The paved lot out front seemed to have soaked up all of the heat of the afternoon and was radiating it through the thin soles of Genevieve's sneakers, even as she hurried into the shade of the royal blue awning above the glass door.

There were blinds in the windows that laid stripes across the shadows, allowing only glimpses of movement beyond. Hemingway shifted inside the crate and made an impatient squawk as she swung open the door and slipped into the dim interior. There were only two people waiting in the front room. The first was an older man with steel . gray hair, tightly curled and matching his neatly groomed goatee, with a cat in a carrier next to him. Across the little waiting area, and holding on hard to the collar of a Labrador retriever mix, was a young Asian woman. The two were exchanges embarrassed smiles as their respective animals made murmured threats across the stretch of tiled floor. Both turned with concern as Genevieve entered, no doubt hoping that is wasn't yet another animal for them to worry about.

A bell chimed with a tinkling metallic sound as the door eased closed behind her. At the long counter and desk, two girls in uniform scrubs dotted with tumbling cartoon kittens and dogs were working on computers. A printer chattered behind them, and after a moment, the blond girl glanced up.

"Hi, can I help you?" she asked, her voice bright despite the end of the day.

"Sure, I'm here to see Dean," Genevieve said quickly, realizing too late she should have referred him as Doctor.

"Oh, right." Her eyes flickered to the crate. "He said you would be coming by. If you just want to take a seat," the girl replied quickly. Her tanned cheeks seemed to gain a little color, and her eyes flickered curiously to the crate again. She smoothed her thin fingers over the wisps of golden hair that had escaped the elastic band, and looked back at Genevieve. "That's your macaw?"

It was a way to start the conversation, Genevieve recognized, and nodded with a little smile. "This is Hemingway," she said, keeping her tone light. This, no doubt, was one of Dean's friends, and for some reason, Genevieve was loath to dismiss her. A people pleaser? Normally that wasn't Genevieve's style. She had an adequate amount of self-confidence, she believed. It wasn't like her to try to impress someone.

"Dean said he was a great bird," the blond continued. "Does he talk much?"

"Well, he's really my father's bird, so whatever he says, it doesn't come from me," Genevieve said quickly, her lips curling into a slightly embarrassed grimace.

"Oh, right," the girl grinned. "Sorry, my name is Becca." She turned to the other girl, "and this is Melissa."

Melissa looked up. As light as Becca was, Melissa was exotically dark. Her skin was like dark chocolate, and Genevieve found herself envying the girl's smooth complexion, especially since she knew her own face was flushed with the heat.

"Hi," Melissa said. She waved her long fingers tipped with scarlet nails in Genevieve's direction. "I sent back a message that you were here," she said. "Dean told us you were going to be by, and he's finishing up some paperwork."

"Thanks," Genevieve said, and slipped into one of the seats. She glanced back toward the two others waiting with their own patients.

"Mr. Beck, they're ready for you," Becca said, standing and walking around to the front of the counter. "Hey, Mr. Mouse," she greeted the cat inside the carrier as she led the way toward one of the line of closed doors. When she swung the door open, Genevieve could see the little room behind the door, the standard

128

vet office with a counter across one wall, some closed cabinets with mysterious jars and boxes on top, and a single chair. During her childhood growing up with Hemingway, she had gone to the vet with him whenever he was due for his checkups. She had watched with rapt fascination as the older vet, his head ringed with a fringe of white hair, the little half glasses sitting on his nose, had toweled her friend and then proceeded to check over her pet. He had been endlessly patient with her questions, showing her the blood feathers as they emerged from Hemingway's pale pink skin, the odd little holes that were his birdie ears, and the bulge on his front, his crop where he stored food just after eating.

Now she watched the door close on the man and his cat, and looked back toward the Asian woman. She looked relieved with his absence, relaxing her grip on the dog slightly as the dog sat back on his haunches, his prey now out of sight. He seemed less interested in the big parrot, and Genevieve was relieved about that.

Another door at the end of the hall opened, and Dean swept out, a white coat fluttering and flapping. He was dressed in neat slacks and a dress shirt. He looked professional and attractive, and infinitely capable.

"Hey!" He strolled to her and grinned, his eyes warming. "Come on back while I finish."

Genevieve stood and before she could pick up the crate, watched as Dean scooped it up, holding it eye level so he could peer inside.

"How are you?" he asked the bird.

Hemingway leaned close to the wired door and cocked his head so one dark eye looked out through the opening. Tiny lines of scarlet feathers striped the pale white skin around his eye, and when he turned, he caught one of the bars in his huge beak.

"Looking handsome as ever," Dean said, and continued down the hall. He took them into an office in the back of the building, the windows overlooking a green space where they no doubt walked the animals when they needed to take them outside. It was more inviting than the front of the building.

Genevieve hesitated at the doorway, her eyes scanning the office. It was a mess. There were papers in untidy piles over every inch of the desktop surface with an additional small table set up next to the heavy wooden desk, a laptop computer placed in the center. Clusters of paperclips, bent staples, pens without tops, and pencils littered the desk as well. Dean walked around to the far side of the desk and began shifting through the paper piles, moving them and stacking, taking time to sort and shift according to a system only he knew.

Dean put the crate on the desktop and turned back to Genevieve.

"So you had something to show me?" he asked.

Genevieve pulled her voluminous bag in front of her and opened it to reveal a notebook, her planner, a tightly wrapped trio of pens, and the envelope with the pictures she had had printed at the drugstore. She had three 8 by 10 glossies, one of the map and the other two shots she had chosen more or less randomly from the pictures she had of Jack.

She pulled out the envelope and slipped the photo of the map out. It was a little blurry from being enlarged, but still would have been legible had it contained any writing.

"So this map, he sent it to you in an email? And there was no explanation?" Dean observed as she put the picture flat on the desk next to the crate.

"No, nothing," Genevieve said looking at the photo spread out now on the desk before him.

"What about the title of the email? Any clue there?"

"I don't recall the title," she said, her eyes straying to the window as she remembered back to that day. "I saw the email, and by then I was already worried about him. I just remember seeing his email address." Jack wasn't much of a technophile, so it was unusual for her to get anything but a phone call. Texts were pretty new for him and if she sent one, she would have to wait months before he replied. Emails were usually things Jack had stumbled across and wanted to send to her. More often than not, they were about birds, funny bird pictures, news articles, and an occasional bird video when he had learned how to do that as well. "No, there wasn't any kind of title that would have told me what it was. I'm almost sure. I remember opening up the attachment and seeing the map and having no idea what it was. I thought it was just a picture."

"Well, it was a photograph. It was just a photograph of a map." Dean was rubbing his chin thoughtfully, and Genevieve could hear the whisper of his whiskers against his palm.

"Does it look familiar?"

He pushed the photograph away from him slightly, squinting to study the picture. "I don't think so," he said slowly. His brows drew over his eyes. "But I'm not sure. I feel like I might have seen it before, but it's not what I would call familiar."

Genevieve sighed. "I hoped you might have recognized the area. Without any more information, I'm not sure how I'm going to figure out what it is." She pushed a hand in her pocket, feeling her phone, still and silent. "And I'm just assuming this is somewhere local. It could be anywhere in the world."

"But the boat is gone." He paused, his hand going to the picture again and picking it up.

"Yeah, and it has been out for some time. Of course, the guys said they knew the boat was out, not that Jack was necessarily on it."

"But Mac has been gone for the same amount of time that your dad has?"

"Yes," she put her hands on her hip in an automatic posture, one she probably used when she was leading team meetings for work.

"Then it makes sense."

There was a shuffle of sound outside the door and a quick rap echoed off the hollow core door.

"Dean, could you spare a minute?"

Genevieve recognized Lillian's lilting voice before she stuck her head in. Her dark hair was tied back in a tight bun and her scrubs were dotted with French poodles with ridiculous hairstyles and bright pink bows.

"Hey," she said, seeing Genevieve. Then she looked hopefully around the room. "Do you have Hemingway with you?"

Genevieve nodded and gestured. Lillian slipped in as Dean stepped out.

"Room 3," Lillian told him quickly, taking his place in the office. "Do you mind?" She asked approaching the crate.

"No, of course not. He'd love the attention," Genevieve said smiling.

Almost before the words were out, Lillian had unlatched the door and the giant bird was stepping out, his feathers fluffed in aggravation.

"He's mad because he had to wait this long," Genevieve said watching the bird climb onto Lillian's arm. His eyes closed blissfully as Lillian fluffed his neck feathers.

"Such a sweet baby," Lillian crooned. She glanced at Genevieve where she stood staring at the photo.

"Is that a map?"

"Yes," Genevieve replied. "Jack sent it to me, and I've been trying to figure out where it is."

"Local?"

"I think so, but I don't know."

"It looks like Baker's Cove," Lillian said, leaning over the picture while she smoothed Hemingway's feathers.

"Where?"

"Baker's Cove. It's a couple miles out from the coast, a little spit of an island. But the cove is beautiful. My friend Luke took me out there once. He had an aerial map since he hadn't been there before. We had a heck of a time finding the cove itself so we could dock. Not that the island is big. He was just stubborn and didn't want to ask for help. I think he wanted to show off." She made a little face and crinkled her nose. Genevieve surmised that the relationship hadn't lasted.

Genevieve leaned closer to the picture, trying to discern if she could tell that it was an island in the picture. It definitely looked like the curve of a coast, the outcroppings outlined in black ink with the bulk of the picture showing the pale blue of water. A few scrawled lines depicted what might have been edges of lettering, and in the distance was the shape of another island, she supposed. The color here was a warm golden brown with rough symbols showing the presence of a wooded area.

"How can we check?" She asked, feeling the fission of excitement creep into her voice.

"If we look on the Internet, we can probably find it," Lillian said. She considered the map in silence for a moment, "why do you want to find it?"

"Jack sent me the picture," Genevieve said thoughtfully. She was bent over the picture now, her finger gingerly tracing the curve of the land. "Maybe you're right." She stood up quickly, her eyes going to the laptop. "Do you think Dean would mind if we borrowed it?"

"Nah, I look up stuff all the time," Lillian replied and tapped a few keys. Genevieve saw the screen blink to life, a screen saver popping into view. It was a picture of the dogs, a pile of fluff and fur settled on the wooden floor in his house, all lolling tongues and bright eyes.

As it turned out, looking up the cove was remarkably easy once they had a possible name. Lillian had already pulled up a few images when Dean returned and sat behind the computer. His fingers flew across the keys, using the mouse to manipulate possible pictures. As he shifted the most promising image, flipping it since they had been looking at the photograph from the wrong angle, they all breathed in a little sigh of relief. It was as exact as any old map could be. It might not have had the precision of modern day mapmaking, but it was clear enough. And even though there was no X to mark the spot, there was a circled area on the coastline. Close enough.

"This is it," Genevieve breathed. "This is the spot from the map. Definitely." She glanced at Dean. His brow was furrowed as he studied the picture, the screen on the computer, and then raised his eyes to Genevieve.

"What are your plans now?" He asked. "You're not going to try to run out there, are you?"

"Well, yes," Genevieve said, her voice firming under his scrutiny. "Of course I am. This is the closest thing I have to a clue to his whereabouts. I have to follow up."

"It's not a bad ride," Lillian said, her voice curious. "Why shouldn't she go out to check?"

Genevieve felt a surge of gratefulness. The other woman was echoing her thoughts exactly. She was already planning the next steps in her head, the ideas blooming like fruit on a vine, very systematic, very clear. How was she going to get there? She would obviously have to rent out a boat and someone to man it. She had been out on the water all of her life, but didn't know if she was competent enough to take a boat out alone. Especially on the ocean. But the problem was easily solved. All she had to do was find someone willing to take her, and all that took was cash.

"I'm not sure you should head out by yourself," Dean began, straightening to his full height.

"I'm perfectly capable of doing this." Genevieve's voice was matter of fact. She refused to be offended. "I'll hire out a boat. I might need someone to watch Hemingway," her eyes turned to Lillian.

"I'd love to watch him." Lillian's dark eyes were alight with a shade of mischief. "I can even give him a bigger place to stay. I have a big cage in storage. I've fostered a cockatoo for a few months while his owner was recuperating from surgery. I still have the cage. I can get it cleaned up." Her gaze went to Dean, "and you can ride along with Genevieve. That way, she has a local with her if she needs any help."

"I'm not exactly a local," Dean murmured.

"I don't think I need anyone else," Genevieve was saying at the same time.

Dean glanced at her, his expression unreadable. "But you know, I think I should go along. After all, your mother wanted me to accompany you here, and I think she would feel much better about you going out on a boat with someone that you know."

Genevieve was looking at him somewhat skeptically. Her mother had wanted her to have someone to accompany her on the long ride here, but she was fine now. And the comment about going with someone she knew was a little funny. Before a week or so ago, he had been a total stranger.

"You're off work tomorrow right?" Lillian was asking Dean.

"Since I'm doing Saturday, yes, I am."

"Then you should find a boat to take you out," Lillian said firmly. "And I know the perfect guy."

Lillian was one of those people that easily drew friends. Maybe it was her warm smile, maybe the flash of her dark eyes, maybe her bubbly personality that shielded a quick mind, but whatever the reason, she had someone set to take them out to the cove thirty minutes later.

"You're going to love Antony," she said as she slipped out the office door. "He said he can be at the marina by six."

Lillian had left then to finish with their last patient, and Dean had slumped in the chair by his desk.

"That was nicely done," he said a smile just tilting his lips. His eyes looked a little tired, lines creasing the skin at the corners. He looked a little less the beach bum with the white lab coat.

She stifled her own smile. His lab coat, although it was in name the same, looked different than her own. Hers was pressed, usually starched, and spotless. The pockets held a pen and small notepad, sometimes business cards when she was out and about in the building, but generally just that.

His was wrinkled with fraying cuffs. The pockets had been stuffed full and were ripping at the seams. A blotch of blue ink stained the front just below his embroidered name.

"What was nicely done?" She asked, finally letting the words sink in.

"Lillian. She usually gets her way. She has some reason for us to go together, and she's not likely to be put off by anyone."

"Really?" Her attention was now fully focused on the comment.

"Um," he muttered and stood. "I have to help close up. You want to grab dinner after?"

"I have Hemingway," she said, gesturing to the crate still sitting on the desk.

"We'll head over to Lillian's first. I'll help her drag out the cage and get it ready for him. It'll be better for him to be in a bigger cage anyway. That crate has got to be getting uncomfortable for him."

She felt a surge of guilt. She hadn't had the bird out nearly as often as she wanted, but she was confident of his behavior with strangers. And she wasn't like Jack, letting the bird stay on his shoulder all the time.

"Okay, that's a good idea." She hesitated and caught the handle of the crate. "Maybe I should swing by the hotel and grab some of his other supplies."

He turned, one tawny eyebrow lifted. "We're at a vet office. We have plenty of supplies to last him the night, or longer if we need to."

"Well, okay."

"You can just hang around in here for a few. I'll get some things done and then come back and get you. You can use the computer if you want. Maybe you might learn why your dad sent the picture to you."

Chapter 15

Genevieve settled in at the desk, swiveling the chair so it faced the little table to the side where the laptop was open and humming softly. She felt comfortable with the computer in front of her, the lighted screen responding to her keystrokes. The Internet was a wonderful thing, she thought fondly. It took only a few searches until she found a few old articles that were specifically about the Cove.

Baker's Cove was named after the first recorded settler of the tiny island, Christopher Baker, originally from England. It was primarily a vacation spot for Baker and his companions, a fishing spot with only a rough split log cabin as residence. It was one of hundreds of islands that dotted the Florida coast, some of them still uninhabitable.

The island had gone from father to son, and eventually Bakers' son had handed it down to a nephew when he had himself been childless. The inheriting family had used the cabin sparingly, and when squatters had settled in the summer, an article was written to tell the story of how the current owners, now several generations away from Christopher Baker, had tried to reclaim the land.

The article wasn't that interesting, but the interview with the remaining Baker ancestor was more intriguing. This one claimed there was more to the island than the fishing, and whatever was found there belonged to his family. Of course, family meant him, Thomas Baker Knox.

The picture of Knox was a wrinkled yellow-toothed man who looked to have drank a few too many alcoholic beverages to support a healthy lifestyle. Even in the black and white photo, Knox looked ruddy in the cheeks with watery pale eyes.

When asked what he was referring to, Knox quickly changed his tune, and according to the reporter who had had the misfortune to interview the man, Knox had insisted there was nothing of value on the island.

"So there's nothing on the island, but he wanted it," Genevieve said thoughtfully to the bird as he clung to the door of the crate.

She ran a few more searches, but found nothing more to the story. She would need to have some help to get other information, such as what had happened to Knox. And perhaps why he wanted to keep the island. And what of value he thought was there. Either he had been under some illusions that there was value to the land, or there was something else on the island that no one else was aware of.

When Dean came back in, he was shedding his lab coat. "We're ready," he said briefly. "Bet you're glad about it, huh, boy," he said to the bird as he dropped his coat over the corner of his desk.

"I'm sure he would like to get out," Genevieve agreed.

Dean grinned. "Then let's go," he said. "I'll drive this time."

"What about my car?"

"We can swing by and pick it up after dinner," Dean assured her. "We can't exactly stay out too late. Lillian has us heading out at six in the morning."

"You don't like the early mornings?" Genevieve couldn't resist teasing.

"I'm okay with that," he said eyeing her. "But on my days off, I prefer to sleep in."

"You don't have to go," Genevieve said feeling a twinge of guilt.

"Are you kidding?" Dean was back to smiling. "A treasure map and a beautiful lady by my side! This is going to be great!"

Rachael Rawlings

Lillian's home was a rambling sided building Genevieve suspected had once been someone's tiny home combined with shed or outbuilding. It was not large and appeared to be made up of a series of single rooms and held a trailer sized kitchen, a fold out bed that transformed into a stiff couch in the living room, a tiny bedroom with a single mattress and dresser, and a bathroom that would better fit children than grown adults, especially one of Dean's height. Genevieve could hear him muttering through the doorway as she and Lillian installed the last of the borrowed perches.

"Are you sure this is going to work for you?" Genevieve asked. Her eyes went from the too large cage now lodged somewhere between the old television set and the little dining set. "It doesn't look like there's enough room for this cage."

"It's fine," Lillian said blithely. "I already live in a jungle." She gestured to the cages opposite the window curtained by flowered fabric Genevieve suspected were sheets.

Genevieve walked slowly toward the other cages, amazed at the inhabitants. She was accustomed to Hemingway with his array of multicolored feathers and huge black beak, but these birds were something else entirely.

In one cage were two birds with little spikes of feathers on their heads, crests that bobbed with enthusiasm as they moved and whistled inside the cage. They were both in shades of gray with pale white scallops, soft papery feathers making rustling sounds. Genevieve knew that these were cockatiels. She had seen them in local pet stores and recognized the size, the body type, and the cheerful orange patches on their cheeks. They hovered close to the door, and Genevieve assumed they were begging for attention just as Hemingway did when she entered the room after an absence.

In another cage of approximately equal size was a bird colored a deep green over his back and wings, with round black eyes that sparkled with mischief. He wasn't as loud as the cockatiels, but he tumbled in the cage, running up and down the bars and hurrying to the floor to pluck at twig and straw toys before scurrying back up. She thought he was a sort of conure, the smallest of the line, and watched with amusement as he danced in the cage.

The most brightly colored in the group was a slightly larger parrot with a bright green back, a white belly, and yellow marking on his head and face. This one she wasn't sure about, but she thought she had seen one in a pet store in Florida. She didn't know how common they were in Kentucky, though, because she was sure she hadn't seen any in their local pet stores.

"Hey little guy," she said as the bright one plastered his feathered body against the side of the cage in invitation.

"That's Skittles," Lillian said glancing their way. "He's a caique. Very friendly."

"He's beautiful."

"He's a handful," Lillian confessed. "He's a great little bird, but I think he's like Dean. Attention problems."

"Hey," Dean protested from next to one of the other cages. He had already opened it, and had the little conure sitting on his shoulder.

"Watch Crackers there," Lillian warned him. "He bit hard enough to draw blood last time I tried to put him away."

"You wouldn't do that, would you Buddy?" Dean crooned to the little bird.

"I don't think I know much about these little guys," Genevieve admitted. Skittles was climbing down to the bottom of his expansive cage, making a funny whistling sound that reminded Genevieve of the mole on Winnie the Pooh. As soon as the bird reached the floor, he put his head down and started for the corner of the cage. There was a small plastic ball with a bell in the center on the floor in front of him, and he caught it up in his beak. With obvious pleasure, he tossed it up in the air, catching it and throwing it again, until he tumbled to his side with the ball in his clawed feet. Like a puppy, he rolled on the floor with the ball while Genevieve watched, amazed. She had seen Hemingway play, but never with this much abandon. "He's great!" she exclaimed grinning as the bird continued to run around the cage floor, tossing the ball and rolling around to his back to play with his feet every few minutes.

"Those birds are more like dogs than any I've ever met," Lillian said happily. "I've had him for five years. I got him from a breeder when I helped her out in her business. I was still in college and trying to make some extra money, but when she offered him instead of cash, I couldn't resist."

"That I believe," Dean said, the little conure hidden in his pocket.

Genevieve stepped to the other cage with the two cockatiels in it. She stood for a moment to watch them before an insistent squawk from behind her had her turning around.

"Jealous," Lillian said chuckling. "Hemingway doesn't like not being the center of attention."

"Probably," Genevieve said and went to the crate.

"We might as well get him transferred. Then we can grab something for dinner." Dean was gently tucking the little green bird, apparently unscathed by the sharp beak, back into his cage.

"Sure," Genevieve agreed and swung open the crate door.

Hemingway was a perfect gentleman and went into the borrowed cage without so much as a ruffled feather. Genevieve had to admit that all of the traveling had made the macaw more flexible in his behavior. He was willing to go from cage to cage, from location to location, with only a minimum of complaints. It was turning out to be a good thing since she figured he wouldn't have been happy to have been left in her mother's care while she went in search of Jack.

"Okay, Lillian, this is your neighborhood. Where do you recommend?"

"For dinner?" Lillian looked up at Dean. "I have a few ideas."

Genevieve went to bed that night feeling uncomfortably full and a little lonely. She tugged the stiff sheets up around her and balanced a paperback novel on her lap. It had little gouges in the pages, remnants of an argument she had had with Hemingway. She had gotten used to having the bird with her in her room, and had grown accustomed to talking to him as she prepared for bed. Not to mention how many times she had traded treats with him, taken him into the bathroom while she showered to watch him fluff and preen in the mist, and settled him into the bed next to her. She stretched out her legs restlessly and scolded herself. It was not that she wanted the bird or would be happy for him to be a permanent companion. She still knew he was too noisy, too pushy, too destructive. But it made her reconsider her rather sterile life. Maybe she needed a pet to keep her company. She shook her head and pushed the blankets back, smoothing them even though there weren't any wrinkles.

She huffed out another sigh and frowned. She hoped Hemingway was settling in okay. But he had seemed content when they had left. The cage hadn't been fancy, but it had been plenty large enough for him, which was saying something. Green wing macaws were one of the larger macaw species, not as big as the brilliant blue hyacinths, but still enormous creatures. A cage to accommodate one had to be pretty significant. He had been enjoying some pellets and treats the vet practice kept on hand for their occasional overnight avian guests when Genevieve had bid him a reluctant farewell.

Dinner had been at a family owned diner that served Puerto Rican cuisine. Lillian had assured them that the food was as close to homemade as you would find without heading to the source. Genevieve had agreed the food was delicious and tried everything since they shared most of the dishes between the three of them. Then they had run by the vet office to retrieve her car, and Dean had insisted they would follow her to the hotel to make sure she made it back safely. It was a ridiculous gesture, but he was determined, and Lillian told her to give up on the protest since he was unlikely to change his mind. At the parking lot, she had climbed out of her car and gave him a quick wave before he could switch off the engine and walk her to her room. She didn't need any additional guidance. She was fine to go to her room alone. She slipped through the open door of the hotel, stopping only a moment to look through the glass to see the car pull away. She had been a little startled to see a second car pull out just behind them. Strange since the rest of the lot was only a fourth of the way full. She had shaken her head then, feeling a little paranoid for even entertaining the idea that the second car had been following Dean.

That had been almost two hours ago, and she was having trouble getting to sleep. She kept thinking of Jack, of the map, of Dean, and Baker's Cove. Since she knew Jack had sent her the picture, she also was sure it was at least something he had been interested in. She could easily picture him standing over an old map, aiming his cell phone camera that luckily would focus automatically, his finger clumsy on the little gadget, and snapping a picture. She could almost see his grin, his shaggy beard splitting to show his surprisingly white teeth. My Genevieve girl would like this, he would say, his eyes sparkling with inner excitement, his mind moving faster and faster.

But what had he been thinking? What story was he chasing? She had known he and his buddies went off on some pretty wild tangents. She had known them to travel far and wide to search for some special, little known antique that they wanted, no, needed, they would insist, to add to their collection. So what was it this time? The sight of the island and the sandy cove, made her think of pirate treasure. Could it be that obvious? Had they found some shipwreck, some tall tale, which made them think there was something buried on the shore or sunk just off the coast?

She sat up and pounded on her pillow. She needed rest. She reached out and pulled her cell phone close. She checked the alarm, unnecessary, she knew since she had just set it a few minutes ago. And the battery would be full in an hour, so it would be powered up for the boat trip in the morning. She looked at the lighted screen and sighed. She needed sleep. This was unusual for her. Normally she could nod off without a thought, her purse and briefcase packed and ready for the morning.

Even now, she had her clothes laid out in neat stacks and ready for the next day. She knew her sunscreen was on the sink with her makeup, her sunglasses in her purse, her photo of the map tucked in her bag.

She fell asleep mentally listing her supplies with a slight smile on her lips.

"If Lillian hadn't recommended this guy, I'm not so sure I'd be boarding right now," Dean murmured into her ear as they approached the dock. When she glanced his way, his lips curved up slightly, and an eyebrow tilted up just a bit.

"She said he was a friend of the family, right?" Genevieve asked.

"Yep," Dean said as they drew close, "but she didn't guarantee the boat would stay afloat," he quipped.

"Funny," Genevieve muttered, and headed toward the side of the swaying boat.

Truthfully, the boat was not unlike the boat Jack and Mr. Macintosh had bought from Topper's nephew. However, the resemblance ended as soon as they climbed aboard. Not surprisingly it smelled of fish, but the underlying scent of mildew was more off putting. The rest of the boat was more of the same: slightly shabby, slightly stinky, and hopefully seaworthy.

Genevieve obediently put on the life jacket despite the fact she was a good swimmer and the weather was sunny with minimal breeze. There was just something slightly suspect about the boat.

Antony was thin but looked strong and wiry, his face shaded with a stubble of beard, silver strands standing out against his sun-burnished skin. When he smiled, his teeth were straight and impossibly white. Genevieve suspected dentures.

She hadn't drunk any coffee; she held a huge cup from the local 7 eleven ready to go. She was holding out though, waiting until they had settled before allowing herself a sip. For now, she was walking in a sleepy fog, letting Dean do most of the talking.

The boat was well stocked with other drinks and snacks too. Antony had provided, with only a slightly increased fee, a large cooler with plenty of ice and some generic sodas floating among the cubes. In a bag next to the cooler were single serve packages of chips, crackers, and granola bars. It wasn't fancy, but it would do fine. The trip out to the cove would only take a short amount of time. They had the boat for the day, and she had promised Dean dinner when they returned. She owed him for taking a whole day to chase down Jack's map.

The engine of the boat roared to life and Genevieve felt the thrum of it beneath her feet. Harsh exhaust was fanned onboard by the breeze. With it came the scent of the sea, and Genevieve found herself tipping her face up to the sun. Yes, it was early, and yes, she was tired. But wow, there was something about being here, on the water, in the warm glow of the early morning sun that made her feel good.

As the boat pulled away from the dock, Genevieve turned to look back toward land. Dean had driven and his car was parked in the lot closest to the boats. He had insisted he wanted to drive. He didn't want to leave her nice car sitting there so close to the harsh salt spray. Now she was grateful for that.

The boat moved at a leisurely pace as they pulled away from land. Antony was propped up at the wheel, his back curved in a comfortable sl

"Lillian says you have a map of the cove? That you're looking for a particular place?"

"I have a picture," Genevieve said. She pulled out the printed photo and presented it to him.

He took it without hesitation. His eyes scanned it. "Old one," he said his eyebrows rising. "This is an old map, looks like." He paused and his eyes, dark brown and slightly bloodshot, landed on Genevieve.

"I don't know the history," Genevieve admitted. "I got the picture sent to me from my father. I'm just following up."

She suddenly realized she was reluctant to admit she was chasing down her father without any better reason than the fact that he had left without explanation.

"Not too many go out to that one," Antony said, his tone casual and conversational. "No facilities, decent beach, little dock that should handle us just fine.'

"My father was looking for some fishing places. Somewhere that is not as well known." The lie was sour on her tongue, but she was hesitant to admit to anyone that she had no idea why Jack had sent her the photo. And if she was wrong? That was a distinct possibility. The email had been sitting, unopened, in her inbox for some time before Jack had taken off. There may be no relation between the email, the map, and Jack's disappearance. And if the trip yielded nothing? She turned her face up into the sun again and closed her eyes. She hadn't planned that far ahead.

"So you know Lillian?" Dean was standing next to Antony, his eyes going from the horizon beyond to the figure of the older man as he gently steered the boat.

"Mm, know Lillian, know some of her friends. She hangs around my girl Maria." He looked over at Dean. "Maria is finishing up at the university in another couple months. Going to be a teacher." There was a warm tinge of pride in his voice.

"That's wonderful," Genevieve said meaning it.

"She's a good girl," Antony agreed. His squinted eyes focused in the distance. "Might see some dolphins on our ride."

"Oh, I haven't seen them in such a long time," Genevieve said wistfully. She was thinking again of when she went out in Topper's boat so many years ago.

"They like the morning. And they like to play in the wake. Like dogs." His words were being scooped by the wind and thrown behind him, but Genevieve could catch the words.

She slipped closer to the side of the boat, leaning over the side. The wind tore at her hair, strands of it whipping against her cheeks. Her eyes skimmed the shallow trough of the wake, the edging of foam. She was staring off into the water when Dean called her name.

"Did you see one?" She turned towards him.

"Over here," he said, and she edged to the other side of the boat. Close to the bow was a disturbance in the water and after a moment, she saw the sleek charcoal gray back of a dolphin as it arched out of the water.

"There!" She cried out, excited like a child. "I can see one! Did you see it?"

"I did," he said, but he wasn't looking at the water. His eyes were on his face, his lips quirked in a thoughtful smile.

She looked back toward the water trying to stifle her embarrassment. Dolphins were cool. And it was perfectly reasonable that she would be excited about seeing them, especially since she wasn't a Florida native.

"There!" she said, seeing another back arch from the water. The forms seemed to glide just beneath the surface of the water, moving fast, with little effort. A minute later they were gone, and Genevieve rushed to the back of the boat, trying to follow their progress. After another few moments she saw the bodies emerge again. She could see the curve of their spine, the fin splitting the water, and then the side of their faces, a dark eye seeming to study her with interest as much as she studied them.

"Amazing, aren't they?" Dean was asking. He had come up next to her as she was staring into the water.

"They are," she agreed. "This was one of my favorite parts of going out with Jack on the boat."

"I only studied marine biology in a limited way in school," Dean admitted. "In Kentucky we didn't have a lot of dolphins as patients." He shrugged. "I always thought it would be cool to work with some of the more exotic species, but I wanted to go where there was a need."

"So if you had gotten a marine biology specialty, would you have to live by the coast?"

"Unless I found something at a zoo or aquarium." He shrugged. "But I like what I do, dogs and all." He was smiling again, his teeth showing against his golden skin, his eyes squinted in the sun.

They settled into silence for a while, watching the Florida coast shrink. Antony gave them an occasional update about where they were in relation to the islands, pointing out the occasional rim of land in the distance that was another island. Genevieve finished her coffee while the wind blew the heat from her lips. From time to time, she would admire the diving seabirds as they fished in the pewter blue water. After another hour, Dean called her over to see the dolphins again as they resurfaced like their own aquatic tour guides.

"We'll get to the island in another thirty minutes or so," Antony told them. He seemed utterly content to be letting the silence and the surge of the sea take over.

Genevieve nodded. She knew the general direction of the island, but nothing about how long it would take to get there. And she honestly had no idea of what they would do first once they made it to the cove. She supposed they would settle at the dock first, and she and Dean would head out. The island wasn't big enough to get totally lost on. And Antony had said he would wait for them, wait as long as they needed.

"Almost there," she said, more to herself than anyone else. "And Jack, you'd better be okay," she whispered.

Chapter 16

The island was a double hump in the distance as Genevieve approached the bow to watch the boat close in on their destination. On this side, the island seemed to be made up of a spit of beach and a sizable grove of evergreens. There was no sign of habitation from what she could see, and she felt her heart plummet. What if? What if they had come all this way for a plot of abandoned land and nothing else?

The boat skirted the coast for a few more minutes on approach, the engine gradually reduced to a steady throb. It was another fifteen minutes before the boat grew closer to a makeshift dock. It seemed to take a painfully long time before the boat was finally moored at the rough planks, and Antony enlisted Dean's help to tie up.

"Okay now?" Antony asked as they clambered onto the weathered wood.

"Sure," Dean said, his hand going under Genevieve's elbow to help steady her.

She nodded her thanks but stepped away. "We'll go looking around for a bit," she said to Antony.

He had stepped back into the boat. He quickly swung the lid of the cooler wide and dipped one hand into the icy soup, fishing out a soft drink. "I'll be here," he said briefly. Then he swung the can and ducked his head toward the beverage, "you want one?"

"No, we're fine," she said. She looked toward Dean, and he nodded his agreement. "We'll be back soon enough," she said.

"I'm going nowhere," Antony responded cheerfully.

Together she and Dean traced their way down the dock feeling the wood sway beneath their weight. Genevieve glanced into the water and saw beneath the swirling sand that it was still deep at this point. Despite the appearance of a sloping beach farther down the coast, it was apparent that this area was less easily accessed.

"So I guess we're heading this way," Dean said, turning toward the right where a path appeared to be carved in the vegetation. Genevieve glanced in the opposite direction. The wall of trees appeared to be pretty dense that way, so their decision was made for them.

"Sure," she said on a sigh. "Let's go."

They moved on, Genevieve turning once to look a little longingly at the boat. Antony had slumped back in his seat behind the wheel, a second soft drink in his hand and the thin strains of music catching on the breeze.

The land was weedy with tough woody vines that snaked across the path as though planted by some angry wood sprite trying to catch intruders unaware. Genevieve was glad she had chosen the sturdy canvas shoes rather than the sandals she usually wore. As it was, she turned her ankle once, and a little down the trail, caught the toe of her shoe on a stray root, making her pitch forward only to be caught by Dean before she hit the ground. She reddened with embarrassment. So much for seeming like she was comfortable with the hiking. Although, she had to admit, the hiking she was used to was on cleared paths with hewn stone steps in public parks, not in the wilds of some isolated island. She was sagging behind Dean a little, but she kept her eyes on his back and then the ground, careful where she stepped. When she watched him misstep, she was relieved to see she wasn't the only one struggling. She saw him stumble a little, more than once on the dark trail, and utter a mild curse when a limb smacked back, hitting him squarely in the chest.

"Sorry about this," she said, feeling guilty.

"Yes, you should have gotten out here and cleared the path before you brought me out," Dean quipped, throwing her a smile.

"I thought about it, but then thought I'd rather sleep," she agreed. She felt the sting of an insect bite and slapped her hand to her neck. "Bug spray," she exclaimed. "I knew I forgot something!"

"Yeah," Dean muttered. He was slapping at his arm and frowning at the smear of blood. "I forget the mosquitos sometimes, and then I go somewhere like this and think, I can't believe I complained about these buggers when I was in Kentucky."

"They're bigger here, aren't they?"

"And meaner. Much more bad tempered."

"And fast," she bit the words out as she smacked her arm, grimacing at the smear of black and red.

"That too," he agreed.

The path widened ahead and she could see the beach was spread out before them. She breathed a sigh of relief. Going closer to the running water might help with the bugs, she supposed. And at the very least, the breeze would help the heat. She was sweating, and not just a little bit. She could feel droplets snaking down her back and between her breasts. She longed to feel the wind. It was stifling in the trees. And the shade was doing nothing to help.

"Finally," Dean breathed, voicing her thoughts. She wondered how long they had been pushing through the paths, and then thought with dismay that it didn't matter. They would have to go back the same way, no matter how far it was. And her face was already stinging with sweat and the itchy bumps that were rising where the bugs had dined.

"I think I hear something," Dean said, putting out the flat of his hand to stop her progress out of the shelter of the trees.

"Something?"

"A radio. Voices. Something."

She stopped next to him. It took her a moment for her heart to slow. She tried to still, to listen. And then she heard it, the buzz of voices.

"I hear it too, I think," she said, now whispering.

"A radio?"

"Something like that."

Then she heard something else, something plain and familiar, and she set off jogging, not listening as Dean hissed behind her.

150

"Jack!" she shouted as she emerged from the woods and saw them, saw the little camp, and saw her missing father.

Introducing Jack to her friends had been a joy when she was young. His big booming voice paired with the extravagant beard and broad grin had been alarming at first to other more timid kids, but had endeared him to them as they grew to know him. In middle and high school, some of the charm had worn off. By then, Genevieve had realized the differences between her parents and the parents of her friends, realizing with a pang that most fathers stayed at home instead of traveling constantly, returned to the house after work for dinner and share stories of their day in the office, at the construction site, at the store, wherever their regular job might be, and watched sports on the TV in the evenings and on weekends. These other fathers were a steady, if sometimes irritating presence in their daughter's lives. But not Jack. And as she reached middle school and then the trials of high school, she had changed her tune about her eccentric father. Jack might be Jack: unpredictable, colorful, and outlandish, but that didn't mean she had to like it. After a few of her new teenaged acquaintances had cast disbelieving glances at Jack when they had stopped by her house to pick her up, she had stopped introducing them. Eventually, she had stopped having her friends by her house, embarrassed by the slightly shabby look of the place, the gardens wild with pervasive herbs, the bees buzzing contentedly in the far field.

She had remained that shallow, self-conscious twit for a couple of years before she had grown out of her own petty pride when she made it to college. Now she introduced Jack with a sense of stubborn loyalty. He was her father, after all, and it was fine for her to criticize him. But no one else could. No one. At the sight of him, she was suddenly angry at herself, angry that she had been so small minded to resent him.

Now as embraced her father, her heart still pounding, her face against his broad chest, she felt almost weak with relief. It was only in the periphery that she was aware of Dean's approach.

With the sight of him, she pulled away from her father and glared up into his face, reddened from the heat of the Florida sun and the surprise of seeing his only child on what appeared to be a deserted island.

"Where have you been!" She burst out, her voice high and loud.

Oh, God, he looked good, all hale and hearty. She hadn't been aware of how she had prepared herself to find him broken, to see him hurting. She had been sure that if he had left unexpectedly and with no word to either she or her mother, he was surely now in a coma in some far off exotic locale.

But no, he was here before her looking his typical self, his khaki workpants stained and sagging, his work boots dusted with sand and clotted with mud on the heels, his shirt clinging to his broad back in the heat. He had a bandana around his head, no doubt to protect him from further sunburn, but beyond that, he looked much the same as he had the last time she had seen him.

"Genevieve, my girl, I have been here!" he exclaimed, his sweeping hand encompassing the makeshift canvas tent built on the edge of the beach. Her eyes skirted the details, the set-up of chairs in the shade of the tent, the buzzing of a radio playing some ballgame, the cooler closed but holding a couple of open cans of beer on the top, their sides glistening with condensation in the heat.

The anger rose up in her like a wave, a black wave so strong, so dense, she could barely see through it. She was barely aware of the stretch of beach as she stalked past her father, away from his still open arms, and away from the little campsite.

The nerve of him! Here he was, perfectly healthy, perfectly happy, as though there was nothing going on to cause her to worry, to worry herself sick. She fumed silently, walking in fast strides, until she reached a grove of trees, which seemed to signal the end of the beach and the beginning of more trees. She stopped there and turned toward the ocean. Her arms and legs were unbearably itchy with bug bites. Her feet hurt from walking over the uneven surface of the island trial. She was pretty sure her face was either sunburned or wind burned, but none of that was registering. All she could think of was her feelings, and beyond the anger, well, there was a lot more anger.

"I suspect this is not what you had expected." Dean's voice was deep and calm. She thought about turning on him, tossing a few barbed comments, but had enough control to avoid blaming someone who was completely innocent.

"Not exactly," she said shortly. She bit her lip, letting the wind from the water blow the sticky strings of hair off her face. She forced a long sigh.

"Are you going to be okay?"

"Is there another choice?" she said, but her voice was less pointed, less full of sharp edges. She turned toward him, seeing over his shoulder Jack's tall shape as he stood watching their exchange. "Look, I'm sorry. It looks like this has been one big mistake. Here I was concerned about him, worried sick, and he's been taking a tropical vacation." She clasped her hands tightly together so that she didn't make any reckless moves and possibly throw something at the figure of her father in the distance.

"It's not a vacation," Dean said softly.

"What?" She hadn't anticipated the comment, but then, she was being pretty masterful at jumping to the wrong conclusion.

"Your father. He's not here on some kind of vacation. He's working. On what, I don't know, but he's definitely not here for the fun of it."

She took a deep breath, shaking her head and crossing her arms in front of her chest protectively. "He's always got some kind of plan," she said on a sigh. "I don't doubt he thinks that he's saving the world, or finding some kind of long lost hidden treasure, but the truth is, he's here for his own adventure." She found herself glaring at Jack again and deliberately refocused on Dean's face. "I'm sorry Dean. I'll just talk with Jack for a second, and we'll head back to the boat. I've taken your whole vacation day."

"It's been a nice day, um, besides the bugs," he said smiling.

"You are being too generous," she said, her eyes going down to her shoes, caked in mud and now crusted with sand.

"I am not," he said, "and I think that you need to go talk to your dad."

"I suppose," she reluctantly agreed. "But you get to come along."

Dean's eyebrows lifted.

"Well you were crazy enough to come with me, so it's only fair you get to see the total story. Trust me, you'll love to hear Jack's stories." The last she said with a shade of bitterness.

She strolled back along the waterline, not because she could feel the chilly surf through her boots but because it gave her something to focus on besides seeing her father up ahead. Shells littered the golden sand like so many jewels tossed by wind and waves. The high sun threw shards of light off the ever moving water, and she kept her eyes directed toward that, just that.

She saw her father's good friend Mr. Macintosh sitting in one of the low folding chairs under the shade of the tent. She realized that in her periphery she had seen the older man as soon as they had arrived, putting to rest the other source of her concern, for here was the other missing man, and no doubt the missing boat. She nodded briefly at Mac as she grew closer, and a smile played around the corner of his lips, an inconspicuous gesture so like the gentleman. She presumed he had risen when she had approached, his manners were impeccable, but had sat back down when she had stormed past. He was a wise man, and he would stay out of the discussion until he knew the air was cleared.

She walked past Jack as he stood at the shelter's edge, and slipped into the shade. This close to the water and with the breeze, it felt pleasantly cooler. Not that it wasn't still in the 90's out there, but it didn't seem to hit as hard.

"Mr. Macintosh," she greeted Jack's friend, feeling suddenly guilty for not acknowledging him earlier. She had been raised better. Well her mother had raised her better, she thought with a bitter stab. She stilled and watched as Mac rose to his feet, taking a few extra minutes to leverage himself up with one hand. He wasn't getting any younger, and Genevieve felt a pang of alarm. Why had Jack brought him here? This certainly wasn't Mac's type of place. She had been in his house several times, venturing through the sleek modern décor, always clean and tidy, antiseptic almost. The sand and the sun did not fit this man who routinely wore a silk vest with his dress slacks. He was much more of an academic then either her father or Topper had been.

"Genevieve, my dear," he said warmly, and she felt herself soften. He had reminded her of a kindly grandfather since she

154

had met him almost fifteen years before, and he continued to do so. He was somehow ageless in that gentlemanly, antiquated manner. "Do not be angry with your father," he said, startling her from her thoughts. "This whole endeavor was my idea, my fault completely. Your father only came so that I did not go alone."

She merely stared at him. Her eyes skated over his warm brown eyes, crinkled now in the harsh light, his slightly rosy complexion shaded slightly by a truly outstanding mustache, his thinning hair mostly covered by a totally uncharacteristic fishing cap. "Your idea?" She said at last.

She felt a heavy hand on her shoulder and turned her head slightly to see the sturdy figure of Jack behind her.

"After I stumbled over the map, the map I had been searching for, for so very long, I felt I hadn't a moment to waste," Abraham Macintosh began in his best scholarly voice. "There are plans for this island! It is in litigation just now, but if the current owner gets his way, it will soon be overrun with construction workers and then tourists in a matter of months," he shook his head, his face seeming to sag with the weight of the thought. "And the chance will be lost."

"What chance?"

"To find the secret!" he exclaimed, his voice excited but pitched low.

"The secret?" She found herself whispering too, and felt ridiculous for it.

"The Madman's treasure," her father intoned from behind her, and she felt the shiver then, the feeling she had mostly forgotten, the feeling of something impending, something big, something that might change her life.

Chapter 17

Twenty minutes later, she was ensconced in a folded chair in a sad little cabin just up from the beach. She suspected that this was, with many generations of renovations under its belt, the original Baker cabin. It had no plumbing or electricity; in fact, it had no glass in the windows and had only nets that had been stapled to the window frame to keep out the worst of the bugs. It was rough living in its purest form, and it was only the spectacular view of the ocean and beach, paired with the steady breeze from the sea, that kept it from being totally intolerable. Instead, Genevieve was reminded how it must have been for vacationers back in the day, before the invention of efficient air conditioning, when only the placement of the buildings and their corresponding windows, would let in enough of a breeze to prevent suffocation in the heat.

The one-roomed shack had just enough space to fit folding chairs for each of them around a plastic folding table, two makeshift cots that held only one thin blanket each, and a larger and sturdier cooler that probably had most of their food for their stay.

The table was almost completely covered with papers, sketches and notes, some sheets yellowed from age and many stained, and some showing signs of fresh inking. Her father's characteristic broad strokes showed on a few pages, and Genevieve felt sure the neatly printed columns were done in Mac's hand.

Rachael Rawlings

The map of which she carried the photo still in her bag was most prominent. It had been pinned to one of the wooden walls, first backed by some sort of sturdy wax paper, and hung with care away from direct sunlight.

Genevieve could see the photo she had was only a bit of the original map. The one on the wall was four times the size of hers showing more of the Florida coast, the adjoining islands, and sketches of looping handwriting.

Dean had made a quick introduction as they had climbed the path through the undergrowth, another breach in etiquette Genevieve was bothered by, but she was busy avoiding low lying limbs to take up the introductions. The path was better, this one much more defined than the route they had taken from the beach, and now they sat around the table with drinks in their hands. Genevieve was acutely aware of the time. She wasn't sure what she had anticipated, but it hadn't been this. She hadn't thought that they would find her father here. Not really. And now that she was faced with Jack, and Mr. Macintosh's admonition that he had been the instigator of the journey, she was paralyzed with indecision. Antony was sitting with the boat waiting for their return. She figured they had only a few hours before they needed to be back to him before he began to wonder about their absence. And if there was one thing Mr. Mac had made very clear, it was the fact that this whole situation was to be taken with the greatest of discretion.

"No one, and I mean, no one, needs to know what we are doing here."

The soft drinks had grown warm as they listened to Mr. Macintosh's story. There was something mesmerizing in the way he spoke, the rise and fall of his words, the emotion behind his voice.

"This island predates the Bakers, their family and all those little skirmishes by thousands of years. Just like all the other islands around here, they have been used for ages as homes for native people, stopovers for boaters, hideouts for pirates, the occasional accidental destination for wanderers. They have a rich but little known history. And this island is just like the others.

But there was an accidental meeting here that made this place special.”

He took a draw on his soda and shifted in his chair, pulling it closer to his listeners. Genevieve had heard him like this before. His speech slipping into a lecture, his excitement rising with the subject.

“In the 1930’s, there was a collision of worlds here on this little island. Hamsdale Williamson was a trader and amateur explorer. He was originally from England, from a family that had traveled a far way themselves and settled in South Carolina. His father and grandfather were fisherman, so Ham knew how to handle a boat. He had made money in the transport of goods, not bulk things but small specialty items, from one end of the coast to the other. It fit his life and he made a little money as he went along.”

Genevieve saw Dean stretch out his legs, absently scratching one of the multiple bug bites on his calf. He was listening though, his eyebrows drawn down as he focused on the older man.

“So the story goes that Ham had stopped by what he thought was an uninhabited island when he saw some activity on one of the beaches. He had enough common sense to know that approaching a group like that might lead to something he didn’t want to get involved in, so he just laid low and watched.”

“And what do you suppose he saw?” Jack’s eyes were wide and expressive, his shaggy brows winged upwards as he looked from Genevieve to Dean.

“Pirates,” Dean said immediately. “Pirates burying their treasure.”

Genevieve found herself nodding even though she had no idea if the story was going to go down that ridiculous path.

“That’s exactly what I thought,” Jack said, a grin splitting his beard.

“That can’t be it!” Genevieve burst out. “It was in the 1930’s for Pete’s sake. Pirates were long gone!”

“True for your ‘aye mates’ type of pirates, but there are true pirates still active today, and no doubt there were some in those days as well,” Dean said gravely.

"Okay, I'll give you that, but I doubt more modern day pirates bury their treasure on desert islands."

Dean grinned. "It would make a good story," he said, eyes alight with amusement.

Genevieve grunted but didn't argue.

"Oh, no," Mac said, taking up his story again. "Not pirates. Ham watched for a good long while. He managed to creep up a little closer until he recognized something. These guys were in suits and ties. And they were doing a lot of standing around and talking."

"Why would anyone be out on a deserted island having some kind of meeting?" Dean said, his voice tinged with disbelief.

"And that's what Ham wanted to know. All he could tell was that they were there, and they looked to be busy doing something." Mac scraped his hat from his head revealing more bald skin than Genevieve remembered him having and dropped his hands back to his lap, his fingers bending the stiff material of the brim.

"So let's summarize this a little," Jack said gruffly.

"So the truth is stranger than fiction. As Ham watched, he saw the men venture into the woods just off the beach, just this area." Mac made a decisive gesture to a spot on the map, then turning to gesture with a sweeping his hand out to include the area beyond the window. "He was totally stunned when he saw they had been digging out here. The spot showed all the marking of a study being done, like an archeological dig, with stakes and strings and little flags marking some spots. He swore he saw them uncover some stone ruins from the earth."

"So the men were archeologists?" Genevieve looked at Mac still confused.

"Ham didn't know. All he knew was that he felt sure he shouldn't be there. So he scuttled back to his boat as quickly as he could and headed off the island. He made plans to return, but not before he took notes about the whole event in his journal."

"And he did go back," Jack said from his seat next to the door.

"He did," Mac agreed. "Almost three weeks later, he approached the island again. This time he came to the main dock, where you yourselves arrived. As he was tying up, a man came out to greet him. This guy was dressed for hard work," Mac nodded to a stack of photocopied lined pages on the table. "All of this is from Ham's journal as well. Turns out that this man was Baker who claimed that he owned the island."

"Oh," Dean said thoughtfully. "And would this be 'Mad Baker'?"

"It would," Mac said. "Unfortunately, the journal doesn't describe what conversation they had, but it can be assumed they discussed what Ham had seen that night. Later, it seems they went out to the site to see what had happened with the dig. But the journal did note that there was nothing left of the strangers' work. The place was bare of vegetation, someone had been there, that's for sure, but there was no other evidence that anyone had been staging an elaborate dig there." Mr. Mac again gestured toward the map. "And together they took an old map and marked it up, adding the exact spot where they had seen the dig so they could find it later."

"So Ham and Baker believed someone had been doing some digging on the island. I still don't see how this had you all rushing down here like this," Genevieve protested.

"That's what I was getting to," Mac said mildly. "The two men left the island together to start doing their own investigation. It seems they contacted a more scholarly man named Eric Levinson, a professor from a college in the northeast. He was studying the Native American artifacts found on some of the other islands in the vicinity. His belief was that there was evidence that prior to the settlement of the Seminoles, there were signs of the tribe of Tequesta Indians who died out centuries before and had spread out over parts of Florida and onto some of the surrounding islands."

"This is where the story gets interesting." Jack was leaning forward, elbows on his knees, totally enjoying to the tale.

"So Baker and Ham persuaded Levinson to come with them back to Baker's Cove to have a look at the area. And according to Ham's journal, Levinson agreed readily, and the three of them met again two days later. By now, Levinson was pretty fired up. He was going to be able to check out some private island with the permission of the owner, but he had something else going on in his head. I think he knew exactly who those other people had been."

Jack nodded sagely in agreement.

"Ham reported amazing findings from their trip and subsequent dig. Levinson knew what he was doing, and managed to get a fair area cleared with the help of the other two men. I'll have to show you the list of found artifacts later, but it included stone carvings on great slabs of stone planted in the soil, large basins to hold some unknown liquid, skeletons of some marine animals as well as several human skeletons, and bits and pieces of copper and precious stones. Many of the items they found were not from the area, showing that somehow, the natives had acquired the materials from far away, continents away. Another mystery there."

"According to Ham's records, Baker wanted to go public with the information. He wanted to tell everyone what they had found. But Levinson hesitated. He said they didn't know who had been out doing the initial digging, and he didn't want to risk it until the site had been more thoroughly explored and cataloged."

Now Jack leaned forward again. "But you see, that never happened. Just three days later on his way back north, Levinson was killed in an unexplainable accident when his car careened into a lake while he was on an outing with his wife. Neither survived the accident. There were a few letters that we found in some of our papers that alluded to the fact that the other men were now afraid, but the journal ended so abruptly, we didn't know the whole story. So that was when we went looking for what had happened to Hamsdale Williamson." Jack's voice went deep and rough. "It seems he was found brutally murdered on his boat."

Genevieve felt a little sick at the thought of the crimes. "So Baker?"

"Baker became a more of a recluse, interacting with just a few trusted people. He didn't want to stir up any more news until he could get someone to believe the story, and someone to help work at the site again." Jack was shaking his shaggy head as Mac added this point. "But as he got older, he became more brash, coming out to the media, claiming that there was something buried on the island. Something valuable enough to kill for."

"But no one believed Baker," Mac continued. "They all thought he was trying to gain publicity for his little island so he could make some money in the sale of it, or he had gone insane with age and drink. He couldn't get anyone to come and check out dig, and eventually he stopped trying. Mother nature had helped destroy their original work, with storms and floods dissolving their careful markings and causing cave-ins where they had cleared the earth. And then the map disappeared."

"How do you know what happened to the dig?" Genevieve asked, distracted. She was absently rubbing her arms, feeling the swelling of a dozen mosquito bites.

"There were a few articles by the local papers, mostly side articles enumerating the madman's claims," Mac said. "I poked around some before we headed out. I wanted to make sure the site hadn't been excavated at a later date. There was a quarter of a century that separated Hamsdale's death and Mad Baker's claims. I wanted to see if anyone had come out and worked the site in that time."

"And they hadn't?"

Mac shook his head, once again putting his hat on his head and pulling it into position, a little tilted toward the back of his skull.

"But what happened to all the evidence? All the metal and bones they found? The artifacts?" Genevieve was caught up in the mystery now, and couldn't stand the thought that it would end like that, fizzling out into nothing, just a tall tale. She forced herself to drop her hands from her arms and clasped them in her lap.

"Disappeared," Mac said sadly. "All of the objects they had unearthed and identified had been stored in this building. It stated that in the journal. And the day after the murder of Ham, it all vanished." His frown carved lines in the corners of his lips. "That was from one of the local papers. Baker tried to have the cops come in, but his reputation was never good, and they thought he was fairly touched, making all these wild claims." Mac leaned back, hands on his middle like he had just completed telling the longest story ever and was weary from it.

"I'm sorry to be butting in, but there is something I don't I understand," Dean said, looking at the men. Genevieve was struck by the seriousness in his tone, but she was grateful. Surely she wasn't the only one that thought this whole thing was just a little too farfetched? "Everyone knew which island it was. Everyone knew the rumors. Why are you getting involved now? After all of this time, I understand you found the map, but what does it mean?"

"The map finally shows just where the dig was," Mac said victoriously. "Baker had gotten so confused in the end, he lost track of where on the island the men had dug. The journal gave hints, but no specifics. After all of this time, by using the map, we know where the artifacts might be found. Don't you see?" Mac's voice was deep and sonorous. Now he looked like a professor, his eyes so sharp and direct despite the scrunched hat shielding his balding head. "This island had once been inhabited by the Tequesta Indians. That makes it a significant archeological site. It would be full of information about their culture, and beyond that, the other items that were found might reveal how much trading from other parts of the world was happening right here on this little island. But digging up the remains and destroying them, well they were changing the history of the place. For some reason, someone didn't want it to be known that the island had been a former site. And I think it was the men in suits. I think it was the people Ham first found on the island. It was stifled then and it's worse now. Because now, they have a reason for it to be covered up." His voice had risen with intensity.

Genevieve frowned. "What do you mean?"

Jack took a long drink from his soda and crushed the can in one strong fist. "They want to make this place into one of those damn resorts for the rich and famous. They've already been in talks with the remnants of the Baker family who are only too happy to get their hands on cash. They don't care to see what their ancestor was complaining about. It was too many years ago, and his reputation has probably been a skeleton in their closet for a mighty long time. As soon as the sale goes through, they'll be wealthy and rid of it, and the island will be virtually raised to make it suitable for a golf course and resort buildings. They plan on major excavations to allow for more beachfront. And what you see here, all this woodland, will be taken down and repurposed for the needs of the tourist. In a few months, you won't recognize this place."

"So that's why you're here? You're trying to find the site where they excavated and see if you can find anything yourself?" Genevieve looked from one lined face to the other, reading the determination in their eyes, the set of their jaw.

"That's exactly why we're here," Mac agreed.

"You know us," Jack said his voice surprisingly gentle as he looked at his only child. "We can't just leave this alone. We can't let them win." Jack had taken her hand. "Now you can see why we had to come. We had the map from Ham's things. And we had the journal. We had to see what they had discovered here. We have to stop them from building up some resort if there was an ancient Indian settlement here."

"You couldn't call a university to look into it?" Genevieve said, grasping at what might have been a logical step in the investigation.

"We didn't want to go to anyone just yet. We wanted to see what we would find, gather some evidence before we brought in any professionals. And at this point, I doubt we have enough proof for them to be interested." Jack looked at her hesitantly. "There is something else. We know someone is actively trying to stifle the story. The map was almost destroyed. The files it came from, part of the Baker estate, went missing shortly after we went there to look for it. Most of the letters between the men disappeared. You see, we just recently got the notice that the family was planning on cleaning out some of their ancestor's belongings. There were several old pieces they had put up in a local auction. They hadn't even bothered to clean out the old cabinets and desk. When Mac found out who had bought out the lot, we went there and asked about the papers. We were lucky. They had already pulled the map and sold it to us for a song. Not a day later, we went back when we realized what we had found. But the rest of the papers were gone. Someone had snatched them right out from under the shopkeeper's nose."

Mac looked at them, his mustache twitching. "We just need to buy a little bit of time until we can find evidence to stop the construction," he said firmly.

"But why didn't you tell me where you were going?" Genevieve said turning back to her father, her voice a little harsh. "Why the disappearing act?"

Jack looked at her for a moment and then leaned over and squeezed one of her hands in his two big palms. "I would have told you everything if I could have," he said gravely. "I would have told you and your mother in person if I could have stayed. You know that." He hesitated a moment. "But that's why I sent the email. I wanted you to be ready when I sent Hemingway to you."

"The email only had a picture of the map," Genevieve argued feeling confused. "How was I supposed to figure out what it meant?"

"That's what the other email was for," he said insistently. "I explained to you about the island and the chance that it had been an archaeological site that was being destroyed. I wanted you to understand why I couldn't call you. Our phones are almost useless out here."

Genevieve hesitated. "Jack, I got an email with the map. I didn't get anything else from you other than those pictures from your last trip to Mexico."

"That Mexico trip was months ago. I put the explanation in the first email." He rubbed his hand through his wiry beard, his brows meeting over his eyes. "I sent the map second. I didn't want to put them together. Just in case someone was checking in with me. I wrote out the instructions first."

"I only found one email," Genevieve said slowly, her thoughts getting twisted as she pictured the email she had read. There had been only the title, she was positive. But had there been another email before that? No, she had looked through them all, especially after finding the map. So what did that mean? "It must not have gotten to me," she reasoned still frowning. She looked at Jack directly. "I've been having some trouble with the emails coming in from you anyway. The one with the map disappeared from the server just after I opened it."

"Disappeared?"

"I didn't delete it. I'm sure of that. I had seen it on my cell phone and opened it. Then when I checked again, it was gone. So when I couldn't find it on my computer or my phone, I pulled up the server from the Internet." She saw her father's confused look and waved her hand. "Don't worry. I just mean that my business uses a larger memory cache and it's run differently from my personal email address. It takes a little more work to erase it from there. I'm sure they want to make sure there are plenty of backups in case of accidental deletions of important documents for the company." Unconsciously her hand went to the cell phone in her pocket. It was a company owned gadget too, but one of the best on the market. They believed in keeping their employees plugged in at all times and were willing to pay for the equipment needed to do so. "But when I looked on the server, your email was erased from there as well. There was no trace of it I could find. I was just lucky I had opened the map on my cell phone, and it had saved the attachment in the pictures gallery. When I found it there, I sent it back to myself and enlarged it. Without that, I had no idea what had happened to you!"

She could see the realization dawning in her father's eyes. Jack and technology didn't always mix well, but she could see it as he processed what she was telling him. She saw in that moment he hadn't known that she was unaware of his location. Apparently he had written a note to tell her where he was, and had believed for all of this time she had been informed about what he was doing and why. Or maybe he had skipped the 'why' part, but he had told them he was going to be incommunicado for some time.

"Oh, my girl, I had no idea you didn't know where I was!" Suddenly he was on his feet, pulling her up to envelop her in a warm tight hug, smelling of sunscreen and perspiration. "You came all the way out here with no real idea that I was on the island. You were hunting me down!" When he pulled away his eyes glowed with something like pride. "And that's my smart girl! You figured all of this out yourself!"

"Not by myself," she said awkwardly pulling away. "I had a lot of help."

"So all you had was the map? How in the wide world did you track us down?" Jack's face had slipped from pride to concern as he thought of her journey.

"I had the map and I had Hemingway, so we drove down," she began, but predictably, he interrupted.

"Hemingway! Where is that old bird?"

"He's with one of Dean's co-workers. He's safe."

Jack's eyes sharpened. "Who?"

"Lillian is very capable," Genevieve said sternly. "She works in a vet's office!"

"Is she a vet?" Jack was still in his interrogation mode.

"No, I'm the vet and she's my assistant." Dean was listening to the conversation with interest and a little bit of amusement. Genevieve realized she was recognizing it in the quirk of his lips and the one eyebrow that was creeping up.

Jack's eyes swiveled toward Dean, and he looked at the younger man with interest. "A vet, you say." Jack seemed to be thinking fast now. "And how exactly did you end up on this island?"

Genevieve huffed a sigh. "Dean's mother and mom are friends. Dean came down to keep me company on the ride. And it's a good thing that he did. My car was damaged on the trip down, and I got held up in a small town in Northern Florida." She crossed her arms in front of her chest, feeling a little like she was defending her decision to have Dean with her. "Since we've gotten to Florida, Dean has helped me a lot."

"Well, then." Jack looked back at Genevieve. "So you left Hemingway with this Lillian, and you followed the map?"

Genevieve's lips twisted. "It wasn't that easy. I first asked Casper to see if he knew where you had gone. He said he didn't." She studied Jack to see if he flinched, to let her know that Casper might have been deceiving her, but Jack's expression remained impassive. "Then I went to talk to Mac, and happened to see his neighbor."

Mac's head came up and his mouth opened slightly under his slightly drooping mustache. "Who was that?"

"Your next door neighbor. She knew you were going to be gone. She said she was watching your house for you." He was nodding slowly, his unsettled expression calming.

"Then I went to the marina. I could see the boat was gone, and they were able to tell me how long it had been gone. Only that, but they had no idea where you might have taken it."

"We didn't tell anyone where we were going," Jack declared. "That was on purpose."

"I know that now, but at the time, I had no idea where you were or what you were doing!"

"Well, now, girl, I'm not complaining. Since you didn't get my note, I can see why you felt like you had to track me down."

"But if she can do it," Mac said slowly, his lips curved down, "then someone else might be able to."

"It wasn't that easy," Genevieve argued. "I happened to show the map to Dean and Lillian, and Lillian recognized the coastline of the island."

"Wonder how many other people would recognize it?" Mac was stroking his moustache thoughtfully.

"I didn't show the picture to anyone else. After I found it the first time, and the email was deleted from my computer, I didn't even know it still existed. It was only when I was in Florida that I found it again."

"You said the email disappeared?" Mac's eyebrows crept up his forehead.

"I couldn't pull it up again," Genevieve explained. "I found it once, but when I searched again, it had been deleted off my mail email account."

"And the trash had been deleted too?" Dean was listening closely, his face tightened with concern.

"Yeah, and that was strange for me. I don't usually empty it until they send out the reminder to help clear the server. The last time they did that was probably six months ago. I generally remember when I do that. Clearing out my email takes some time, and it's generally a pain."

"Who else could delete it from the server?" Mac had his chin in his hand.

"Just me or one of my coworkers, I suppose. I mean, I have it password protected. But it wouldn't be too hard to figure out. It's not like I worry about them and what they might be getting into." She found herself chewing her lip thoughtfully. Now this was getting outlandish. It was one thing for Mr. Macintosh to

168

worry that someone might be tracking them down trying to prevent them uncovering the possible dig site. That would be someone local, and probably someone who had a stake in the island or the development of the resort. After all, there were people out there who didn't want the resort to be impeded. It would put quite a snag in their plans if real artifacts were found. But that was far removed from her father's notes to her sent by email to her company address. And farther still from her co-workers who definitely had no reason to interrupt her mail.

"It had to have been a computer glitch. Or maybe someone in corporate decided to clean house." She sat back. "I'm not going to worry about the email any more. Now we just have to figure out where to go from here."

"What are you doing about the dig?" Dean asked, glancing out the window.

"We've been poking about," Mac admitted, "but the truth is, that many years can change an island. The coast has been greatly affected by storms, by normal erosion, and by some man made tampering. The place that was marked on the map may be quite a ways inland, or could be under the ocean. We're just not sure until we are able to get some more recent aerial maps."

"I could get some," Genevieve blurted before she had thought out what she was going to say.

"What?" Jack's lips were turned down, his chest puffing up in the father knows best posture.

She thought about it for a moment. "You can't go back to land without getting a whole lot of questions. At least, you can't easily. And by me asking around, I've got extra people looking out for you. Not that I think anyone else is aware of what you are doing here, but in case you're right, in case someone is trying to keep the island from being explored, you might want to lay low. So while you poke around here, I can go back to the mainland and look up the information you need. I can bring it back out here tomorrow or the day after and bring any supplies you need." She glanced around the little cabin. "Surely you have to be running out by now. How long have you been here, anyway?"

"Well, some time now," Jack said. "And we probably have run a little low on a few things."

Genevieve looked between the two older men. "Or maybe you both should go back for a little while," she said worriedly. "I mean, you may need a break from the heat, the bugs," as though to accentuate her thought, she felt the sting of a bug bite and slapped at her calf.

"No," Jack said quickly. "We don't plan on leaving here until we have some sort of evidence to stop the construction. If we head out now, it would be like giving up, and that is not going to happen." His voice had firmed into that familiar stubborn tone Genevieve and her mother had heard many times before.

"Dad," Genevieve said softly.

Jack heard the tone of her voice and his face eased into a gentle smile. "Now girl, you know me. The heat doesn't bother me, and the bugs don't bite me. Too full of vinegar. I could live out here another year without a problem."

Genevieve looked around the cabin, unconvinced.

"We have a boat. We've been back to the mainland a few times since we came out here. It's not like we're stranded out here," Jack said. "When the weather gets bad, we just head out. I might be a stubborn old man, but I'm not reckless."

Genevieve sighed, but before she could argue, Jack continued.

"You're my smart girl. You go back and get that picture for us. You look around and see what you can dig up. Then you come back here. We'll keep up our work here."

"What about bringing in someone who might know about the history, or at least how to handle a dig like this?"

Jack shrugged. "We're working as carefully as we can. If we find something that looks promising, we'll bring in the professionals. But for now, Mac here knows a fair amount about this kind of thing, so we aren't bumbling around and tearing apart possible evidence."

Genevieve's eyes snapped to Mr. Macintosh. It didn't surprise her he would have some experience in archeological digs. He was a true Jack-of-all-trades. She had forgotten what skill sets he seemed to have.

Finally, she heaved another sigh and stood. The rest of the little party eased from their chairs as well. "We should head back to the boat. I'll try to look into the pictures for you. And I'll be back tomorrow or the next day." She was talking sternly to Jack, but including his friend as well. She didn't like just leaving them out here like this.

"And that would be splendid," Mac said. "I'll start a list of supplies."

Genevieve nodded her agreement and turned toward Dean. He was standing still, his eyes directed out the screened windows. "Are you ready?" she asked, and then felt stupid for asking. Of course he would be ready. Typical of living with Jack, her life had taken a strange little diversion. Dean was nice enough to come along for the ride, but she suspected he was ready to get off the crazy train.

"I'm ready whenever you are," he said gesturing carelessly. "This has been absolutely incredible. I can't wait to get more information."

She gaped at him and then quickly tried to hide her surprise. "You're planning on following this craziness?"

"Well, of course," he said, grinning now. "I wouldn't miss this!"

Chapter 18

The bath was absolutely delicious. Genevieve had bought some special medicinal bubble bath to help sooth her dozens of bites. She laid her head back on the edge of the tub and closed her eyes. A cloud of steam, scented with a tangy herbal essence, enveloped her.

He's out of his mind, she mused, her thoughts going to her father, living on the island contentedly in the heat and the sand. There was no possible way she could do what he was doing. Of course, he had been known to stay in worse places. His hair raising tales of past trips, living in tiny hovels in Eastern Europe, in frail cottages on the rainy expanse of some Scottish field, and flea infested tents on some distant plain.

This little island seemed to be fairly mild in comparison, but Genevieve was only too aware Jack was aging, as much as he tried to deny it. And was he different? He seemed pretty healthy when she had seen him. Perhaps his age wasn't such an issue with the day-to-day survival on the island.

She slowly raised an arm from the tub water, looking sourly at the red welts dotting her shiny flesh. It wasn't age that had gotten her, that was for sure. She wiped a damp strand of hair away from her face. She would know a few things to add to her packed bag when she went out to the island the next time. She huffed out a breath and climbed to her feet. After pulling the plug, she stepped from the tub and wrapped herself in one of the bleached white towels provided. Not very soft, she thought frowning. Her tidy motel, so generic in every way, had just the minimum of comfort. She missed her own bed, her own soft towels, and her own fully stocked medicine cabinet with anti-itch cream.

Genevieve hung the towel back on the rack and reached for her nightclothes. Distractedly, she finished dressing and went to climb into her bed. She saw a stray feather, bright red at the ends with a paling toward gray near the shaft, still sticking to the bed linens. The hotel staff hadn't caught it. And now it was her only reminder of Bow, Hemingway, she corrected herself. She would have to call Lillian in the morning. She took the feather and somewhat reverently laid it on the nightstand next to her charging phone.

She was going sleuthing tomorrow. She had a few ideas where she might get a copy of the map printed, but found she was anxious to look over some of the information Mr. Macintosh had found, not that she wanted to cause too much of a stir. She wasn't sure she believed someone was out there trying to sabotage the site. Was there truly some shadowy figure out there trying to prevent them from finding the evidence of the Indian settlement?

She tugged the blanket over her, smoothing it flat with both hands. She was tired. She needed sleep. But her mind was spinning away, sketching mental visuals of ideas just to quickly disregard them. There was something afoot, she thought wryly. She just hoped it wasn't all in Mac's head.

She grabbed her pillow and fluffed it with a little too much force. The days were slipping past, but she wasn't nearly ready to pack up and head home. She had called her mother as soon as she had gotten into her hotel room. She couldn't say much, but it was enough for her mother to know her father was safe. Genevieve was slightly alarmed at how easy it had been to dodge her mother's questions about her whereabouts. She was getting a little too good at this evasion. She pulled out her phone and checked the email account for work. Just a few messages. The guys were handling most things without her, but she could see Bob's gentle hand in the questions. He wanted her to know he still wanted her involved. They might not need her like they had before to make the project go, but they weren't about to do anything without her.

She laid down again and pictured them. Bob was a truly great boss. He had the wisdom to let them go where they needed to, to follow the leads and thought processes that had moved the project on to its eventual success. And the three of them, Dr. North, Dr. Morney, and Dr. Glass, well, they worked pretty smoothly. Granted, Rick tried to take the lead occasionally. He seemed to care a little too much for the glory of the job, but she could handle him. Larry was just a big teddy bear. He was the glue, the great intermediary, the man in the middle. When she had told him she was going on this trip, he had been predictably unflappable. She frowned. Rick had been a little upset about it. Just a little. He hadn't actually said anything, but he had looked uptight, like he was thinking of something that troubled him. But he hadn't complained, and then her plans had gone through, and on their last day, both men had seemed comfortable. Hadn't they both asked after Jack, telling her to not worry, that they were sure she would find him perfectly healthy and happy?

And they had been right. Well, pretty close to right. She had found Jack, and he was fine. But he wasn't in the free and clear. He was involved in something up to his whiskered chin. Like usual. Another adventure that may or may not bring a payoff. He wasn't actually looking for that this time, though. This wasn't for the money. This was for the sake of history.

She turned on her side and flicked off the light. She could stand behind Jack on this one. If there really was history to be preserved, then she wanted a hand in helping. She slid off to sleep with a slight smile on her face.

The logical first step was a library. Where else were there copious amounts of books, atlas, and periodicals that would trace the history of a spot with as much precision? The closest branch was just a few miles away from the hotel, but like the hotel, was a generic shadow of what a library should be. It had the mandatory selection of fiction books, mostly hardbacks wrapped in crisp plastic, many in large print for the growing elderly population. Genevieve was amused to see a fair number of seniors already filling the library seats, many of whom were tucked behind flat-screened monitors. Who ever said you couldn't teach an old dog new tricks? They looked pretty comfortable with the technology.

She strolled down the rows of books, finally giving up when she realized that this branch was going to be too small to have the information she needed. At the desk, a young woman with oversized glasses was bent over a stack of new book, carefully applying the protective covers. Her head bobbed up and a smile bloomed on her face when Genevieve stopped by the desk.

"Can I help you?" she asked, long fingered hands stilling on the book.

"I was looking for some information, and I'm afraid it might not be here," Genevieve said slowly.

"We're just one of the smaller branches, but if it's a book you're looking for, we can always have it transferred here. Do you have something on hold?"

"Oh, no," Genevieve clarified. "I was looking for maps and some historical data."

"I see. You need research material? Like for a paper?"

"Yes, more like that," Genevieve agreed.

"Then you'd be best to go to the main library." The librarian ducked under the counter and emerged with a photocopied paper. On it was a street map with blocky buildings marked as the other satellite locations of the library. "You're probably going to need to go ...." She traced a snaking road and pointed with one slender finger, unpainted nails neat and short, "it's only about a twenty-minute drive from here, and their collection is much more extensive. Especially for the non-fiction and periodicals." She went on to traced the best route, her voice patient, stopping to show the final destination, which she circled with a yellow highlighter. "Here are the hours," she continued, highlighting a notation that stated the address.

"This is great," Genevieve said, smiling in relief. It would save her a lot of aimless driving if she could find the maps all in one location. "Thanks for your help."

The young woman pushed her glasses up on her nose more securely, showing bright green eyes that crinkled with amusement. "Not a problem!"

The Macaw Muttered

Genevieve grabbed a hamburger on the way to the other building, sitting in her car in the shadow of a grove of palm trees, her window cracked to let in the sultry breeze. The air smelled of exhaust, of heat and cooked pavement, and just the faintest hint of the sea. Still, it was better than going into one of the eating establishments where the toddlers were running full force, sticky hands outstretched. Lunchtime in a fast food restaurant wasn't relaxing in the least, and here she could just think.

Her mind seemed incapable of slowing anyway. The whole situation was patently ridiculous. Not that she would expect anything less from her father. If there wasn't an adventure to be had, he made one up. And this time, it seemed he had willingly followed Mr. Mac into the adventure, lured by the whiff of historical scandal and unsolved mysteries.

She frowned as she crumpled her burger paper and dropped it into the slightly greasy paper bag. She wiped her fingers on one of the paper napkins and carefully scanned the car for any crumbs or debris. She needed to get the car cleaned. It wasn't like her to let it get as dirty as it was, with the dusting of sand and salt dulling the exterior, and the stray feather or bit of food left from Hemingway's occupation of the back seat.

That would have to wait. She gathered her purse, the bag of garbage, and keys and slipped out into the heat. With a quick flip, she locked the car up with the remote and dropped her keys into her purse. She found a trashcan on her way into the library and dropped in the bag. She noted without alarm that a gray sedan had pulled in a few spaces from her, and a man with dark sunglasses was sitting behind the wheel, his expression unreadable. She shrugged. He seemed vaguely familiar, but she didn't know many people in Florida, so it was doubtful she had ever met him. With a final glance back at her car, she slipped into the library through the glass doors and into the super cooled interior.

Genevieve liked libraries. She liked the old ones with the dusty books stacked on wooden shelves, their split spines showing years of wear and enjoyment. She liked the new ones with soaring rooflines that took advantage of the space to add the newest computers, the most efficient use of soundproof cubicles to allow for the optimal use of high tech audio equipment, video, and the like. She even liked the ones built somewhere in the 70's that sat awkwardly in the architectural fallout, ugly things that did their best to be serviceable, to provide the room needed to house the books, just waiting for a more elegant update. And as a comforting bonus, all the libraries were bound by common organization, structured in the traditional Dewey Decimal System that made the type A part of Genevieve's mind sigh in pleasure.

This library was no exception. In contrast to the branch that Genevieve had visited earlier, this one had a little more age to it. The center portion of the building had no doubt been built decades earlier, but the Florida patrons had been generous, and the added wings dwarfed the original space. It was dominated by a central desk, so new and updated that Genevieve was surprised the price tag wasn't still attached. Behind the desk, a middle aged woman with a name badge hanging from a beaded lanyard, Jeannine according to the blocky text, was clicking busily through the screens on her computer. In front of her was a stack of books, either on their way into or out of circulation. Genevieve was tempted to stop and browse, especially when she saw a brand new copy of her favorite author's release, but forced herself to stop at the desk.

"Maps." The woman's eyes lit up behind stylish glasses at the idea of a quest. "So you need to research the changes in the coastline? And what area are you looking into?" She had already slipped from behind the counter and was starting across the carpeted floor, her sneakered feet making no noise against the marble tile.

Genevieve explained about her interest in the island and tagged after the woman, glancing with fascination at the murals on the curved walls as they jogged up a set of stairs that led into the second floor of the right wing of the library. In the upper floors, the non-fiction area opened with journals of all types and topics, leading into some reference books. Genevieve knew she could have just as easily looked up some of the information on the computer herself, but felt like she owed Mac to make the most thorough investigation. So yes, she would do it the old fashioned way.

A few hours later, Genevieve sat back, her fingers massaging her temples where it felt like a miniature mariachi band was playing merrily in her head. The pounding was not improving, but she felt a definite sense of accomplishment. There they were. Neatly photocopied with the help of the librarian, Jeannine, and her infinite patience, the stack of diagrams and maps were labeled and paper clipped, ready for the false research paper Genevieve had said she was preparing to write. Sure, she hated lying, but what choice did she have? There was no way she could explain why she actually needed the maps, the fantastic satellite photos, the diagrams of wind and waves and erosion, without sounding like she was crazy. The little white lie gave her a good reason for wanting the information and had piqued the interest of the librarian, who admitted she had been something of a research nut when she was in college. She had definitely gone out of her way to find additional information that Genevieve, by herself, would have never dug up. With a few phone calls and some electronic files sent from friends in other libraries, Jeannine had pulled strings that were far-reaching and expansive, and Genevieve had ended up with success.

"I don't know how I can thank you enough," Genevieve said earnestly, the papers held tight to her chest.

"No need. This was fun. It's been a slow day, so it gave me a chance to dive into something interesting." Jeannine pushed a strand of pale blond hair behind her ear. "Let me give you my card. If you find out you need something more, you can call me." Jeannine produced a business card, not for the library, but for a side business based on elaborate crafting projects. The heavy cream card with elegant lettering had her cell phone number sketched out in looping text. They had discussed the business, and a multitude of other things, as they had waited for files to print and copy. Genevieve pocketed the card feeling a surge of gratefulness. She probably wouldn't need any more information about the island, but she might need more help later. She just wasn't sure what the next steps would be.

178

"I will make sure to call you if I find out I need something else," Genevieve replied. "I wouldn't trust the project to anyone else!"

Jeannine smiled, her eyes pinning Genevieve from above the frame of her glasses. "You know, I suspect that this project has more going on than just a research paper," she said mildly.

Genevieve's eyes widened in alarm, but she kept her voice even. "Really?" she asked, her voice deliberately casual.

"I've helped lots of students with papers. I've done college thesis, high school papers, even some professional ones for journals. But this feels different to me." She put a hand out and laid it gently on Genevieve's arm. "I'm not saying anything to anyone. I can tell you want to keep this to yourself. And from what I can deduce, whatever you're doing means no harm. So I'll just put it out there. If there is anything else I can do to help, you come to me, and I'll do what I can."

Genevieve was surprised into silence. It wasn't just that the other woman had seen through her deceit so easily. It was that despite that, she was willing to help. Genevieve cleared her throat and gave a little nod. She was a little afraid if she spoke, her emotions, always hovering just a little too close to the surface lately, might spill into her words.

"Okay then," Jeannine said, a smile once again blooming on her face.

Her cell phone rang as she was sliding into her car seat, now superheated by the sun, and she yelped as her skin hit the leather. She fumbled for the phone, pulling it free of her pocket after setting the stack of papers on the seat next to her. She had almost expected to see Jack's number, which was foolish, she knew, since there was no way he could get reception on the island. The thought had her muscles tightening involuntarily. His inability to use his cell phone while he was on the island was just one of the reasons he had been so difficult to track down. It explained why she had gone for so long without hearing from him, although it had been a typical Jack move to assume she would have gotten the email and immediately understood the situation. She squinted at the lit screen for a moment. The display showed a slightly fuzzy picture she had used as part of her caller id. It was a photo of Dean she had snapped when they had been stranded with her car, a shot of him wading through a puddle at a distance, head down, a lock of hair falling attractively on his brow.

She fumbled with the slick screen to answer the call and then held it to her cheek stuttering a breathy hello.

"Genevieve?"

"Dean, hi," she responded settling in her car, still wincing at the heat against her skin.

"Hey, did I catch you at a bad time?"

She realized she was wheezing a little and made a face. "No, it's fine. I just got into the car. I've been at the library for most of the day. I've got the maps." It was nice to be able to talk to someone who would understand the statement without going into any backstory.

"Already? Great! You must be good at this research stuff."

Genevieve was tempted, just for a moment to take the credit, but couldn't do it. "Not my doing. I met the best librarian and she had plenty of time. So she helped me find everything. I've got the maps, articles, pictures, a whole stack of information."

"That's great. So now what?"

She hesitated. That was a good question, she realized. She had a lot to read, and she had absolutely no desire to do it on the island with her father and Mac, no matter how picturesque it might be. There were bugs on the island. There was no air conditioning. There were no bathrooms. And there was sand. Lots and lots of gritty sand, seeping into every corner and every crevice, sand that would stick to everything.

"I'm not sure what my next step will be," she said, shifting in her seat now that the heat wasn't so stinging. "I guess I need to read over all of this stuff."

"Want some company?" His voice was that warm buzz and she smiled to herself.

"That is a great idea," she agreed.

"Then I'll see you later," he responded, and her smile split into a grin.

Chapter 19

She went to Dean's house that evening for an early dinner. As it turned out, he was a pretty decent cook, although he insisted it would be difficult to mess up his mother's personally canned spaghetti sauce. He had stopped on the way home from work to buy some salad and garlic bread, and Genevieve brought the wine. She wasn't sure if he even drank wine, but it seemed just too awkward to arrive empty handed except for a stack of work, so she picked out a red from a locally run vineyard and hoped for the best. She bought a chocolate cake to go with it. If he didn't like wine, at least she figured she could appeal to his sweet tooth. He had already done so much for her she felt like she needed to do something to show her appreciation.

But perhaps that wasn't honestly the reason she arrived bearing gifts. Just maybe she wanted to impress him, please him. And why not? He was a handsome man with a charming personality and he liked her parrot. What more did a girl need?

She pulled into his driveway, noting that his car was already pulled up next to the house in the shadow of a grove of palm trees. She drove up in front of the house and parked her car, locking it up after she stepped out and closed the door. It was still grimy looking, the paint job looking dull in the waning sunlight. And that was unusual for her. At home, she regularly took her car in for a wash and wax, meticulously vacuuming the interior and wiping down the leather with special polish recommended to her by the dealer. But this was Florida, this was vacation, this was a step on the wild side. However, the mess still grated at her just a little.

Apparently the sound of the car door closing had alerted the dogs of her presence, because a flood of fur seemed to erupt from the back of the house, headed straight for Genevieve where she stood, cake balanced in one hand and bottle of wine in the other, her purse hitched up on her shoulder. A piercing whistle had the dogs freezing in their tracks and turning toward the noise, and Genevieve noted in relief that Dean had come to the door. He was wearing an apron. She stifled a smile and headed towards him, the dogs preceding her but turning over their shoulders with hopeful goofy grins.

"That is an excellent look for you," she exclaimed as she slipped by him, smelling the subtle scents of his soap mixed with garlic and oregano.

"Thank you. I like it," he responded. "Don't mind the guys. They've been a little lonely today, and when I told them you were coming, they got just a bit too excited."

"I'm surprised they remember me that well."

"You're memorable," he assured her, taking the cake from her and sliding it onto the kitchen counter. He had gone for the cake first, she observed, thus proving chocolate was the way to a man's heart. Or at least, that was her guess.

"The spaghetti will be done in about fifteen," he said. "Do you want to put your purse down?"

She was holding the bag in her hands, but the intrigued expression on the fuzzy faces was making her hesitate. She didn't want her nice bag filled with hours of research material to be chewed and or slobbered on by the dogs, no matter how cute their expressions. "Where?" she finally asked.

"If you want to put it on top of the counter, the hoard won't get to it," Dean assured her.

She nodded and put the bag in the recommended place, the added wait making her more aware of the stacks of papers inside that they would need to wade through later on in the evening. For now, though, she wanted to enjoy a little time not thinking of Jack and the island. She watched with amusement as the smallest of the dogs, Barney if she had heard correctly when Dean had been bellowing at them earlier, led the other two through the kitchen and into the living room. Like a breathing carpet, they collapsed on the cool floor in puddles of canine contentment.

"So you said your mother made the sauce? Does she like to cook?" she asked, striking up a casual conversation while she studied the kitchen. It was much like the other rooms of the house, full of dark wood and plain cabinets, a smoky gray countertop that might have been poured concrete and contrasted nicely with the glossy floors.

"She loves it," Dean admitted. "And my dad and I loved to eat what she made, so it was the perfect combination."

"And what does your dad do?" she asked off handed, thinking that although she had heard stories of his mother, his father seemed like a seldom discussed topic.

"He was a cooperate manager. He passed away two years ago," Dean said, his eyes on the boiling water as he stirred it slowly with a spoon, not paying attention to the task.

"Oh, I'm sorry," she said, feeling a pang of dismay at his expression.

"It's been some time now," he said, clearing his throat as he took the spoon from the pot and placed it carefully on the counter and wiped his hands on the apron. "That's why I had decided to come home this last time. I wanted to be with mom for the anniversary."

"Two years isn't much time when you lose someone," she said softly.

He looked over at her, head still bent. "Umm, yes, I agree." He straightened. "Mom has taken it well, but there are some times that are more difficult than others. Special occasions, holidays, birthdays, and, of course, this time."

"I'm sorry," she said again, this time feeling more meaning in the words as emotion colored her words.

"Yeah, so am I," he agreed. "Losing dad was like, I don't know, it was like losing part of my childhood, part of myself. I still can't believe he's gone sometimes."

Genevieve thought about how irritating Jack could be. How the eccentric fly by the seat of your pants upbringing she had suffered through had made her what she was. But she wouldn't have had it any other way. And as much as Jack made her crazy, she wouldn't have changed him. Not for anything.

"Was it unexpected?" she asked.

"Heart attack. He was at work. He went really quickly, and he wasn't alone." Dean shifted the lid from the saucepot and stirred slowly, placing the spoon next to the pan and turning from the stove. "How about we open the wine?"

"Sounds good," she agreed, and watched as he rummaged in the drawer and brought out the bottle opener, deftly using it to release the cork.

"I don't actually have wine glasses," he said, opening a cabinet and pulling out two glasses that could only be left over jelly jars. "Think of it as casual dining," he said lightly.

"Works for me," she agreed, and watched as he filled the glasses half full and handed her one.

"What should we toast?" he asked, his eyes so intense and lovely.

"To our fathers," she declared.

"So why Florida?" she asked as she took a nibble of bread and slipped a crust under the table to a willing scavenger. She heard a grateful pant and crunch. The two smaller dogs that could fit under the table had settled at their feet, but Duke, with his long legs and huge feet, was content to lay by Dean's side on the floor, moving only his eyes and bristling eyebrows, ever hopeful of a crumb that might slip off a plate.

"We used to come here when I was a kid. When I had to think of somewhere I wanted to live, I just kept thinking of those long days, hanging out on the beach, walking in the waves. It seemed so relaxing, and I needed something like that, so I started looking in the area." He smiled and put the fork on his empty plate, his eyes crinkling with laugh lines at the corners. "From there it was easy. I found the job opening in one of my professional journals, called the practice, and sent them my information."

"And I'm sure they jumped at the chance to get you," she teased.

"They were perfectly willing to take someone who had a minimum experience, but a good education." He glanced up, that lock of hair falling over his forehead again. "Besides, I was cheap, and they needed help."

184

"And you're happy here," she stated, feeling like it must be true.

"I have my days, but yes, in general, I'm happy. The practice is thriving. The patients are great. I get along with the other staff. So yeah, I like it." But his smile had melted some and a subtle tightening of his jaw made her think there was more to the statement.

She frowned a little. "You don't sound so sure," she said frankly.

He sat back in his chair and almost immediately, Duke dropped his head in Dean's lap, warm brown eyes rolled up in gentle pleading.

"I like it here. I mean, the place is great. I live minutes from the beach! The weather is always warm; the atmosphere is pretty relaxed." He wiped a hand over his face his palm making a gentle scratch as it rubbed over the whiskers on his jaw. "But I do miss home. I miss living closer to my mom. And I miss the seasons, the autumn colors, and even though I hate to admit it, I miss the snow."

"Do you think you would want to move back home?" Genevieve asked, surprised at the little surge of happiness this idea gave her.

"I don't know. I can't say it's out of the question though." He shrugged, his hand resting on the dog's head, absently stroking his gray ears. "But for now, I guess we have work to do."

Together they stood and carried plates into the kitchen, loading the dishwasher while they refilled wine glasses. The dogs weaved in and out in a subtle dance, but were gentlemen and didn't try to jump up or snatch any food that wasn't offered. Dean washed the pots and pans and Genevieve dried, amused when he put the apron back on for the job. He offered her a second one to wear, which she refused. The warm water was enough to send her hair into a mild frizz; she didn't need the added look of an apron.

Once the dishes were all put away, either in the dishwasher or the cabinet, Dean switched off the light and they headed into the living room where the large coffee table would offer ample space for them to spread out their stacks of papers. The dogs accompanied them there too, Barney leaping gracefully onto the couch, circling one small pillow and tucking his sleek form into a doughnut of fur and sleepiness, eventually dropping his chin on his own tail. Henry had found a bone and was contentedly chewing by the back doors, alert for any traveling squirrels or birds outside that he might need to bark at. Duke chose to stay with the humans, sitting upright for a time, looking almost like a third to their little research group, his large nose dipping to sniff the papers disdainfully. He finally flopped onto his belly, his head on his paws, his eyes following their movement.

"We can put the map pictures in chronological sequence," Genevieve began. "Then we can look at comparisons." She flipped through the stack, tugging loose a couple of sheets. "I also have several different articles that go along with the maps; things like big storms that might have impacted the coastline and the rare mention of the island in a news story."

"You were certainly thorough," Dean observed, paging through some of the maps and laying them out on the table.

"I wish I could take credit, but I really can't," Genevieve admitted. "If it hadn't been for the librarian, I would have walked away with two maps maybe."

"Well this looks good," Dean assured her.

Together they compared the information, making quick notations on the margin and finally writing out some of their findings on a legal pad Dean scrounged up.

"So when are you headed back out to the island?" Dean asked Genevieve as she absently tucked a pencil behind her ear.

"Probably day after tomorrow," she responded. "I have to get in touch with Lillian so I can get the boat hired again." She was looking thoughtfully at one of the older maps. "I think I have most of the information I need, if we can just figure out how all of these fit together."

"Are you going anywhere else tomorrow?"

Genevieve looked up from the article she was reading. She felt a surge of excitement and leaned over to show him the paper. "You know, I think I'm going here," she replied, pointing out an address in the article. "It looks like they might have some evidence of the lost tribe, the Tequesta. That should give me a good idea about what I am looking for." She hesitated, feeling

186

her cheeks heat. "Umm, what Jack and Mac are looking for, really," she amended. Since when was she excited about the search, the possible dig?

Dean took the article and skimmed it. "Assuming the exhibition is still active, you're right. This might show us exactly what we need." His eyes were crinkling again. He thought it was funny, but Genevieve didn't comment. Her eyes went back to the papers in front of her, but she was smothering a smile, ridiculous that his expression should make her so happy. She refocused on the article. The picture at the top of the page showed a wide glassed case with dozens of preserved objects couched within.

"Right," Genevieve said. "Hopefully this show will give us a good idea of what is buried out there on the island, assuming that some of it is left, and how it came to be there." She stressed the 'us' with her eyebrows raised.

Dean looked from the article to her. "If you can wait until three," he said, "I'd like to come with you. It's not every day I get to play Private I."

Genevieve nodded. "Sure," she responded, but had to stop herself from grinning. She looked at the stacks of papers spread on the table and sighed. "And now, maybe we can have a piece of that cake."

The sun was starting to set when Genevieve glanced out the window. The cake had been a nice distraction from their work, but it had been finished an hour ago. She repressed the urge to stretch, to pop her joints to relieve the pressure, but the yawn was irresistible. Dean seemed to catch her in the sleepy gesture and then follow her gaze out the window because he smiled a little ruefully.

"You can't say I don't know how to entertain a lady," he quipped.

"It's not your fault," she said, embarrassed to be caught sleeping on the job.

"You want to take another break?" Dean asked, eyebrows raising and a quirk tilting his lips.

"What do you suggest?" Genevieve replied, letting the sheaf of papers drop back to the table.

"When was the last time you got to watch the sun set over the ocean?" he asked.

Genevieve thought back to the visits with Jack, the evenings on the swaying deck of the boat feeling the water move beneath them in undulating rhythm, the sun staining the sky red and then deepening until the sea and sky met in a thin line of gold. "Not for years," she said honestly.

"Then let's take the dogs to the beach." He said standing quickly. "We have a few minutes before we miss it."

"The sunset?" Genevieve asked, still feeling a little hazy after so much reading. What time was it anyway? And what time did the sun set?

"Of course," Dean replied, pushing back his chair and standing. In a gallant gesture, he put out a hand toward her. "This is something you cannot miss."

They took Dean's car even though Genevieve insisted the drive couldn't make her car any grimier. Dean just shook his head as he loaded the three dogs in the back seat and told them firmly to sit.

"You wouldn't want these guys to be in your car," he corrected her gently. "They're good, but not that good. A little drool and sandy paw prints would take that nice car to a whole other level of lived in."

"Then you drive," Genevieve said, her voice gentle. "And I'll just relax here with the gang."

Dean winked. "See, there you go. Just relax for a bit, and the guys and me will show you a good time."

They rolled down the windows and grinned while the dogs pushed their noses out the cracks and snuffled loudly. Barney had made his way to the front seat and was resting warm and solid in Genevieve's lap by the time they could see the flash of the ocean between the buildings by the beach. Even though they could have walked, Dean was afraid they would miss the spectacle on their way, so the drive was wonderfully brief. He parked at one of the public access lots, and Dean leashed the dogs one at a time before opening the door and letting them free. He handed Barney's leash to Genevieve, and they headed down the narrow path that led to the sand.

The wind was a steady brush against her skin, the waves a gentle rush. It was, Genevieve realized, just what she needed. She felt her muscles loosening. She took a deep breath and smiled down at the dog. Henry's deep eyes were focused on the water, and he shifted his body so that he was that much closer to Genevieve's bare legs. He didn't like the water, Dean had said. As they got a little closer to the surf, the other two dogs seemed to lose their evening languor and when Dean released the leashes, Duke ambled into the water, his giant head ducking to allow the salty water to soak into his beard and pearl his scraggly brows with beads of liquid.

Barney raced toward the water with reckless abandon, skidding on the wet sand, going in only as deep as his chest before arrowing back out, howling with exhilaration. He repeated the routine, snapping at the waves with yips of excitement while Duke watched, his old man face a study in embarrassment.

"Barney can't help it," Dean said mildly. "He's the clown of the group around water. No dignity."

"And Henry?"

"Henry prefers to watch. He doesn't like to get wet on a good day, and sand just makes it worse." Dean bent and cupped the dog's head with his hand, stroking the golden ears. "I found him left on my doorstep when I was brand new at the practice. I didn't know what their policy was, but I sure didn't want to take him to the pound." He straightened. "I told them he was my dog that I was bringing in to keep me company. I decided it was better to lie and get my hand slapped then risk Henry here." He was smiling at the dog with obvious affection. "By the end of the day, he was my dog and he came home with me. He still goes back to the office to visit pretty often. They all do."

"And what about the other two?" Genevieve asked. It didn't seem to be much of a stretch that the man would have multiple dogs. He was a vet and therefore had to have a general affection for all things finned, feathered, and furry. She just wondered if he made it a habit of bringing home strays.

"Barney was an owner surrender. He had to have heartworm treatment and the guy that had him didn't have the time or money to invest. Not a bad guy, just not meant to have an animal." Dean shrugged. "The treatment was done and Barney tolerated it well. By the time he was back to being healthy, he was the office pet. For a while, we took turns taking him home, but since then, some of the other staff has gotten other pets and he's fallen into my group more consistently. He still goes for occasional visits though."

Genevieve turned to watch the dog in question leaping into the shallow waves. "He won't get washed out to sea, will he?" she asked a little fearfully.

"Um, no. He's done this plenty of time. He never goes deep enough to lose his footing. His first owner lived on the beach, so he's done this since he was a puppy."

Genevieve watched the smaller dog dodge around Duke as he danced in the waves, his fur going from gray to black as the water soaked in.

"Duke was a puppy whose owner had a pure bred show quality Irish wolfhound. Somewhere along the way, a visiting mongrel managed to get into the yard. He and his 6 brothers and sisters were the result. The owner was giving them away to good homes and asked for help with finding families to take them. We thought Duke was going to be the runt."

"The runt! How big were the rest of them?"

"They all grew up to be within 10 pounds of each other. I still meet up with a few of the other guys that adopted. We usually go to a park. No one wants more than one of these big lugs in their house at a time." The sun had started its gentle slide toward the water, and its rays sent shards of light, like curved pieces of glass to reflect on the salty surface of the sea. Genevieve had to squint up at Dean's face as he spoke, noticing not for the first time how wide his shoulders were and how straight he stood, firm and reliable.

Dean turned and let out the sharp whistle that had Henry's ears pricking and the other dogs bounding from the water's edge. Dean gave a gesture and the group of them shuffled into place. And they walked.

The beach was a long stretch of warm sand and salt, of laughing children and lazy adults soaking up the last rays of a vacation spent in the sun. Genevieve and Dean were stopped frequently. Everyone was a dog lover, it seemed, and everyone

190

had a favorite of the three dogs. Duke allowed sticky fingered toddlers to lay pink cheeks against his flank while their siblings bent to coo about Barney's big eyes and lolling tongue. Henry had his tail tugged, but looked on with supreme patience. Even the adults in the crowd liked to give the dogs a pat on the head or a stroke down their back, each having their own story of their favorite dog, long dead or left at home, still missed.

By the time they had gotten out of eyesight of the beach access, Dean had taken Genevieve's hand and they were walking toward the waning sun in companionable silence. As the sunset began to send out blood red and neon tangerine, Genevieve dug out her expensive cell phone and took a few pictures. She snapped the dogs playing in the surf, Dean standing in the brilliance, and the sun as it made its final showy exit. When shadows started curving from the water onto the beach, Dean whistled to the dogs again and put on the leashes. They turned back the way they had come, the wind blowing at their backs.

Genevieve had lost track of where they were. She couldn't have found the car or the beach access without much help. But she felt the weight of thought lifted as she enjoyed the few moments of peace. Dean paused and gestured vaguely toward inland.

"We're here," he said, reigning in the dogs until they huddled in a comfortable little bunch, flopping on the sand.

"I'm really glad we came," Genevieve confessed, letting the breeze blow her hair away from her face. At this angle, she couldn't see Dean's expression. The light had died out fast, leaving his face a palate of sharp angles.

"I am too." His voice was husky and pleasant. She felt the brush of his fingers as they reached up to trace the curve of her cheek. "I'm glad I came on this whole adventure."

"Are you sure?" she asked, her voice light and playful.

He didn't answer, but when his lips brushed hers, she figured she knew his feelings about it.

Chapter 20

The hotel was the epitome of unsatisfactory, she thought to herself as she sat up in bed and pushed the balled up blankets to the foot of the bed. The air conditioning had failed sometime during the night, and she was sticky and disgruntled. She didn't want to complain to management, it just wasn't the way that she normally handled things, but she was in Florida, and there was no way she could function without air-conditioning.

So her night had been close to miserable. On the other hand, her evening had been absolutely amazing. She could still feel the heat of Dean's kiss even hours after she had left him standing in his driveway surrounded by his furry entourage.

She found herself humming despite the heat as she slid out of bed and headed to the shower. She had made plans to meet him this afternoon, but she had plenty to keep her busy. She needed to call Lillian to get another boat ride arranged. And she had to admit she was feeling like a neglectful sister to Hemingway. Jack would be disappointed in her. She hadn't checked on him at all since dropping him off with Lillian and the rest of her feathered menagerie. Not that she was concerned. Lillian was obviously a great choice as a bird sitter, with her love of the exotic pets and her work experience, but there was no excuse for Genevieve's apparent neglect.

So she would call Lillian as soon as she was done getting ready, and then head out to the library again. This time she wouldn't be looking into ancient history. She was after some more recent information, and although she was capable of using her laptop to check out the websites she would most likely need, there was no way she was going to stay in her sauna like room any longer than she had to.

After stepping out of a cool shower, she quickly toweled dry and chose her clothes with more care. Was it because she would be seeing Dean later? She disregarded this notion as soon as it entered her head. She had far too many things to be concerned about without the added stress of worrying about her love life.

When she had finished applying a light touch of makeup and put her hair up in a knot off her neck, she gathered her computer in its bag, her purse, and keys. She would have to decide at some point whether or not she wanted to stay at the hotel. For now, she would leave her belongings. She had extended her reservation for the room for another week, but she wasn't sure if she could follow through with those specific plans. She wouldn't stay another night in the heat that was for sure.

At the desk, she noticed a buzz of disgruntled patrons, other tourists and business people with eyes dull with fatigue. The woman behind the desk looked no less irritable. A harried younger man was standing next to a phone that was ringing with frightening frequency. When the man picked up the receiver, his face paled as he listened to the barrage of ire from the other end, a fine sheen of perspiration gathering on his upper lip, whether from the berating or the heat, Genevieve couldn't tell.

"Yes, sir, we are aware of the problem," the man said in a burst of speech as though trying to wedge his words into a second of silence. "Yes, the air conditioning is out all over the building." He was nodding as the voice on the other end began a prolonged rant, audible through the line.

Genevieve had thought she would consult with someone at the front desk to ask about the estimated time the air conditioning would be repaired, but now that she had seen the crowd of people already gathered, and heard the ringing of the telephone, she suspected it would take her some valuable time to speak with someone about the issue. And that was time she knew was better spent outside of the stifling building.

She slipped out the automatic door, and hit the door lock for her car, listening to the beep with satisfaction. She climbed in her vehicle, pleased she had thought to park in the shade of some overgrown palms, rather than let her car heat up in the morning sun. Once she had the engine on and the air conditioning blowing cool sweet air, she took out her phone and dialed Lillian's cell phone.

Lillian didn't answer so Genevieve left a message, explaining what she needed and leaving her own phone number for Lillian to return the call. If she were lucky, she would be able to stop by and visit with Hemingway sometime during the day, or perhaps in the evening if Lillian had a full day of work. She would feel much better seeing Jack if she had also gotten to see Hemingway and knew he was doing well in his transplanted abode. She knew well Jack could read her like a book and would know if she hadn't seen his feathered friend.

Her next stop was going to be breakfast. She hadn't eaten anything since the heat had robbed her of any appetite, and the idea of hot coffee had been abhorrent. But now, with the prickles of cool air stroking her skin, she was feeling close to human. Food first, then research, and then Dean. It was a good plan.

She chose a Starbucks that was close enough to the library that she wouldn't be going out of her way to make her quick stop. As she shut off her engine, she saw a few other drivers had the same idea. A bright red jeep pulled in next to her, a dark gray sedan next to them, both drivers blanketed in the glare of the sunlight. Inside the building, the place had a few patrons already set up at wooden tables, their coffee cups at the elbows and their laptops open before them. Seeing this, Genevieve decided to change her plans a little. She could start her research here. She only needed some reliable Wi-Fi anyway, and this seemed at least as comfortable as the library would have been.

She ordered a tall regular coffee with room for cream, and then added a shot of caramel as an afterthought. If she was going to be here for a chunk of time, she wanted to enjoy her stay. She chose a slab of banana bread for her breakfast and then headed to her seat. She left her laptop on the table and went to add cream to her coffee, watching the steady ebb and flow of people.

With all of her research tools in hand, including her much needed caffeine, she slipped back to her seat. Her laptop had a full battery and would last for hours. She booted up the machine, listening to the whir of the fan as the screen blinked to life. She checked her email first. Drat. There was a message from Rick and he sounded none too happy. He had been the one who had seemed most put out that she was leaving for the trip, so she wasn't surprised he would be the one to criticize her that she wasn't on hand for every little question that arose. But really, most of the hard work was done, and the project would lay dormant for a few weeks while some of the administration waded through regulations. She still had enough time to tie up this issue with Jack before she would be needed back home to start the second phase.

She sent back a brief response and checked the rest of the messages, finding cooperate information, a few housekeeping messages, and some spam that managed to sneak through their tight industry filters.

That finished, she switched over to the Internet and tapped in her search words. She still had some questions about the island, and their plans for the resort, and she figured the quickest way to get answers was to act interested in investing.

The website for the construction was already up. Genevieve looked in amazement at the proposed hotel plans, the lush gardens, the golf course, the beachfront restaurant, and the expanse of shopping. It was a lot for the little island. It was a lot for any resort, very upscale, very expensive looking, and very developed. They must have spent some substantial time on the plan.

She looked with something close to disgust as she saw that the natural vista had been sliced and diced, sectioned out with cabanas and golf course lanes until she could barely recognize the island.

She sighed and pulled up the site search again. There were a few brief articles that had been posted as though in an afterthought in the local paper. Most had just a brief mention of the planned construction. A name kept cropping up in her searches, the Monroe Group, headed by Kenneth Monroe, who appeared to be spearheading the project. This was the developer, the one that held the reins, that made the wheels spin, that brought in the money. She made a mental note to look up some more information about the Monroe Group and the rest of their holdings. Perhaps they were some small firm just making headway into the area. Maybe they didn't know anything about the history of the island. And maybe, just maybe, if they were informed, they would do the responsible thing and have some professionals called in to investigate the site before tearing it to bits with massive equipment and hundreds of workers.

Of course, the opposite was just as likely. They might be desperate for the work, determined nothing stand in the way of their progress. If that were true, no pie in the sky argument about a possible historic link would slow the inevitable wrecking ball of progress.

And perhaps both of those ideas were wrong. Perhaps the Monroe Group was a massive conglomeration that cared little for the community and knew only the scent of money. Maybe they already knew about the rumors, the possible history they were about to demolish, and had decided it was worth the possible backlash of scholarly outrage if the destruction was to be made public.

In any scenario, Genevieve felt the likelihood of a confrontation was inevitable. And for some reason, the idea was almost appealing.

Genevieve noticed the traffic of patrons had changed. There were fewer young professionals with laptops and tablets, and more of the older generation, a few ladies looking like they were ready for the meeting of their book club, and another couple who had skeins of yarn between their knees. Knitting and coffee. Not a bad idea, Genevieve observed.

Her eyes drifted over the faces of the other customers. Most hadn't been there when she had arrived, but one man, sitting off by himself in one of the cushy corner chairs, had walked in just after she had and was still there. He didn't even have a computer with him. No book, no newspaper, nothing seemed to distract him from his steadily scanning eyes. There was something cold in that dark gaze. But no, she was being foolish after looking over the research, finding enemies when none existed.

She was thinking about getting a refill when the glass door opened and a familiar figure slipped through. It was Jeannine from the library, her glasses pushed back to anchor her blond hair in place, her tennis shoes making a soft scuff on the floor.

196

Genevieve watched as the older woman went to the counter to give her order. She wondered if Jeannine would recognize her. How many people did the librarian meet per day? Of course there couldn't be the too many that took up all the time she had in her intense research session. Genevieve had looked back up to the counter when Jeanine turned around and caught her eye. The smile that spread over her face showed she remembered Genevieve.

"Hello," she greeted. Jeanine observed the open computer and the stack of papers at her elbow. "Don't tell me you're still doing your research!"

"I am," Genevieve admitted, "but your help was absolutely invaluable."

"So you think you've figured out how the island has changed?" Jeanine asked. Her voice was oh so casual, but Genevieve could see the curiosity that lit up her eyes.

"Mostly, but I'm trying to find a little more information about the island anyway. You know how they are planning on making it into a high priced resort? I was looking more into that." Most of the articles Jeannine had helped Genevieve find were several years old, but there had been a few that covered more recent developments.

"Oh, sure! I knew they had several articles in the local paper about it a few months ago. I read most of them. A lot of fuss. There were a few protests, but mostly people were curious to see what was happening. It's not one of the more visited islands, really. At least not now. Looks like that will be changing."

"I suppose," Genevieve said slowly. "I was looking at the articles myself." She gestured to the screen where the ruddy visage of Monroe filled the screen.

"That's Kenneth Monroe, isn't it?" Jeanine was leaning over, looking more closely at the photo-shopped picture showing Monroe in a pale blue polo with the stitched M of his company over his left pectoral muscle. His skin was just a shade too pink, his eyes just a little too blue. He looked plastic in the picture, Genevieve thought critically. "I've seen him speak before. He's quite the one to sponsor the urban renewal." Jeannine made little air quotes around the phrase urban renewal, and her tone was wry.

"Urban renewal?"

"He likes to tear down old neighborhoods and replace them with something concrete and glass. In fact, he likes to change the look of whatever he lays his hands on."

"Oh," Genevieve felt her interest pique. "So he makes it a habit of taking property to develop, even if some people might not think it needs to be improved," she said slowly.

"That's precisely what he does," Jeanine said tartly. "But I don't think that's what the situation was here." She was gesturing toward the computer. "The island has been sitting out there, barely visited except for an occasional angler or some teenagers wanting to have a party. It's just a little too far off the coast to be much of a draw. Maybe this resort will be a good thing."

Genevieve had immediately leapt to the most obvious thought. It was the perfect explanation. This Monroe was an unscrupulous businessman. He wanted the resort, and when he thought the idea would be scrapped because of what they had found on the island, he had taken it upon himself to get rid of the evidence. Or perhaps he was too good to actually get his hands dirty. He might have had someone else go out to the island to destroy the site.

"Pity about his recent problems," Jeanine was saying, and Genevieve found herself pulled back into reality with some difficulty.

"What?"

"Oh, he was in a car accident about two months ago. His whole business has been shut down, it's basically in limbo, until he's back on his feet."

Genevieve could almost see her idea slowly disintegrating and she sighed. The accident didn't necessarily mean he hadn't been involved with all of the trouble, but it made it less likely. But the idea was perfect.

"So say something was found on the island that might make it much more difficult to build on," she said glancing sideways at Jeannine, "who would be the most upset?" It was a little risky, bringing in Jeannine on what was a no doubt a shaky idea, but Genevieve suspected the other woman was pretty plugged into the community. She kept up with the news. She might know information she wasn't even aware of.

"What do you mean?" Jeannine had slid into a seat across from Genevieve, and now she put her cup on the table and leaned forward.

"Say something was found on the island that made it impossible to build over. Not the whole island, but part of it might become inaccessible. Maybe not forever. Maybe just as long as things need to be investigated. But it would definitely shut it down." Genevieve was looking at Jeannine, watching the other woman's face to see a shift in her expression. But she didn't look like anything was ringing a bell, like she understood what Genevieve was alluding to.

"So if there was something that prevented the building," Jeannine was saying, picking up her coffee and looking over the rim, "who's nose would be most out of joint?"

Genevieve smiled at this description. A nose out of joint would be putting it mildly, she thought, if what she was proposing was true. If the archeological site had the power to shut down construction on the island where they had already gotten the drawings prepared, the fees paid, the companies hired and booked to start work, who would be willing to sabotage the dig to prevent it?

"I suppose the Monroe Group would be the first to be affected," Jeannine said, squinting thoughtfully. "And second would be all the people they had hired."

"The people they hired?"

"Sure, as soon as a job is proposed, they go through all of the red tape to get the government permission, the documentation. Then they have to hire the actual builders. That would include the architects, engineers, construction managers, and all the people that come with. I think one of biggest contractor's is with Justin Nazerine. He's a big mover and shaker in the local business community. Or at least he used to be. He has to be getting up into his 80s by now."

Genevieve blinked. Now she had another name to go on her list. And what a list it might be. She had seen the website. Why hadn't she thought about the scope of the project? It would take far more people than just the Monroe Group's employees to get the project off the ground. It would be a major undertaking.

"And I don't think the island would have any kind of utilities. Who knows what's involved with getting electricity, fresh water, transportation to a place like that?" Jeannine seemed to be warming to the idea. "Why, to get all those buildings constructed they would need to have an army of people helping! Nazerine Construction would be just the tip of the iceberg."

Genevieve felt her stomach fall a little. Her possible suspect pool had just become something closer to an ocean. And if she didn't know who was trying to stop the discovery of the Indian site, she was going to have a much harder time keeping ahead of them.

Chapter 21

Genevieve ended up going back to the library with Jeannine to finish what she had thought was an already finished job. She left the building, stepping out into the super-heated sunshine with a few more articles printed out and ready to go in the manila folder where she was keeping all of her research information. She had just enough time to run by the hotel to check herself in the mirror before she was to meet Dean.

The air conditioning was not fixed. As soon as she walked into the lobby, she could feel the heaviness of the air. Already, the place was feeling empty, and she suspected most of the tenants had left, looking for somewhere with coolant and a comfortable bed.

She approached the desk feeling frustrated. She didn't have time to call around to another hotel, but she wasn't going to be staying here. Her choices were limited, she realized. She would need to find somewhere to stay rather quickly if the utilities weren't going to be fixed by that evening.

"I'll tell you like I told the other lady, the guy won't be out to even look at the unit until tomorrow afternoon," the harried young man at the desk was telling a little group in front of Genevieve. The daughter had her thumb stuck in her mouth and her sandy feet scuffing at the tile flooring, her long hair hanging in sticky damp strands around her pink cheeks. She looked all of four years old, hot and tired, and Genevieve felt sorry for both her and her mother as the frustrated woman held the little girl's other hand, a baby propped on her hip.

"Another day and night? There is no way we can stand that," the husband said, his face a little flushed, whether from heat or anger Genevieve didn't know.

"There is nothing I can do about it," the hotel worker said in a defeated voice. "I have these complimentary breakfast coupons we provide."

"You have to be kidding me! Breakfast." The husband was disgusted, and Genevieve felt the same. She couldn't tolerate another night. But she doubted there was anything this poor man could do about it, so she headed up to her room.

It took her fifteen minutes to totally pack her room, and another ten to check out of the hotel. She must have been among many to abandon the hotel, because the staff didn't question her leaving before her reservations were up.

Thirty minutes after that she was pulling into Dean's driveway. This time, the dogs were already put up and Dean was waiting on the porch, the sun dropping dappled splotches of lemony light on the lush green of the yard. The sun glinted off Dean's hair as the wind caught a lock, blowing it in an arc across his forehead he brushed at unconsciously.

"Do you want me to drive?" he asked as he pulled her passenger door open.

"No, of course not," she said quickly. "As long as the dogs aren't coming along, I don't see why you would need to." She tossed him a quick smile.

He grinned and climbed in next to her. "I thought about bringing Duke. Maybe putting a hat on him. He sits really well in a chair. I'm sure the museum wouldn't even guess he wasn't a normal patron."

"I'm not so sure about that," Genevieve replied. "And I'm not sure he would have fit in the car."

Dean looked into her back seat, blowing out a breath when he saw her bags. She hadn't reorganized her trunk yet, so the bulk of her belongings were in the seat.

"What happened here?" he asked. "It looks like you're moving out?" He sounded concerned and Genevieve wondered if he was more worried she might be going home or that she might have decided to stay out on the island with Jack.

"My hotel lost its air conditioning last night, and it won't be fixed until tomorrow at least. I can't live with another hot night, so I'm looking for another place to stay."

She had deftly turned the car around and was heading out to the main road, watching as Dean fastened his seatbelt and then stretched out in the seat.

"You can stay with me," he said, his voice casual.

She felt the flush rise before she could even stop herself from thinking thoughts that were better not revealed.

"Oh, no, I'm fine. I'm going to try to find something closer to the marina anyway."

"Then at least let me help you find something."

She glanced at him, her lips quirking. "Maybe I'll let you this time," she teased.

The museum had been built in what appeared to be a defunct strip mall. The front windows were blanked out and the separating walls had been knocked down to allow a long and surprisingly wide hall lined with exhibits. Unfortunately, the exhibits were sparse with blank tables and empty glass cabinets at intervals, dust covering the surfaces with fingerprints making ovals of clear glass. At the populated shelves and tables, it appeared that informative papers had been scotch taped to the exhibit to show content. Not the most professional set up. Great. It didn't look like she was going to learn much. Looking around at the condition of the place, Genevieve had serious concerns as to whether the artifacts would actually be accurately documented or even the genuine piece.

She turned back toward Dean and made a vague gesture forward. They might as well try. At the front of the space was a Formica counter with various photocopied sheets that described some of the exhibits in the hall. The papers were unfortunately in black and white and the only photos they contained were gray scale and grainy. The third sheet down had "The life of the Tequesta Tribe" boldly printed across the top. Beneath the title were five small pictures of different artifacts, almost impossible to distinguish from the background of the black and white photo. Beneath each picture was a brief description of the object, and then a long paragraph as a summary of the tribe's history, way of life, and culture summarized from what might have been a textbook entry.

Genevieve was paging thought the various stacks when a back door creaked open with an audible alert, and an elderly man scuffled out. He was a tall man with a shock of graying hair and brows that had overgrown to meet in a tangle over his somewhat bulbous nose. He smelled strongly of black coffee and cigarettes and his voice attested to these vices when he grunted a reluctant greeting.

"May I help you?"

It might have been a question but it sounded like an imposition. Genevieve wondered what the purpose of the museum actually was. Surely they weren't there for the entertainment and education of the public. Not with this guy as the figurehead and greeter.

"I saw your advertisement about this exhibit," Genevieve began holding up his own photocopied information for him to see. "I wanted to see if it was still on display."

"Got the papers, don't I?" he responded, his brows raising to show pale blue eyes with a yellowing cast.

"Yes," Genevieve replied, her tone even.

"The Tequesta stuff is toward the back. Second to last on the back wall. Don't touch anything. We've got video cameras."

Genevieve had to force herself from commenting on the last statement. Surely they weren't the most disreputable people he had seen coming by to view the museum. Or perhaps he was this delightful to everyone who dared stop by. In that case, it would explain why the venture did not look like a success. He would frighten off even the most passionate historian.

Instead of responding to the comment, Genevieve pulled out her wallet and looked around for a sign that would hint at a possible admission fee.

"It's five dollars each," the man said, eyes sharp on the bills in Genevieve's hand. She handed over the two fives and waited as the curator stuffed them into his pants pocket. Without another word, he turned away from the counter.

Genevieve nodded to herself, clearing her throat with discomfort and started down the room, passing glass cases full of old paste jewelry, shelves with china dolls, faces cracked and glass eyes staring blankly. Here and there were pieces that looked like they might have been museum quality, but Genevieve dealt in chemicals, not history. It could be crowded with flea market junk for all she could tell.

The display of Tequesta art, on the other hand, was almost surely real. As described in the article, the pieces included pieces of weapons carved with elaborate scrolling patterns, some fragile bones of sea creatures and human's alike, disarticulated and laying in straight lines across the glass shelf. The pottery pieces were still dusted with what looked like sand and had prominent notches decorating the rims, but were mostly just fragments. There were also displayed shells and bits of bone, bone pins according to the paper about the exhibit, that reflected just a piece of the ancient tribe's daily life.

"I may try to take some pictures of these," Genevieve breathed to Dean, keeping her voice down so the dour old man wouldn't hear her comment.

"They may not allow flash photography," Dean whispered back.

Genevieve gave him a wide-eyed look and he grinned.

"Okay, so maybe it isn't the most reputable of places, but he seems like he'd like to catch us at something. I really don't want to give him a reason to kick us out."

Genevieve nodded in agreement. "I'll just use the camera without the flash. My phone does a pretty good job in low light." She pulled the slim cell phone out of her pocket and quickly snapped a few pictures, keeping her back to the front desk just in case the man would get curious and come over to see what they were doing.

They spent a few more minutes wandering down the opposite end of the building looking at what appeared to be a collection of jarred two headed animals, some obviously fakes, a large trunk filled to the brim with old umbrellas and parasols, and a rack of dusty women's clothes. The hats had ratty feathers that caught a draft as the front door opened and a man and woman came in, both in knee length shorts and Florida t-shirts. A second later, a shaft of light spilled a bar of gold across the scarred floor as another man came in. Genevieve glance toward him, and then looked again, feel a chilly shock flicker over her skin. It was the man from the Starbucks. She was almost sure of it. She remembered his pressed pants, his pale dress shirt sleeves rolled up to reveal darkly tanned skin. And the dark eyes, the sharp assessing way he had squinted as he looked over the long rows of shelves and cases, hit her with clarity. It was the same man, and he was following her!

She kept her face averted and drew closer to Drew. Was she being ridiculous? What reason would anyone have for following her? Should she tell Dean? But then again, her life already had a generous helping of crazy, and she didn't want Dean to think she was losing her mind on top of everything else.

"Are you ready?" Dean kept his voice down and Genevieve gave a little jerking startle. Was she ready? Almost certainly! They had seen what they had come to see. And now that more people were there, and conveniently blocking the view of the lurking man, she saw an opportunity to slip out without the unknown man following. The old worker had come shambling back out and was giving the other couple a gruff welcome as his eyes studied the stranger who had paused by a particularly hideous stuffed alligator.

"Sure," she agreed, her voice pitched low. "Let's go." She caught Dean's arm and led him around the back of one of the cases, moving a shade too fast. When they emerged, the museum manager was bearing down on the stranger, no doubt to ask for payment. Genevieve pulled at Dean's arm until they escaped through the doorway.

The harsh sunshine was a welcome change from the dusty interior and even the damp wind felt good. She maintained a grip on his arm and tugged him toward the car. His eyes were curious, but he let her pull him into the parking lot. When she noticed the door of the museum had stayed closed and no one had followed them, she felt herself relax slightly. Could it have been her imagination? Was she going crazy?

"Okay, so what was that about?" Dean asked as they slid into their seats and pulled the doors closed in unison.

"Um, maybe nothing," Genevieve said evasively. Dean was studying her intently when her cell phone buzzed.

206

After she finished her call, Genevieve turned back to him, forcing a smile. "Looks like we're going to see Lillian and Hemingway," she announced, and unlocked the door.

It seemed that on top of being smart and lovely, Lillian could also cook. Although she preferred to make decadent desserts, she had taken the time to fix them a full meal, just like her mother would have made, with tamales so hot they made Genevieve's eyes water. She couldn't stop eating them, however, they were so good, so she kept a tissue to dab at her watering eyes and grinned through the meal.

Dean was less effected by the spicy fare. He had eaten there many times before, and noted that Lillian had also been known to bring in dishes for lunch when they had staff meetings. When they settled at the little table in the kitchen of Lillian's house, Genevieve was amused to see that Hemingway was invited as well, perched on an enormous t-stand Lillian admitted she had borrowed from work.

"He eats almost anything!" Lillian exclaimed, handing the bird a pinch of her dinner.

"He's bad about begging," Genevieve admitted. "I think it's partly my fault. He's figured out that if he complains enough at the hotel, I'll give him something to quiet him down. I didn't want them to come and tell us we had to leave. It's not like dog friendly hotels. There's no sign saying they accept parrots on the premises."

"He's smart enough to figure that out," Lillian said smiling, her brown eyes lit up with amusement.

"So the next hotel you go to will have to be pet friendly," Dean said casually.

"You're changing motels?"

Genevieve looked at Lillian. "The one I was staying in had problems with the air conditioner. I just couldn't stand to stay there one more night."

"You could stay here," Lillian volunteered.

"Oh, I don't want to impose," Genevieve said, grimacing when she heard the stiff sound of her own voice.

"It wouldn't be a problem. And you wouldn't have to worry about Hemingway." Lillian seemed to warm to the idea. "I have the extra couch that folds out into a bed I keep ready for family when they come by to visit." A small wrinkle marred Lillian's brow, "unless you don't think it would be comfortable."

Genevieve felt herself weaken. She liked Lillian and she didn't want the other woman to feel like her home wasn't nice enough to stay in. Genevieve was at ease in the tiny house, and the other birds skittering in their cages delighted her. Besides, she was full from the big dinner, and the lack of sleep the night before was making her feel even more tired.

"I wouldn't want to get in your way," she argued half-heartedly.

"Oh, this will be fun! Just a girl's night and we can gossip about Dean!"

"Hey, wait," Dean said, with an exaggerated pained expression. "I think I should be invited too!"

"Humph, no way," Lillian said briskly. "But you can help do the dishes."

It was late by the time Dean was bundled out to the car, a foil covered plate with tamales balanced in one hand.

"You're sure you trust me with your car?" He said, smiling.

Genevieve was grinning back. She had drunk one full glass of sweet red wine, enough to take the edge off, but was completely cognizant of what she was doing. She was sure a man who loved her car so much would take good, if not better care than she would.

"Come get me tomorrow. We should have figured out by then what time we can head back out to the island."

He grimaced, but even with the expression on his face, the wash of moonlight was flattering. His eyes seemed to catch the light like a cat's.

"Okay, if you're sure," he said reluctantly.

"I'm positive," Genevieve replied.

She saw his eyes slide behind her and knew he was checking for the door. Lillian had disappeared back inside, the door making an unmistakable creak and slam as though punctuating the fact that she was giving them a little time alone.

"Then I'll see you in the morning," Dean said softly, and drew just a little closer to her.

Genevieve felt the heat of the wine, or perhaps it was the blood heating her cheeks, as he leaned in just a little closer. He smelled of pine and spices, and he tasted of wine.

Chapter 22

Genevieve took a sip of coffee as she was finishing up an omelet filled with an abundance of fresh ingredients Lillian seemed to have just waiting in her refrigerator, a miracle in Genevieve's opinion since her own fridge tended to be filled with flavored water, wilting vegetables, and coffee creamer. She heard the characteristic purr of an engine and knew Dean had arrived right on time. Lillian was busy plating his omelet and laying out a big mug of coffee, talking all the while.

"So I told him if he needed something removed from the snake, he was going to have to do it himself." Lillian smiled as the door swung open and Dean stepped in. "And there's the snake wrangler himself!"

"That story again? How big was the snake this time?"

Lillian laughed out loud and placed the mug and plate at the table. "Sit down. I've already talked to Antony. He's saying eleven o'clock is the soonest he can go. But we need to watch the weather too."

"I had noticed," Dean observed, nodding his thanks and digging into the omelet with a fork. "Seems like we have a few storms heading our way."

"All the more reason we get out to the island soon," Genevieve said firmly. "I don't want them out there if there are hurricanes in the forecast."

"Agreed," Dean said. He turned to Genevieve where she sat sipping coffee. Lillian's caique, Skittles was busy playing with her fork, hopping around the table like a hyperactive toddler, making high-pitched chirps and squeals of delight. "Do you think we are set with where we're going to start the dig to search for artifacts?" he asked Genevieve. "I know we were still figuring it out the last time we went through the paperwork."

She nodded in response. She had spent the evening with Lillian pouring over the maps and diagrams of the island again, trying to judge how the landmass had changed over the last century or so. The coastline had shown some movement, that was true, but it hadn't been changed enough to make guessing a dig site too difficult. Besides, she knew her father and Mac may well have found where most of the artifacts were located and may be uncovering them now. She knew from where she had seen them searching they weren't far off from the site she and Lillian and pinpointed.

"I think we have a pretty good idea of where we want to look. That's provided Jack hasn't found anything new by the time we get there. I know he and Mr. Mac had been looking too."

"Hmmm, then the only thing we need to do is get supplies for our trip," Dean said. "Are you two up for shopping?"

A few hours later, they returned to Lillian's house, ready to pack up their purchases to take to the island. The weather continued to be mild with the usual robin's egg blue sky softened by billowing clouds making shadow shapes in the sky.

The evening was reported to bring rain, but it was only the usual Florida shower, a 'toad floater' as Dean might have said, coming in fast and hard but leaving just as quickly. Storms were still stirring out to sea, but the weather forecasters were keeping close watch at their developing low pressure systems, the rise of their winds, and the possible trajectory of their approach long before they hit land.

Lillian had to return to work in the afternoon, a late emergency had turned up and she was meeting one of the other vets to help with a procedure to remove a corncob from a Doberman's stomach. The dog's family was hysterical with worry, and the poor creature was miserable. In addition, it was

Lillian's turn to go in and take care of the animals being boarded at the veterinary office and handle the few appointments they had during the weekend hours. She would be meeting the rest of the skeleton staff at the office before noon. Genevieve could tell she was a little miffed that she couldn't join the group going out on the boat and wished that scheduling could have allowed it. Genevieve would have enjoyed her company, and she was sure Jack would have loved Lillian.

Genevieve dreaded the day when Dean and Lillian would have to return to the practice for full days. She was spoiled by the freedom of the weekend, which was fairly ironic considering how devoted to her own job she was. These days, she almost reluctantly checked her email accounts and voicemail, dreading that she would hear their boss or one of the other scientists alerting her that it was time for them to begin the second stage of work for their project.

In the hot Florida sun, she was helping Dean as they lugged out some of the supplies her father had requested for his continued stay on the island. Genevieve had hoped she could persuade him to come back with them for at least a week to wait out some of the predicted storms, but she knew Jack well enough. The chances were not good he would be willing to leave, and even less promising if they had happened to find anything on the island that resembled the artifacts they had been looking for. Of course, the threat of a hurricane would mean all bets were off and he and Mac would be forced to come back to the mainland. Even the two older men weren't foolish enough to remain on the island in the face of that sort of weather phenomenon.

"You know, we need to find someone who knows how to do this the right way, an archeologist or something," Genevieve said, adding the last shovel to the mound of supplies in the trunk and appreciatively watching the play of muscles on Dean's back as he closed the lid.

"I might actually be able to help you on that one," he said, a half smile tilting his lips.

"What do you mean?" she asked, climbing into the passenger seat.

He grinned at her for a second, but said nothing.

"Hey," she prompted as he buckled his seatbelt.

"Patience," he said, glancing her.

"That's not fair," she exclaimed, but despite her bickering and begging, he remained close-lipped for the drive.

At the marina, they pulled the car close enough to Antony's docked boat that they would only have a few short trips to deposit the supplies in the hold. Antony was already on board, running checks and generally looking busy in preparation of their departure. As Genevieve was leaning into the backseat to gather her bag containing the important research papers, sealed in a waterproof pouch, she saw a pair of canvas tennis shoes pause next to her car door. She slowly straightened, her eyes following the line of the visitor's shape until her gaze rested on the chocolate brown eyes of a stranger. He was beaming, showing a line of bright white teeth contrasting with his warm brown skin. His skull was smooth and hairless, completely bald, but he had a well-manicured beard that almost, but not quite, reached the dimple in his cheek.

"You must be Genevieve!" His voice was deep and warm, just a hint of a southern accent.

"I must," she said, puzzled.

"Hey!" The shout came from Dean as he came around the boat, his long legs eating up the distance. "Noah!" Dean clasped him around the shoulders giving him a quick one-armed hug.

Genevieve stood aside, her arms full, watching the men with amusement.

Finally, Dean looked over to her and his smile widened. "Genevieve, my love, let me introduce our archeologist."

Genevieve was so caught up in the 'my love' comment she almost missed the archeologist part. "Our what?" she said, her voice just a little high.

"Genevieve, let me introduce you to Noah, my old friend who is still slaving away at school," he paused, "in archeology." The last was said with the sound of victory in his voice.

"Really?" Genevieve asked.

"I'm two short months away from finishing my degree." Noah affirmed. "And it's nice to meet you."

"Noah volunteered that he would go out with us to help us look at the site. Free of charge except for a few beers I owe him."

"Really!" Genevieve exclaimed. "That's great!" Her eyes went back to Noah. "We were so worried we might mess something up."

"You were worried," Dean corrected. "I doubt Jack was."

"You might be right," Genevieve conceded, "but I'm still glad we will have someone who knows what they are doing."

"I'm not guaranteeing anything," Noah said hands out in a warning gesture, "but I am interested in seeing what you all have found. I've even looked up some information on the tribe, so I know better what we might be looking for."

"Noah has been doing field work on some other Native American sites," Dean continued. "And he speaks a few languages…"

"I speak Spanish and French, a little German, but let's not get carried away. I don't think my classes in Latin are going to help much either." Noah looked uncomfortable at Dean's enthusiasm.

"You said you were working toward some Native American languages too," Dean protested.

"Trying, not fluent," Noah corrected.

"Whatever, man. You're better than a vet and a chemist, I imagine," Dean said, gathering the last of the bags.

"Ah, I love it when you tell me I'm better than you!"

The bantering continued as they climbed onto the boat, Noah aiding in their departure, freeing the lines with the ease of a man born to water. He was familiar with the ocean, his sea legs much more natural than Genevieve's, and she sat and watched the curl and lap of the waves as they passed.

Armed with sunscreen and bug repellant, Genevieve found this second visit to the island was much more pleasant than the first. They had plenty of food, additional batteries and rations for Jack and his partner, and some fresh clothes and towels Genevieve insisted they bring. He might be living the island life, but there was no reason for Jack to be totally uncivilized.

To Noah's great relief, the two older men hadn't started trying to dig up any of the landscape while they waited for their backup workers. He had fretted a fair amount on the boat ride over about the hazards of amateurs ruining the site with careless digging. It happened too frequently when overzealous and starry eyed diggers tore through valuable layers of history in search of what they considered the mother lode.

Between her exhaustive research with the help of the talented librarian, Genevieve and Noah were able to find an estimate on where they would like to start the dig. They had started in the little building, laying out the papers on the table while Noah referred to the map still pinned to the wall. After they had finished their comparisons, they went back out into the heat, now looking with critical eyes for some landmarks that might help them know where to start. Noah had brought his own supplies, including tools of the trade, which he handed out with some trepidation.

"Ordinarily, we would have some training on how to handle a dig like this. Any unnecessary jarring could completely destroy these pieces we might find. Remember, we are talking about things that could be hundreds, if not a thousand years old." He had lost some of the college boy ease from his demeanor, and his face looked much more serious now that they were discussing his passion. "If you find anything you even suspect to be of value, call me. Don't touch anything further if you have any inkling it might be old. Better to move fast and carefully."

"Understood," Mr. Macintosh intoned. With his past experience, he was elected to do some of the delicate work, while Jack and Dean were assigned to move the heavier loads. Genevieve would dig as well, but was given the job of documentation too along with what Noah was tracking. She had her cell phone camera ready as well as several tablets of paper.

The work was not glamorous. They started by clearing out the vegetation, the limbs and detritus that had built up over the decades. Noah carefully choreographed their next steps, with stakes and lines to demarcate areas. As the digging began, most of the talk diminished to soft grunts from the men as they carried away the excess soil to be reexamined later. Sweaty, sandy, and still bothered by bugs despite the help of spray, Genevieve sat back a few hours later. Dean and her father had taken another load of sand away, but Dean had come back to the dig and was crouched next to Noah who was bending close, looking at the uncovered square of earth. Noah noticed her expression and gave her a rueful grimace.

"It takes months sometimes to find what we are looking for in places like this. Sometimes years."

"I know," Genevieve said sighing. "It's not that. I just feel like there is something hanging over our heads. Like we need to hurry."

"Are you worried about the weather?" Dean's eyes shifted toward the sky, still a startling blue dotted with whimsical cotton candy clouds.

"Well, yes, Silvia is coming in hard," Genevieve said, reflecting on the news reports she had read earlier. The tropical storm had seemed to be picking up speed and strength. "But I keep having this crazy feeling like someone is following me, tracking me. You know how it feels when you think someone is watching you? That's how I feel now. Like we might be, I don't know, the subject of some kind of surveillance."

Dean looked puzzled, but Genevieve couldn't explain why she felt that way. When he had asked about their hasty departure from the museum, she had decided not to share her worries about the stranger. Just because she might have seen him in two different places she had been didn't mean he was stalking her, did it? She shrugged and looked down the path toward the beach. Perhaps in the back of her mind she had noticed something more, but what could it be? Something strange at the marina? Someone out of place that seemed to be paying just a little too much attention to their little group? Maybe the dark sedan that kept turning up? How many times had she seen it? She felt a little shiver despite the heat when she realized how many times she had noticed the vehicle. It made her wonder how many other times it might have been there and she hadn't seen it. Undoubtedly a coincidence, right? But if she had not been paying attention, she would never had noticed the frequency of it. And what was the likelihood she might have seen the driver as well? A dark man with sharp eyes?

"I'm just being paranoid probably," she said almost to herself, dismissing the thought.

216

Noah's dark eyebrows raised, but the conversation was broken off when they heard a sound from Jack.

"Noah, over here for a minute," he exclaimed. He was standing close behind Mr. Macintosh who had gotten a low chair and was carefully brushing dirt away from a curved object embedded in the sandy soil.

There was no doubt. It was a sizable chunk of pottery, stylistically carved, with a notched rim. Nestled next to it was a darkened shaft of what was almost certainly a human bone.

It was past midnight by the time they started loading up the boat to head back to the mainland. Antony had waited patiently, but now even he was looking a little worried about the weather. The wind was whipping up, making the flames of the campfire sway and stir miniature tornadoes of ashes to skitter toward the sky.

"Are you sure that you want to stay?" Genevieve was looking at Dean as he stuffed an additional rain jacket from the boat into the backpack he would take back to the little cabin.

"After what we found today, I think it's important for us to get as much done as we can. As soon as it's light, I can continue the work until you all make it here. Noah has given me plenty of instructions. With the weather turning, we're going to need to get as much evidence on board your father's boat as we can tomorrow. Hopefully, our examples and documentation will be enough to start a formal dig. Then we can let the professionals take over."

"Dean, this isn't your fight," Genevieve protested. In truth, it scared her to death to see Jack out here on the island. To have Dean here too should have made her more reassured, but Sylvia was narrowing her course and looked to be gusting winds already over a hundred miles per hour.

"This is our fight," Dean said. "This is just doing what's right. And we will be fine. We can get most of the work done in the morning and be long gone by the time the storm hits."

Jack came up to Genevieve and threw one arm around her shoulder. "Get going now, my dear, before it gets any later." He squeezed her. "I'll be seeing you in the morning."

Genevieve shook her head in assent, returned the quick embrace, and gathered of few of her supplies she would take back with her. The rest she would get tomorrow. Her father had a firm arm still around her and was gently guiding her back toward the path through the woods. The wind made the trees shiver as they passed, but it had cleaned out the bothersome insects, which was a slight relief. At the boat, Noah was climbing aboard with Antony helping him with some of their packs. He thrust a life jacket at Genevieve e as soon as she boarded, and she obediently put it on. She didn't want to be anywhere near the ocean without the protection. The boat was already bucking and swaying beneath their feet.

Dean climbed aboard with her as her father had a few words with Antony at the stern of the boat. Dean drew close, his hair catching in the wind, his words snatched from his lips.

"I have my cell phone, but it might not work. Your dad hasn't been using the boat's radio much, but if we need to call for help, we always have that." He bent and dropped a kiss on her forehead. "Tell Lillian I owe her another biggie for taking care of the troops."

"Sure," Genevieve said, feeling the strands of her hair flutter in the wind like a rippling flag. "And I'll see you all soon. Um, don't believe all the stories Jack tells you. He can exaggerate," she forced a smile.

"Not a problem," Dean said solemnly, "as long as you do the same for what Lillian says."

Genevieve watched the figures of the two men, her father and Dean, melt into the blackness. The other boat, Horace Topper's legacy, was moored well away from this more public dock, so it felt as though they were leaving the rest like castaways in the wilds.

It took Antony and Noah some fancy maneuvering before they cleared the dock and some of the shallows. The ocean seemed to be protesting, pushing against the hull in protest, but the wind was at their back, and the journey seemed to take a much shorter time to make it to the mainland. At the dock, Noah insisted he needed to walk Genevieve to her car, a gentlemanly gesture she appreciated. He was planning on coming for the next day's voyage, but he still had a thirty-minute drive back toward campus.

"Then we'll meet out here at six?" he asked, an involuntary yawn stretching his jaws.

"That's the plan," Genevieve agreed. Her car made a satisfying beep as she triggered the unlock, and the light glowed from within the luxury interior. Her eyes were scanning the lot, but she didn't see any suspicious cars lingering in the shadows.

"You'll be okay to go by yourself?"

"Sure, and thanks. I know my way to Lillian's now." It seemed there was no end of men concerned for her safety now.

"Okay," Noah agreed, and as Genevieve slipped into her car, he closed the door for her. She started the engine and waited until she saw he was in his own vehicle, a 90's jeep with mud-spattered tires and a giant sticker of a Neanderthal skull on the bumper. She mused silently that the vehicle looked perfect for him. When she saw his headlights spear the darkness, she pulled out her cellphone and plugged it into the car's charger. It still had 10 percent, but she had to make it back to Lillian's. She was pretty sure she knew the way, but she wanted to reassure her new roommate she was on her way back. The only other exchange they had had that day was in the early evening when the inconsistent connections had allowed her to hastily report on their progress. She explained she was coming in later that night and had plans to go back to the island in the morning. All of this was before they had made their significant find, and she was sure Lillian was going to be as excited as they were. It was incredible. She had seen with her own eyes the bit of civilization that hadn't seen the light of day for almost a thousand years.

The phone was answered almost immediately, and Lillian's voice didn't sound the least bit tired. Genevieve briefly told her she was coming back to the house and Lillian didn't need to stay up if she was tired, but she did have more news to tell. That was met with a quick affirmation that Lillian couldn't get a wink of sleep without hearing whole story. As Genevieve backed out of her space at the marina, she was pretty sure she would be lucky to get in the door before Lillian would start the questions.

Genevieve pulled out of the lot and had gone down almost a block from the marina when a glance in the rear view mirror had her hissing in surprise. There was another car coming, and it wasn't a jeep. This one was big and dark, and when the streetlight hit it with an orange glow, she saw it was a sleek sedan of some type. She felt her skin prickle with unease. It was late, and there were only a few cars on the road. She wasn't one to over react, but the sight of it made the alarm bells sound in her head.

The car followed her away from the parking lot and onto the main street. There were few cars and empty building dotting a mostly dark avenue, so it was easy to keep an eye on it. That, of course, was a double-edged sword, since it would be equally as difficult for Genevieve to lose the sedan if they were indeed following her. She felt her heartbeat accelerate as she turned onto the next street. She didn't know the area well enough to outmaneuver it. She could drive down any number of side streets only to find herself at a dead end, alone and vulnerable.

She had taken two more turns when she saw the dark sedan hit their turn signal and take a right. They weren't following her. Or were they? She continued at a moderate speed, her cell phone in her hand, poised to call 911 if she felt the slightest bit of apprehension. But when no lights appeared either behind or ahead of her, she continued on to Lillian's house. Once there, she sat in the car for another five minutes, waiting in the windy darkness for any nighttime visitors. The street was quiet.

She left most of her supplies in the car, taking only the most important documents and her purse, before plunging into the darkness, racing up the steps and hitting the lock button on her car's remote as she made it to the porch. The front door was unlocked, and she hurriedly yanked it open, slamming it behind her with a little too much force before locking it with shaky fingers.

"Hey," she heard Lillian's voice from the living room and watched as she came around the corner, looking very young in her tee shirt and knit shorts, hair tied back in a long braid. "Are you alright?"

"Just freaked out by the storm," Genevieve said, trying to gather her composure. She didn't want to start in about a car following her back. It was incredibly outlandish to think someone would go to such lengths to see what she was doing. "I'm fine. Really."

"I know you're exhausted, so give me the short version, and I'll let you hit the hay," Lillian said gently. "Come on, you can take a shower if you feel sandy."

Genevieve nodded and dropped her purse on the little table next to the door. "I'll put my things down and plug in my cell phone. Then I'll tell you what happened," she agreed. "This is some story, though."

Chapter 23

The alarm was set for five, but Genevieve heard Lillian up before the phone could sound. She slowly rolled over and rubbed her eyes. She could hear the chatter of the bird around her, but Hemingway's distinct voice came from the other room. She wondered how he was behaving himself. She hadn't even greeted him the night before although she was sure his bright eye had been watching her as she stumbled toward the couch. Now it seemed he had wheedled his way into the kitchen for some early morning snacking.

She stood slowly and grabbed up her bundle of clothes. She hadn't exactly laid them out neatly as was her habit, but they were ready for her, even if they were a little wrinkled. In the harsh light of the bathroom she considered her face as she pulled on the clothes. Pale and sunburned. It was a pathetic combination. She could see every streak she had missed with the sunscreen from the day before. But even considering her fatigue, she felt a steady thrum of excitement. It wasn't chemicals; it had nothing to do with her orderly love of balanced equations and neatly labeled charts, but the promise of history uncovered, of civilizations rediscovered after centuries buried in the sand, was enough for her to feel the buzz of euphoria. There was so much she still didn't know, but so much more she knew for sure now.

As she stepped from the bathroom, she heard the sharp rap on the door and blinked. It was early.

Her first thought was Noah, and the chance he had thought of something else, that he was ready to go early. Then a panicked thought that maybe the storm was coming too early. Maybe they were in danger of not making it to the island on time. She could still hear Lillian puttering into the other room, so she jogged to the door. With the ideas whirling in her head, she swung the door open and looked straight into the featureless faces of darkness.

Genevieve couldn't believe how stupid she had been. To swing open the door as though she was hosting a tea party and letting in these guys without so much as a cry in protest. There was no way the neighbors would realize anything was wrong. She had trapped herself and Lillian with incredible ease. Now they were trussed up like two Christmas packages ready to be dropped in the mail. She supposed she should be grateful that the men only appeared to want them out of the way, incapacitated while they took care of whatever task they had been hired to do. Genevieve was almost sure that was what they were. Hired men to take care of the dirty work. The men in the sedan? She had bet her life that they were related although the man with the dark eyes was noticeably missing.

For the moment Lillian and Genevieve were confined in the little living room, hands behind their backs and lashed to identical folding chairs. It was uncomfortable, yes, but they hadn't been hurt any more than a few bruises inflicted when Genevieve had tried to slam the door closed and been thrust back and into the wall with the force of a man's weight hitting the panel. The gun had come out then, and Genevieve had been silenced, the struggle ceasing when she realized the danger. She had never in her life seen a gun in that way, nestled in the hand, pointed and aimed like an evil eye. Sure, she had seen them behind glass in cabinets, in the holsters of law enforcement, or hunting rifles balanced in the arms of men in camo. But this was completely different and completely terrifying. Her mind spun. The men had tied them up clumsily and were standing close together by the door, talking in low but audible voices to one another. They were still debating on whether they should just leave the house or stay and make sure their job was done.

"Look he wanted them taken care of and they are. Ain't no one going to come looking for them today, and by tomorrow, we'll be done with all of this. We said we'd be to Baker's by noon. Can't wait any later." The speaker was a heavy-set guy with a royal blue skiing mask covering his head. A fringe of dark hair showed at the nape of his neck. His irises were brown, but yellowed in the whites, making him look ill. He moved with a lumbering gait, and his words were slow as well.

"I don't trust them," the skinny guy snarled through the mask. His jeans were dark with smears of some greasy substance and he smelled of sweat and oil. "I don't know that they will stay put."

"I'm not getting paid enough to try for kidnapping. I say they stay. By the time they get free we'll be long gone."

"You say?" The thin man had turned on his partner, the black knit moving as he over pronounced his words. "Well I say different. I think we need to make sure they're not going anywhere." The thin man's voice had gone ugly, the quality a grating nasal sound, and Genevieve felt fear clench her stomach. She had the impression the sight of them bound to the chairs and completely vulnerable was having a frightening effect on the man. He wasn't in a hurry to get out like his partner was. He had other ideas that were shining in his glassy eyes like a drug.

She glanced at Lillian and saw that the other woman was looking pale beneath her golden tan, her mouth set in a tight line. Genevieve tried to breath slowly and lifted her head to address the men.

"We aren't going anywhere now," she said, keeping her voice the cool and professional tone she used when settling a dispute at work. "We can't move from here and we can't call for help. But we do have some people coming over to meet us. We were supposed to be going out early this morning. If you leave now, no one can catch up with you." She was lying through her teeth. "And we can't go after you."

The heavy-set man had turned to look at her. "We know about your plans. You were meeting the other guy at the marina. And now you're not." He shot a look toward the other dark figure. "We have a boat to catch and a meeting of our own. And we can't be late," he said, his voice meaningful for his partner only.

"I think that we could wait for another hour or so," the thin man replied, his eyes, a dark gray shot through with red veins, going again to the women as they sat incapacitated on the folding chairs. Genevieve could see dampness through the mask at his temple where he was sweating freely.

"I think you're thinking with your …" the man's words were drowned out by a loud bang and clatter from the kitchen like a cabinet being thrown open.

The thin man shouted an expletive, ducking and then turning in a jerky motion like a marionette whose strings were wound too tight toward the entrance into the kitchen, his gun drawn and trembling. The other man seemed to shrink away and glared at his loud companion. He made a quick gesture of quiet.

Genevieve felt a surge of relief. Someone was there! Someone must have seen the men break in and had called the police. Whoever it was didn't seem to care if they were heard.

Their captors didn't seem to feel the same. "Shut up!" the larger man hissed, both to the women and his partner. He had backed up toward Lillian, his gun at eye level. His blue mask seemed to be creeping up the back of his head, more dark hair showing in the gap, damp with nervous sweat. He was shaking slightly, his gun hand wavering toward the doorway. He didn't look comfortable holding the weapon, and Genevieve wondered if he even knew how to fire it.

"There's an exit just behind us. The back door. It leads out into the back alley. You can go that way, so they don't see you," Lillian said, her voice soft, reasonable. "You don't want to get caught in here when my cousins come." Her accent had thickened, and in the damp darkness, even Genevieve felt the threat. As though to prove her words, there was a louder clatter and the sound of the birds stirring.

The heavyset man glared at his partner. "I am not staying here and risking my parole. And I'm not a murderer." His voice was a low whisper, and sounded of desperation and certainty.

The other man muttered a rude word, shaking his head. "You are such a…" but he stopped, shoving the gun into his waistband. His eyes were dark, too dark to read, but held so much menace Genevieve could feel their chances of survival dwindling.

Genevieve realized she was holding her breath. Why didn't their rescuers come in? She could still hear some murmuring from the other room. Then the thought hit her like a splash of icy realization. There was no rescuer. There was no white knight coming to their rescue. The voices were not what they seemed.

"You can stay here and let your ass get shot off, but I'm not in it. I'm going to that damn island and getting my cash." The heavy man shuffled his work boots uncomfortably and started backing away from the lighted doorway the gun still held up, but now pointed at the floor. The loud banging from the kitchen was repeated, this time the distinct clang of a metal pan hitting the floor.

A deep voice carried through the tense silence, someone muttering in muffled tones as the sound of metal scraped against the linoleum floor.

"Yo, girl!" A deep voice roared from the kitchen, distorted a bit by the thin walls, and Genevieve felt the air move as the two men startled and backed quickly towards the door. They moved in unison, almost silent, their feet making shuffled noises against the old flooring. In another minute, she felt the damp draft as the back door was thrown open, and then heard heavy footfalls hitting the sodden ground. The men rushed off in near silence, a stifled curse rising once when they reached the corner, probably at the sight of the twisted wire fence.

Lillian sagged next to Genevieve and then wrestled furiously with the rope on her wrists. As she muttered her own curses in a fluent Spanish, their rescuer came strutting through the door.

"I'm home," the big parrot exclaimed, and with a great flutter, landed in Genevieve's lap.

Genevieve switched off the television that had been droning in the background for last fifteen minutes. The weather report was getting steadily more grave which made it even more important they get to the island as soon as possible. Hurricanes were almost always fickle things, but that didn't make them less deadly. It wasn't due to hit the island until evening but even if it was downgraded to a tropical storm, the winds would still pack a wallop. Already reports of weather related warnings were hitting the news. No one wanted to be unprepared when the storm finally reached land.

Lillian had Hemingway safely caged when Genevieve finished grabbing her gear. The rest of the birds were similarly in crates. The other woman appeared to be packing a bag of supplies, batteries, and emergency radio flashlights, and some food items in a heavy canvas bag.

"What are you packing for?" Genevieve asked.

"Oh, there's no way you are going without me," was the brisk response.

"I will have Antony with me," Genevieve said quickly. "And Noah. We won't be gone long. Just enough time to get Jack, Dean, and Mac packed up and out of there. You need to call the police. And get to the vet's office. You should be safe there with the others."

"The storm is only hours away. The ocean is already getting rough. You will need as much help as you can get just to collect the evidence. If the storm is as bad as the predictions, there might not be much that survives." Lillian's tanned face had lost some of its color. She seemed haunted. Genevieve was trying not to think of their moments of terror. She might very well be in shock. But she couldn't succumb to the fear now. "And those men," Lillian continued. "They are going out there just like we are. And if they were willing to tie us up and leave us here, they might do much worse when they make it to the island."

Genevieve had to agree. Their problems had multiplied at an astonishing rate. The relics they had found had lain protected in their sandy grave for so long. But now they were fragile and exposed. It really was their responsibility to get them somewhere safe. But the words of the men hung heavy. They were going to Baker's Cove. They were meeting someone there. And it was a sure bet they were not going to let two old men and a veterinarian stand in their way. Genevieve had decided she had to make it out there as soon as humanly possible. And she certainly didn't want to leave Lillian at her house alone. There was the chance the intruders would come back, perhaps to finish their original goal. The thin man with the black mask had an evil streak in him. So the plan to take the birds to the vet's office had seemed like a sound one, and Lillian could get help there. She would be safe with her co-workers around her, and she could call the police from the office. But now she was insisting she wanted to go to the island instead.

"We'll drop the birds off and tell everyone what happened. Then we need to get to the boat ramp to meet Antony. I already called him to tell him we're late but coming. He said Noah was already there." Lillian's face was set; her usually sparkling eyes were cold. "Those bastards are not going to win."

The rain was washing over the deck with sheets of angry foam, the boat bobbing and diving as Antony pushed it through the waves. The ocean had never seemed so powerful, so frightening, so alien before as it did now pushing the boat around like a child tosses its toys.

Genevieve felt for the first time the tinge of true terror, not for herself so much but for Jack, for her father. She knew with a painful certainty that if something happened to him, something horrible and something that couldn't be undone, that a piece of her would be broken, never to be mended. It was a part of her that was long denied, long ignored and stifled indifference to the reasonable side of her, the controlled side, the steady and reliable side. She hadn't wanted to be like her father. But she knew now it was a mistake. To cut away that part of her that was free, spontaneous, joyful, and full of wonder was to cut away the part of her that could love and be loved with her whole heart. It would be taking away the best of her, and she refused to see that happen any longer. She had lost enough time stifling herself to fit into a convenient box with Wayne and his like. She wouldn't be able to change all at once. She still needed organization and neatness in her world, but just not to control her whole world. She needed the strength that was her father. She knew it in her bones that the love she had for him represented the purest fraction of her spirit.

A heave of the ocean had her losing her seat and she felt Noah's strong hand grasping her arm. He leaned in close, his words in her ear. "We haven't got much farther," he said in what she was sure he thought was a reassuring tone. But the fact that the storm was stealing the words was terrifying enough.

Rachael Rawlings

It was crazy how quickly the winds had risen. The first fat drops of rain had splattered on their windshield in the race to the marina. As she drove, Lillian had sat by Genevieve's side frantically trying Dean's cell phone number. She had left messages, trying to decide how to word it, the fact that two crazy men that had threatened and kidnapped them were on the way to the island to meet someone else, someone who was determined to stop their progress.

By the time they had reached the marina, the rain was coming in earnest, the leading edge of what was still being labeled a hurricane. They had found Antony with Noah already on board. They both knew enough to be gravely concerned about the trip, and about their friends on the island.

Genevieve felt terrible about asking Antony to risk his boat, even his life, to venture out on the ocean in this weather. She looked at Noah's tight expression; his bald head damp with rain, a droplet trembling on his chin, and felt a second surge of guilt. Neither of these men should be here. Worse yet, Lillian shouldn't have been there either. She had already been accosted and bore the beginnings of a bruise on both wrists to prove the abuse. But none of them could be dissuaded to go. Lillian went for Dean, and for Genevieve, and Antony went out of loyalty to Lillian, the child Lillian who had played with his daughter Maria so long ago. Noah was going for Dean as well, but moreover, for the chance to save a portion of the find they had discovered. And Genevieve went for Dean and for her father, for whom she realized she would face the grave for.

The boat shuddered over the swells. The waves were growing, but would get much worse as the time went by and Sylvia came in swinging. Genevieve was too terrified to feel sick. She clung to the rail, turning to look back toward the wheel where Antony stood grimly.

As the wind whipped the words from her lips, she saw the rising darkness of the land before them and almost cried in relief. She turned toward Antony and saw he was leaning over and shouting at Noah, wide gestures drawing their attention toward the dock where they had moored the boat before.

A slightly larger boat, heavier and newer with a powerful thrumming engine was already at the dock. The waves were making it tricky, but the boat was held firmly into place. She wasn't sure how long it had been moored there, but she suspected it was long enough for the men to have disembarked. The boat had to either belong to the men that had attacked them at Lillian's home, or to the man they were slated to meet. There was no doubting that their presence was a sign of danger to her father, to Mac, and to Dean.

Antony had begun maneuvering the boat, changing their course to go toward the other side of the island. Genevieve wondered if the men from the boat had spotted them, but she couldn't tell if anyone was on deck. The bigger boat continued to bob in place as Antony struggled to redirect their craft. It took precious minutes to make it around the curve of the land. In an awkward cove, the sides rising in sandy shelves toward a flat high above, another boat was tied up. Genevieve immediately recognized Topper's old boat, her mind automatically flashing pictures of snapshot memories, her standing next to her father, Hemingway on her shoulder trying to get a beak full of the fish she had just caught, Topper standing at the wheel, laughing at one of Jack's preposterous stories, the rare time her mother had come on a trip and accidently caught a flashing silver fish she insisted had to be returned to the water.

It seemed an eternity as Antony fought to change the boat's course once again, more time slipping by. And then they were pulling in close, and Genevieve could see that hidden beside the other boat was a smaller dock, much more worn than the one they had used before, but still serviceable enough to get them on land. From the dock were steps of sorts, mostly rough slats of wood anchored in the sand where the passengers could climb onto the flat of the island, dodging through hardy clumps of beach grasses and tough vines.

Before the boat was completely tied off, Noah and Genevieve rushed to the side, and with just a pause, leaped from the boat to the dock, sliding a little on the damp wood. Lillian followed, her eyes wide and dark wisps of hair haloing her head as the storm pushed in.

They didn't exchange words. There were no plans made. There was nothing they could do except run as fast as possible to get to the camp-site. They needed to find Jack, Dean and the venerable Mr. Macintosh, and get off the island with whatever of value they could snatch up.

Genevieve saw that they were too late as they approached the camp, heads down in the wind and rain, keeping to the fringe of trees. In the middle of the camp were the huddled figures of Jack and Mr. Mac. They were both seated in their familiar lawn chairs which had been moved away from the beach and closer to the shelter of trees, but were apparently tied securely. Rain had rinsed the blood from their faces, but even at a distance, Genevieve could see the bruise rising beneath her father's right eye, a torn shirt, and the way he was leaning as though he hadn't the energy to remain upright. Mr. Mac had a painfully swollen lip gleaming red beneath his mustache and his upturned face looked raw. Both looked worn out. Genevieve looked in panic around the scene. She could see the older men, but where was Dean? She breathed a prayer as she thought in horror of the possibilities. She had brought Dean here. She had pulled him into the mess. And she had left him last night, hoping he could help her father. What if she had killed him?

Her eyes scanned the scene. She squinted in the damp wind and held her breath. There! She saw Dean moving from behind one of the tents, a bundle of canvas in his arms. Behind him was the thin form of a man, pressed slacks, dress shirt, dark hair blown in the wind. It was almost surely the man she had seen in the coffee shop and the museum. He wasn't observing now. He had his gun out and locked on Dean, and Genevieve felt a fear tighten in her chest. She realized that rather than tie up Dean, they had instead chosen him to do some of the labor for them.

Dean carried the bundle into the edge of the woods and then farther, melting into the darkness, on the way to the other boat. Noah began creeping forward, Antony close behind. The men paused in the shadow of the trees and spoke in inaudible tones. When Lillian began to approach, Antony turned and spoke to her. Lillian looked as though she might refuse whatever his suggestion, but then she nodded and headed away. Antony followed her after a second.

"We have an idea," Noah said close to Genevieve's ear. "We need to get these guys away from your father and Mr.

Macintosh. If we get them to go back to their boat, we can free the others and get out of here.”

Genevieve nodded, watching as Lillian disappeared back the way they came.

“She and Antony are getting something for the distraction,” Noah said softly, his breath warm against her ear. “Just stay down and follow me.”

Down at the camp, Genevieve could see that the artifacts they had found, the precious pottery fragments and bits of bone, the rounded stones that had been caressed by ancient hands carefully preserved and placed on the protective tarps, had been rolled into bundles and were stacked under the only remaining tent. Also beneath the tent was the lone figure of a man, an old and bent shadow, resting with one knarled hand on the curved head of a can. He was dry in the fury of the rain, his leathery face immobile, his eyes squinting bright toward the ocean and the coming storm.

Noah mumbled an expletive under his breath and Genevieve turned toward him.

“What?”

“Do you know who that is?”

She looked at him, more puzzled. “No, should I?”

He slowly shook his head. “It’s Justin Nazerine,” Noah said softly. “He’s the founder of Nazerine Construction.” His eyes scanned the beach. “He’s also distantly related to the Bakers of Baker’s Cove.”

Chapter 24

Genevieve hated waiting. She hated waiting in the rain more. She hated waiting in the rain, terrified for herself, her father, and her friends even more, and the time seemed to pass with unimaginable slowness while the force of nature that was Sylvia danced across the ocean in her destructive waltz.

Genevieve was almost ready to turn back to Noah, to question their clever plan, when a whump of sound and a blaze of flame erupted from behind the far side of trees that separated the beach camp from the big boat moored beyond.

“That’s our cue,” Noah hissed, and he began his steady decent into the camp.

Nazerine had risen from his chair, and using his cane, had made it to the opening of the tent, his face as blank as a new canvas. He stood in utter stillness for just a moment and then began to move, first slowly and then picking up speed, toward the flames.

Genevieve reached Jack just as Noah unsheathed a knife and began to maneuver behind the men.

"Oh, girl, where did you come from?" Jack's eyes were wide with alarm. "You need to get out of here."

"I'm going with you," Genevieve said grimly, trying to undo the knots as Noah cut through more strands.

"The storm is coming. You need to be gone when it gets here. Have Noah take the artifacts. The papers are in the bag in the tent. We'll follow you out."

"No!" Genevieve said angrily. "We are going out together. We have to find Dean."

As though her words had stirred up a spirit when she said his name, Dean came running flat out across the sand, his long legs eating up the distance in great bounds. "Run!" He shouted at them as he approached.

Noah stood and as Genevieve helped Mr. Macintosh to his feet, Noah snagged the rolled up tarp. Dean swiped up the bag from the tent and turned toward them.

"The boat!" he said, his breath catching.

"We're out by Jack's boat," Noah explained. "Lillian and Antony are meeting us there."

Genevieve felt her father's heavy hand on her arm. "Go," he commanded, and she did, running and leaping over vines and snaky roots, running in the rain, running for her life. As soon as she reached the top of the slope and looked over toward the dock, she breathed a sigh of relief. Lillian and Antony must have taken a different route, because they were already climbing rapidly down the wooden slats. Her father and Mr. Mac had made surprisingly good time because a second later they stopped just behind her as Noah led them in a careful descent down the slope.

They took both boats. Antony was steering his vessel with Lillian and Noah, along with their precious cargo from the site, while Dean, Genevieve, and the older men climbed aboard

Topper's boat at its place next to the dock. Antony was the most able sailor, so he cleared the area first, allowing Dean plenty of room to maneuver the old boat away from the land.

"The men, the noise, what was that?" Genevieve gasped, as she clung to the seat and the wind tore at her. She was standing close to Dean to hear his words over the rush.

"Lillian and Antony set their spare can of fuel on fire," Dean said, his eyes focused ahead as he followed the other boat.

"Why?"

"It was on the other boat. Noah said we needed a distraction. And it worked! The guy who was guarding me went running. He had a couple other idiots that almost ran him down looking for help. They were so distracted by the idea of the boat going under that they completely forgot me. So I just ducked into the woods and headed the other way."

"But what were those men doing? The ones with Nazerine?" Genevieve looked back at where Jack and Mr. Macintosh were struggling to keep their seats.

"They were trying to steal all of the artifacts. I don't know how far they were willing to go to cover this up, but the old guy definitely didn't have any reservations about murder."

"Murder," Genevieve held her breath as the boat was rocked by another, larger wave that seemed to push at the hull of the boat.

"He's totally crazy. Demented. He was all but bragging that he had been involved in the first cover up back in the 1930s. He was just a kid back then, but he claimed his father had wanted the land for his own. They were somehow related to the family that owned the island, but his father had his own ideas of how to use it. He sounded like a real winner. Drug running, and God knows what else."

"You mean they were the ones involved in the murders of the professor Livinson and Hamsdale?"

"Nazerine's own father had it hired out according to the what Nazerine said. And it sounds like he got away with it. Sounds like Nazerine's father lived to a ripe old age, sick bastard. But Nazerine wasn't satisfied with letting it go. He feels like he had finally achieved the status of being a reputable businessman. The only problem is that his wealth is based on the blood money and drug money from his father. If the site was found, then people would have to start digging up the past. They would find the link between Baker's secret and the murders. That would lead back to Nazerine. Not exactly the person you would want in charge of building your exclusive resort. So he's trying to erase the past. That had to include Baker's secret."

Genevieve was silent for a moment. The pieces of the puzzle seemed to be slowly falling into place, but the sheer magnitude of their precarious position, the rising waves, the furious wind and the howling maw of Silvia had become her main concern.

As though summoning a demon from the deep, a powerful wave rose before them and Dean shouted, "hold on!" Genevieve grabbed for the seat again as the world flew to pieces around her.

They had to peel her fingers off the railing. A call to the coast guard had police waiting at the marina for them to disembark, but Genevieve was almost frozen in place. As soon as her feet hit the dock, she vomited all of her stomach contents onto the decking, watching with dull eyes as the rain and waves wiped the wood clean again.

The huddled group of them was unceremoniously hustled away from the water. Genevieve had to insist she was feeling steadier and didn't need to go to the hospital even though the young officer with the freshly shaven face and serious eyes had listened to her protests skeptically. Genevieve knew she had to look pretty bad for him to want to take her to the ER, but the officer relented when she promised she would not be staying alone.

The group broke up in the parking lot, still rushing to beat the worst of the weather, Noah driving Mac and Jack to Mr. Macintosh's house where they could recover in comfort. Dean drove Genevieve's car with Lillian tucked next to him in the passenger seat, and Genevieve curled up in the back. They were all going back to Dean's house. Lillian had no desire to go home alone.

Dean drove in tense silence as the rain battered at the expensive car, washing the dust and salt, and pushing through the door seals with chilly fingers. The lights were out all up and down the street, limbs snatched from trees, and great bunches of palms laying in the roadway. He dodged the obstacles, creeping along for safety. The normally short and pleasant drive took nearly an hour, and Dean switched on the radio to hear the steadily rising tension in the weatherman's voice as he called Silvia's every move.

The electricity had failed at Dean's, but the tank still held some hot water, enough for a quick bath only. After rinsing off sand and salt, they all collapsed in the living room. Genevieve struggled to stay awake, there were so many questions she had to ask, and she needed to know that her father was safely at Mac's house. As soon as she heard Dean report that Noah was at Mac's and the men were safe, the exhaustion won the battle, and she was asleep before Dean had hung up the phone.

The news was dotted with snippets of stories between the rising panic of the storms arrival. It was reported that the coast guard had been called out to Baker's Cove. Their mission was to attempt to save several people who were not only stranded on the island but were possible suspects in a kidnapping and breaking and entering case. No one knew the men's names or identities, but it was soon discovered they were not the only people to have arrived at the cove. The wildly successful founder of Nazerine Construction was rumored to have taken his boat out to the cove as well, manned by his primary assistant, Ronald Craig. The boat was found floundering in the ocean, ripped from its anchor near the island's coast and already half sunk. It seemed that there was a possible fire on board the vessel that had been extinguished by the storm but had caused considerable damage. In the storm's wake, which had been downgraded to a tropical storm by the time it had wound its way up the mainland coast, the island had been wiped clean of all signs of human habitation. Even the cabin that had faithfully provided shelter to fisherman over generations of men had been scrubbed.

Nazerine was never found. The link between his father and the horror during the 1930s remained buried with him. None Genevieve's party who had been there during the storm ever wanted to repeat what they had heard, and the remainder of the party that had been with the old man seemed to have been lost as well.

A few weeks later when the scandal of the missing men diminished, Noah had brought the remaining pieces found during the island dig to the university. They had only been able to salvage part of what they had pulled from the sand. It had taken some fancy footwork to tell a plausible story of happening on the site that had already been excavated. But the academics took him at his word, and a formal study of Baker's Cove as part of the territory of the Tequesta tribe was slated to begin as soon as funding was available. Noah had not overestimated the value of the discovery and the historians were thrilled with the prospect. It might take years to be provided grants that would fund the project, but at least something had been done to stop the destruction of the island.

Genevieve was pondering all of the recent events as she slowly packed her bags in Lillian's tiny living room. She wondered if Lillian would ever feel the same about living there. There was something forever changed about the place. It felt stained, like the fear and panic had seeped into the fabric and wood of the house.

Lillian was standing with her back to the room gazing out the window, her expression melancholy.

Genevieve looked at Lillian, feeling concern for the other woman. "You're sure you don't want to go back to Dean's with me? You could talk him into going to dinner with you."

Genevieve was going home. Her father was improving, but it would take him some time to recover from his abuse at the hands of his captors. Genevieve knew only her mother could persuade him to go to the doctor to get an in depth examination of his injuries. She would take him home, him and his crazy bird, and hope they both stayed a while.

"I'm tired. I'm just going to stay here," Lillian said softly. She turned, her face still showing some fine scratches where debris had scraped her tender skin as they raced onto the dock. She had some small burn marks on her fingers, but she considered these battle scars and was subtly proud of them. "I might decide to get a dog, though." She forced a smile that looked more like a grimace. "I don't feel as secure here."

"What about your birds?" Genevieve asked, feeling a little surprised.

"My birds can't protect me, although," she smiled a real smile, "Hemingway did a great job, didn't he?"

Genevieve grinned back, but she wasn't sure it reached her eyes. "He did. I wonder what those guys would have thought if they had known the voice was from a big mouthed bird."

Lillian shrugged. "I know. We're just lucky, you know? Really lucky."

Genevieve zipped her bag closed and went to Lillian, throwing her arms around the petite woman. They had known each other for just a short time, days in fact, but she felt closer to Lillian than she did most of her friends at home. Their fear, their anger, their common goal had knit a great friendship Genevieve refused to give up.

"We are lucky. And I'm lucky to have had you, and Dean and Noah, to help me."

"You won't forget us?" Lillian's voice was small, especially considering the strength of her character.

"Never. And you're coming to visit me soon. I'm going to buy some pans so you can teach me how to cook."

Lillian laughed a choked chuckle and stepped back, wiping at her eyes.

"You go on. Give your dad and Dean a kiss for me," she said.

Genevieve nodded silently and ducked out into the watery sunlight.

She stopped by Dean's house, but only to say goodbye. She would get Jack as she left town. Dean had Hemingway with him, which gave her an excuse to come over.

His house was still dark. The power hadn't been restored to all areas yet, and the aftermath of the storm littered the yard. Giant branches had been cleared from his driveway, and Dean was outside when she pulled up, Duke pacing by his side.

"Hey there," Dean greeted, coming up to open her car door as she killed the engine.

238

"Hey yourself," she said, and noted that her voice sounded pretty natural considering how her stomach had coiled itself into a hard lump.

She stepped out of the car and bent to give the dog a good scratching. She felt a little bit like Lillian. She didn't want to return to her home alone again. She didn't want to be in the silence. She didn't know if she would try to find a dog, or perhaps a loudmouthed parrot, but she knew the trip had changed her in some fundamental way.

"You all packed?" The words were just filling the space.

"Yes, I'm due to get Jack soon. He'll need to be looked after for a little bit. He won't want to admit it, but he'll need my mom and me."

"And he's lucky to have you," Dean said softly.

She looked up at him then, seeing the darkness in his eyes, the light glittering in his hair, the scrape that marred the perfect jaw. Here was another person she had known for such a little bit of time. She knew little about him in normal day-to-day life. She didn't know his favorite color, his favorite music, his most watched movie. She didn't know if he liked rollercoasters or who his first love had been. She didn't know what he feared or what he most looked forward to in the future. But she knew he was a good man, a true man, a dependable man. It was enough.

He kissed her hard. It meant so many things in that moment. Goodbye, I'll miss you, I care about you, and a dozen other messages that went unsaid.

"So I'll call you," he said when he had released her.

"Yes," she said and drew close for a quick hug. "You had better."

She left him standing in the driveway with Duke sitting at his feet.

Bob had left a meeting request on her cell phone, which had been lost in the turmoil on the boat. It was two days later when she bought a replacement phone and transferred all of her information that she got notice of the missed call.

Bob's voice was so uncharacteristically solemn she worried something had gone wrong with the project, some unexpected error she had somehow overlooked in her hurry to leave? Had she rushed off to find Jack too quickly, leaving things undone?

But when she dialed his number and heard his voice, she quickly realized it was something completely different that had him upset.

"I'm afraid we have discovered that Rick has made some unnecessary and almost falsified claims regarding his part of the research," Bob began, his voice troubled. "He seemed to have promised an outside firm some information that shouldn't have been shared. As a result, he has been busy behind the scenes attempting to speed up the process. Larry thinks he has been able to find the misinformation and correct it. There is no real harm to the project itself, but Rick has admitted to breaking into some of the laboratory computers to monitor work and alter dates when he saw fit. It also seems he might have read some information that was sent to you, or to Larry, that was not meant to be shared among the team. He said he had been in your email, as well as Larry's, and deleted some messages."

"But why?" Genevieve said, her mind trying to understand what could have made a talented researcher and scientist throw away his chances by misrepresenting information.

"He was desperate to get the study completed early. He was taking some of the material to another company, and wanted to make sure he could claim the knowledge before anyone else could. He said he deleted anything that might have tempted you and Larry into leaving the team. Unfortunately, that included some private emails you should have received."

Genevieve's thoughts went quickly to the mysterious missing emails. She had just known no one outside of the team would have wanted, or been able to access her account and delete the messages.

"He erased messaged from my dad?"

"He did," Bob responded, "and he is sorry. He said he had no idea that your father might have been in danger. He just believed if you had gotten the notes, you would have felt obligated to go and assist your father. It would have taken you from the team. And he didn't want that to happen under any circumstance." Bob heaved a sigh. "Rick is young, and for all of his brains, has little common sense. It never occurred to him that sharing the information would have such an effect on our business. He thought of just the short-term reward. He knew as soon as the chemical hit the market, there would be copies made. In his mind, it was little skin off our backs if the project was leaked. And as for your father's situation, he did say he was very sorry." Bob's voice sounded defeated, like a father admitting his chosen son had been caught red handed.

After Genevieve had hung up the phone, she sat with it in her hand, staring at the black screen. After the last few days, this cooperate skirmish seemed to be almost laughable. Before this, an event like the one Rick had initiated would have made her furious. It was a personal affront to her work, to her ideas, to her achievements. But now, she couldn't feel the fire of indignation. There were too many more important things in her life. No, perhaps that was putting it mildly. Her life was too important. And now her priorities had changed.

She went back to work the next day. Hemingway had settled back in at her parent's house, and her mother had forced Jack into a doctor's visit that was long overdue. Jack was on a short leash for the time being, and Genevieve was glad for it.

Her first two weeks back streamed by in a fury to put out one minor fire after another. In her absence and Rick's bad behavior, there were certain reports and client meetings that had to be cleaned up. It was exhausting work, but Genevieve felt some relief in the familiar pattern of it.

She dreaded going home. Her home felt a little empty and sterile with the giant cage sitting in the living room, waiting for her to maneuver it back out to the garage. She had thought about getting a pet, a roommate, something. She had spent far too much of her time bent over numbers and test tubes. She needed something else.

When she got home, she didn't notice the car parked on the curb until she walked up to the porch and saw a tall figure rising from step.

"Hey there," Dean's voice was more musical than ever, a symphony of cicadas adding a chorus to his words.

"Dean," she said a little breathlessly, and then gave up the shyness and rushed into his arms. The embrace was perfect, the warmth of him and the thud of his heart easing the tension of the day.

"What are you doing here?" She stepped back still in his loose embrace.

"Is that any greeting?" he teased.

"No, but what are you doing here?" she asked stubbornly.

"I'm here to take you on a little ride," he responded, and steered her toward his familiar car.

"Now?" she squeaked.

"Now. I'll take you out for dinner after," he replied.

"After?"

"Um, hm. And that's all your getting from me."

She let him seat her in his car and close the door. A few seconds later he slid in next to her and closed the door.

"So you're not going to tell me what this is all about."

"Nope," he said.

She watched as they drove down familiar streets, heading down Shelbyville road toward the little town of Simpsonville, Kentucky. The businesses became fewer and more distance lay between buildings and neighborhoods. After he had passed several streets, he turned into a paved drive with a for sale sign posted. The drive lead back to a wide commercial building, just large enough to hold a single office, and a much older house beyond.

"What is this?" Genevieve asked breathlessly. But she knew.

"The veterinarian who owns this is ready to retire. He has a thriving business with lots of already established clients. He needs someone to take over for him. And I need to move back home. I need to be here, for me, for my mom, for us." Dean's eyes were glittering in the dark. "The old house is empty behind the office, so I told Lillian if she came with me and helped me manage the practice, she can live there. She's been wanting to get out of that place she's in now. She's ready to leave Florida, and she wants to be closer to her family. This makes it easier for her to see her nieces and nephews too." He smiled a little. "I put in a bid yesterday, and it was accepted. I'm moving home in just a few weeks."

Genevieve stared at the darkened building, and then turned to Dean. "You're moving back?"

"I need to be here," he affirmed. "I need to be with mom. I need to stop running and settle down. So yes, I'm coming back. And I need to know you'll be here waiting for me."

Genevieve felt tears in her eyes. "I'm here," she said softly.